Covert Awakening

D1519027

JULIANNE HALE

ISBN 978-1-64028-012-0 (Paperback)
ISBN 978-1-64028-013-7 (Digital)

Christian Faith Publishing, Inc.
296 Chestnut Street
Meadville, PA 16335
www.christianfaithpublishing.com

Printed in the United States of America

ACKNOWLEDGEMENTS

To the "Forgotten Ones" and those surrounded by terror,

May you fully encounter His love to realize your value, beauty, and inheritance as part of the Kingdom of God. You will never be forgotten.

Be strong and courageous. Do not be afraid or terrified because of them, for the LORD your God goes with you; he will never leave you nor forsake you. -Deuteronomy 31:6

CONTENTS

CHAPTER 1

New York State of Mind

Walid stepped nervously onto an escalator at the most pristine subway terminal he had ever seen. Holographic advertisements appeared on the white walls next to him, floating along with him up into uncharted territory. For some reason, this comforted Walid—as though he moved in amiable company. He knew this feeling was absurd but didn't care. Anything to make him feel less alone and abandoned, like he was being singled out, raised up into a different world where he would be fighting for survival. He immediately regretted his hotel-room viewing of *The Hunger Games*…

His thoughts raced. Would the destination look like the satellite images he had painstakingly examined for the last several weeks? What if he looked suspicious and somebody noticed? Or worse—what if he forgot his procedures altogether as adrenaline pulsed through his veins? His older sister had always teased him for his obsessive tendency to overthink, and her remarks stuck like a burr to his brain. He pushed the thoughts aside and tried to remain calm. Though he had run point for many of his group's previous operations, none were as crucial as this one.

As he emerged from the subway tunnel, any sense of comfort he experienced proved fleeting. Absolutely nothing appeared familiar and—to further complicate matters—storm clouds were gathering in the direction he need to move. *What kind of sign is this?* Walid wondered, trying to stifle nascent feelings of trepidation.

He took a deep breath. *Remember why you're here*, he told himself. And then his training kicked in. He wouldn't allow himself to be anything but perfectly focused today.

As he walked briskly down the street, he sought to seamlessly blend into the rivers of lunch breakers pouring from busy skyscrapers. They appeared too preoccupied with their discussions or cell phones to notice anything out of place. In fact, there was something almost robotic about the way people passed him, as if they looked right through him.

Waves of spice-rich aromas from nearby food trucks teased him like incense invitations from his home far away in Tunisia. He thought of his mother, who was now alone with his two sisters in the island town Djerba, and how, when he was a child, she would make him the most delectable harissa-spiced lamb dishes. *Focus*, he told himself and pushed forward.

At last, Walid reached a busy Italian café. He sat down at a modern metallic table on the sidewalk and ordered a cappuccino. He glanced at the target, relieved to know that everything was already in place. This type of operation was more sophisticated than most, requiring months of planning. The hard part was over; everything should sail by smoothly at this point. So why did he feel so anxious? His partner, whom he had never met, should arrive at any moment. Walid silently rehearsed the cover terms he was supposed to use to ensure recognition of his partner, even though it was unnecessary; how could he forget a more vital three-sentence exchange?

Walid waited another ten minutes. Nobody had approached him as planned.

What kind of novice am I working with? he wondered, annoyed that anyone could be late for perhaps the biggest moment in their life. Another five minutes dragged on. His all-too-familiar friend, fear, tried to visit him again. *Had something gone wrong?*

"Sir, do you need anything else?" his waiter asked.

"Privacy," Walid snapped unwittingly, lost in his thoughts.

The waiter stepped away quickly, muttering a racial slur. *So much for being inconspicuous.* In spite of his baseball cap and Yankees T-shirt he had assembled for his Ordinary Joe costume, he felt as exposed as a jailbreaker still clad in prison garb. Walid, a forty-year-old physically fit man with dark features, looked like many typical Tunisian men. He never had much trouble blending in—something his group loved about him.

A few more minutes passed. Finally, Walid spotted a young man who perfectly matched the description of the person he would be meeting: someone of Arabic descent, tall and thin, slicked-back black hair, and a gray pinstriped business suit with a bright-red handkerchief protruding from the left breast pocket. This man looked far too young and innocent to be taking part in such a mission. It was almost insulting that he had been chosen for the same operation, and one that would make history at that!

Walid hated that anxiety was causing his old self, which was far more rude and self-righteous, to return. He forced himself to remember the life-changing events that had occurred in the last several months, and that he was here at this very moment for one reason. He was here to stop a catastrophic event from happening.

No pressure. Walid laughed at his own thoughts—a little too loudly. Customers glanced in his direction, amused. Surely they imagined that Walid, who had been ogling the street for at least twenty minutes, was suspicious.

Walid's expected partner came closer, staggering as though drunk, drawing far too much attention to himself. He made eye contact. The man looked terrified, like he had seen a ghost. *Did he seriously get drunk?* Back on the continent, it wasn't uncommon for other freedom fighters, as they pridefully called themselves, to drink or shoot up before an operation that would probably lead to their deaths. It numbed the pain and decreased the risk of any last-minute reneging. But they were in New York City! This was drawing far too many looks.

Walid stood up from his table to pull this man aside, perhaps down an alleyway to avoid drawing a crowd. He looked everywhere, reminding himself of his contingency plans. He had barely taken a step when he heard a young woman's piercing shriek. "He has a bomb!"

How did she know? Walid wondered.

Everyone looked up, only to see the young man fall on his face less than half a block from the Italian cafe. Then Walid could see nothing but a blur of faces and figures running away from the man in every possible direction. It was as though he was viewing the wind and debris fall out from a bomb blast. The entire jam-packed area emptied in a matter of seconds.

In an impulsive decision, Walid threw logic to the wind and sprinted toward his accomplice. He was barely breathing but

10

still conscious. Blood stained his light-pink shirt; Walid leaned over and ripped it open. These weren't like wounds Walid had seen in battles caused by modern weapons. In fact, it looked as though the man had recently undergone an operation at the hands of a very clumsy doctor. This man had very recently been sewn up.

"What happened?" Walid asked, hoping he could manage a response.

As the square further drained of people and their screams dissipated, Walid noticed a discoloration forming directly in the center of the man's stitches. The blood drained from his face, and every sound seemed to disappear. He knew what was happening and that his time was running out. Just before the man fell unconscious, he struggled to emit his final words. "I tried to warn them. It's inside me."

CHAPTER 2

Rain of Fire

Three months earlier:

Gunshots shattered the silence. White tracer rounds darted into the dark abyss of the desert, their flashes intermingling with the flares of distant lightning: pink, red, blue. If the night was a strangely beautiful canvas, then God was painting pictures of trouble. *If there is such a God,* thought Walid.

The beauty of the night sky was perhaps the only thing making a prolonged training exercise bearable. Nobody in the unit was exempt from training, even in the most dangerous weather, which frequently thrashed the North African desert.

Walid had been sent to this hellhole in the southern Tunisian desert by his local commander in Tripoli to teach new recruits about strategy and ideology. His group was a rather different kind of army known as the Islamic State of Dabiq (ISD). While ISD referred to its members as freedom fighters, most people in the world called them terrorists.

Walid had been through numerous training exercises and missions for ISD. Most of them revolved around targeting Western interests throughout North Africa. He remembered those times, when he had felt proud to serve in the elite corps of fighters chosen for ISD's most prestigious operations. For years, though, Walid had grown increasingly frustrated with ISD. Their inability to follow through with promises, their distortion of the Quran, their abhorrent treatment of people—all things he couldn't come to terms with. And after years of writing and teaching the group's operations, Walid felt empty. He wanted more. To top things off, Allah had never responded to his prayers. Was he even supposed to?

The jarring sensation of a recruit falling on top of Walid snapped him out of his thoughts; a rifle's muzzle jabbed his side.

Walid pushed him off. "Come on, man, pay attention!"

He rolled behind a Humvee, hoping to wait out the insanity. *How did I wind up here?*

Walid thought back to the day he was recruited. He had recently defected from the Tunisian Army after serving a mandatory stint. He never wanted to join. After becoming radicalized online by al-Qaida senior recruiter and Imam Anwar al-Awlaki's propaganda, defection seemed like the best option. In fact, Awlaki himself introduced Walid to his ISD recruiter.

"It's the opportunity of a lifetime! You'll travel to exotic places. We'll provide a monthly stipend for you and your family, if you die," he remembered the recruiter saying.

"Really...what more could I want?" Walid had spouted off sarcastically. And yet he had listened for more promises from the recruiter, who sounded like a travel agent. He just defected from the national army, after all—he wanted more assurances than a death bond.

After relating a tedious hour-long inventory of ISD accomplishments, the recruiter finally made his pitch. Recruiters were adept at recognizing each candidate's weaknesses…and Walid knew, after answering a barrage of questions, that he had made his desire for meaning through Islam, money, and adventure—he even referenced James Bond once during his interview—resoundingly clear.

Recruiters would typically sell the organization in precisely that way: appealing to the common factors that marked most young, bored men experiencing unemployment in North Africa—a thirst for adventure, for meaning, and of course, for a paycheck.

The recruiter, whose sunken features made it hard to guess his real age, made up for his less-than-intimidating appearance with wits and manipulation tactics. In a last-minute strategy change, the recruiter had paused, scanned the area, and leaned in slowly, as though about to tell a deadly secret. Drawn by a sense of purpose, Walid leaned in, heart pounding, to match the recruiter's posture.

"You're no fool," the recruiter had said. "In fact, it's obvious to me that Allah has given you a talent that should not be wasted. Walid, I cannot remember the last time someone as clever as you came through my doors."

The recruiter nodded toward the door that Walid had entered through: hidden underground at a mosque that the recruiter implied belonged to him. Though it probably did belong to ISD, Walid was unimpressed with his hubris. He grinned as he sat back in his chair and sipped tea. Though he had a certain fear and reverence for the recruiter, he hoped that sporting the appearance of apathy would provoke greater offerings. He was wrong.

"Listen to me!" the recruiter barked so ominously that Walid leaned forward in anticipation. It was like something had taken over the recruiter's body. His features appeared to grow darker and sink even deeper.

"The emir does not typically waste time with people who display such contempt. Completely unteachable." He took a moment to collect himself. "However...we have a mission that could change the course of history. If you're successful, I guarantee that your face will light up every major news network. Think of our teacher, Bin Laden. Don't you wish to achieve that level of renown?"

"What's the mission?" Walid asked.

"I can't tell you here. It's too sensitive." The recruiter pushed a piece of paper to Walid. "Here's what we can pay you." Walid gaped; this was far more than the Tunisians could ever pay him. "Think about it quickly. Remind yourself of the rewards you'll receive in heaven. They'll be far greater than anything you could hope to achieve on your own, inshallah. And another thing... if you speak of this meeting to anyone, even your family, your meeting with Allah, and theirs, will be moved up."

The recruiter had left a napkin with a date, time, and location on the table and swiftly departed the mosque. After hesitating for only a moment, Walid had grabbed the napkin and tried to catch the recruiter to ask more questions—but there was no sign of him. It hadn't mattered. He was sold.

— — — — — — — — — — — — — — — — — —

Walid never thought he'd return to Tunisia after that, but here he was. All that mattered now was getting through this never-ending night and avoiding the sporadic gunfire of ISD's more careless new recruits. Their targets were nearly impossible to see through the cloudy night sky. *Whatever idiot monitors the safety of these training exercises should be fired*, Walid thought, as he did a quick tuck and roll to avoid a younger fighter's gunfire. Apparently, there was no time for teaching muzzle awareness.

Earlier that week, upon his arrival from ISD's Libya head-quarters, Walid had examined the training compound. A man with little personality and desert-camouflaged fatigues gave him a tour that was over almost as soon as it had begun.

"This is where you'll live for the duration of your time here. It could be a while. I suggest you get used to it," he said.

Walid had looked at the makeshift barracks, which were worse than some huts he had seen in the impoverished districts of Libya. The compound had six large buildings: two barracks, a dining area, two warehouses for weapons storage and equipment, and a small, unmarked, nondescript structure that nevertheless drew Walid's attention like a magnet.

"This is your safe house. In case of enemy penetration, you will report here without hesitation."

Walid peered in. The safe house was empty, save for several stepladders descending through large underground openings and wooden slabs that lay ready to cover those escapes. "Sir, what's reinforcing the structure?" Walid asked.

"Excuse me?" he said incredulously. Clearly, he was not used to being questioned.

"Those slabs won't stand up to an attack, right? Is it still under construction?" Walid asked, trying not to sound smart.

The man ignored his question. "Tour's over. Get to work."

Walid had grabbed the man's arm as he turned to walk away. "Excuse me, but I'm not one of your recruits. This place needs work if you want anyone making it out of here alive."

The man pulled his arm away. "And just who do you think is gonna attack us in the desert? Gimme a break! The boss sent you here to brief the recruits on strategy, not building construction. As long as you're here, you're still under me, the camp leader, in case you forgot."

Walid dodged another bullet. Watched a tracer round come too close.

Despite being in the middle of a desert, seemingly worlds apart from any enemy forces, Walid had never felt more unsafe. He couldn't help dwelling on how ineffective such a bunker would be against even a moderately successful attack. Yet he knew all too well that camp leaders rarely had the time or will to reinforce mobile camp structures. And frankly, recruits were expendable. ISD leaders had more important things to spend money on, like weapons or lining for their pockets.

Walid dove away from another recruit's buttstock that came far too close to his head for comfort. He wasted no more than a single bullet on the absurd exercise. His impatience intensified, as did his anger, insulted that ISD had sent him to this place to begin with. He was a strategist after all, not a new recruit. Walid retreated behind a water truck and planned to confront the camp leader the moment this ended.

Several men started shouting. They sounded panicked. All gunfire stopped at once, recruits scrambling to understand the commotion. Total chaos. Walid looked in every direction. A short distance from the camp, he saw smoke rising from the fire of an explosion. His eyes grew wide as he reasoned what this must mean. Nobody had seen where it came from, but Walid surmised that it had to be a failed airstrike…and airstrikes rarely involved a single shot. The attack might not be over.

A siren unleashed a long lament. This was no longer a training exercise. Recruits sprinted for the underground bunker, many leaving their weapons on the ground.

Walid sprinted in the opposite direction of every other recruit. His only plan was to put as much distance between himself and the camp as possible. He instinctively looked up, knowing that ground incursions are highly unlikely to occur at night in the desert for safety reasons enforced by the local military.

And there it was, just as he expected: a brilliant white streak of light with a glowing red tail speeding toward the camp. This one looked as though it wouldn't miss its target. Walid forced himself to keep running without looking back. There was no cover in the desert and no light to see more than a few steps in front of him. He expected his life to flash before his eyes, but there was nothing he wanted to remember. Instead, he just had questions: *How does someone with my with my upbringing end up here? How can this be Allah's plan for my life? Where is he anyway? Why is he letting this happen?*

Walid's body was hurled to the sand by the force of the missile's blast. His ears rang; it sounded as though he was underwater. He forced himself to stay facedown, shielding his eyes from the blaze, which was hellfire hot and bright as the sun at midnight. Pain throbbed in his left leg.

He prayed a quick prayer to Allah to spare his life, which was interrupted by searing pain on his back. He looked up to see fire raining down from the skies—embers pouring down from the strike. Walid got up and ran once again. He limped as the pain in his leg grew worse but refused to look at the damage. He pulled his shirt off and tried to shield himself from the embers.

"What do you want from me?" he screamed to God as he ran. "Are you even there? Why do you never answer me?"

Walid cried out as something massive fell within a few feet of him. A piece of the training camp? He didn't care to look. Though physically fit, he was losing stamina. The midnight sky still appeared brightly illuminated by the strike. Finally, the embers were fading. He was free now of the fiery rain. He could risk a look back. Walid dropped to his knees. Debris from the camp was strewn across the desert floor. Bodies lay closer to the camp, unmoving. Walid let out a scream like a lion ready to devour his prey. He hardly recognized his own voice. He felt more alone and abandoned than he ever had before. In this moment, he felt nothing but anger and emptiness.

Was this it? he wondered. *Or will there be more airstrikes?* Moments felt like hours.

Walid strolled back to the camp. His hearing began to return as he limped through the cold desert sand. He finally looked down at his leg, which was stained with blood from a piece of shrapnel that had pierced his thigh. As he grew closer, he heard a few men moaning and yelling for help. Walid imagined this is what hell must be like.

He saw two men lumbering like zombies into the camp from different sides. Walid postulated they had probably run away just as he had. One of them was holding a bloodstained shirt over his hand while the other seemed to have escaped with nothing more than a few minor burns. The men walked in silence toward the bunker. The structure had completely caved on impact, and there was nothing recognizable left in the hole. The smell of fire and charred flesh was overwhelming. Staggering like zombies, they approached a vehicle that remained intact.

Walid's mind grew still. All that remained was his anger. Anger at God for allowing this to happen; anger at his recruiter, his leaders, and his fellow recruits, for reasons he couldn't even comprehend. Walid slumped in the driver's seat and, after several failed attempts, brought the engine to a roar. Without any words, the three men drove into the night. Walid was determined to bring the perpetrators of the strike to justice. Somebody would pay for this, and it would happen soon.

CHAPTER 3

The Unachievable Task

Walid lay on a small bunk in a military-style barracks in northwest Libya. This was nothing like the austere, prison-camp quality of the Tunisian training compound. This complex had everything from electricity to Wi-Fi; from recreational buildings to gymnasiums designated for more serious training.

The compound had been recently renovated by the Libyan Army before being captured by a local militia with strong ties to ISD's senior leaders. After staying at the facility for a week, Walid found it difficult to imagine that most of the country outside of the capital experienced less-than-desirable living conditions. Corruption was a way of life for the region's elite. And ISD was now part of Tripoli's elite due to its captured resources. Citizens were cognizant of the situation but chose to ignore it. What could they do about it after all?

Walid reached for the Quran on his bedside table, but stopped after remembering that it was covering his American classics: Star Wars and Harry Potter were his current favorites. He shared the room with another Tunisia survivor who might find this to be sacrilegious. ISD had forced the two of them to confinement in the barracks to recover from their injuries.

The other survivor—Bashir—was Libyan, short but built like a tank, with a kind demeanor that Walid was drawn to. Walid marveled at the deep affection in Bashir's voice when he spoke of his family. He had once spoken that way too.

Walid was thankful for the unlikely friendship that was forming. Tunisians typically hated Libyans from the north, marking them as wealthy party animals with no respect for religion. Furthermore, many Libyans would steal much-needed business in Tunisia from impoverished locals. Bashir must have thought Walid was extremely rude when they first arrived, chatting up their doctors but ignoring the man he bunked with. It took Walid a full day to speak with Bashir due to his preconceptions of him. However, Walid was a talker, and finally caved.

"So why were you there?" Walid asked.

"Tunisia? I was supposed to be a trainer," Bashir said.

"Me too. Strategy."

"Ideology. Studied religion at university. I guess we would have been partners!"

"Maybe."

"Maybe that's still the plan. How great would that be?" Bashir changed his tone, as though trying to hide his enthusiasm. "I mean, you seem smart enough."

After speaking with Bashir for six days, Walid could sense that his roommate was far from his comfort zone among hardcore jihadists, though he tried to hide it. Walid wanted to laugh at his attempts to appear tough and callous like other freedom fighters. It clearly went against his very nature.

"The French were right on our tails, but I knew the territory like the back of my hand!" Bashir said as he finished regaling Walid with his most recent war story. "I led them right into an ambush. Just like in Sun Tzu's *Art of War*. Not one of them made it out alive."

"Sounds like a movie scene. Never heard ISD talk about that one."

"Well, it was pretty recent. It happened."

"I believe you," Walid said, though he really didn't. It didn't matter though. Despite his terrible stories, Walid quickly recognized Bashir's intellect and moral principles. He felt drawn to him.

They continued telling stories of previous missions and accomplishments, bonding over their similar values and mutual hatred for the joint US/French operation that nearly took their lives. And hatred of the West writ large.

Walid told a story about one of his missions to attack Western embassies in Tripoli following the NATO-led strikes in 2011.

"I was there too. Still trying to pay them back for 2011," Bashir said, trying to stifle tears. "They deserve to die for that."

"What happened?"

"My wife was in the wrong place at the wrong time. Shopping, of all things! It happened in a complex controlled by one of Qadhafi's militias. Errant missile strike. Worst part is that they denied it."

"Of course they did."

"That's all they ever do. They've convinced the world they're helping, but BBC, CNN, and all the others…they don't show what's really happening, do they. They shape the world's thoughts. It's a powerful position to be in."

"That's why we're here, my friend. To repay them for all the evil they've done."

"Yeah, one day…Anyway I threw myself into my studies after that. If nothing else, I can do my part in shaping young minds."

"We're making a difference, Bashir."

Despite his encouraging words, Walid felt truly hopeless on the inside and suspected he was in like company. But this wasn't the time to discuss the truth.

One morning, someone knocked on their barracks door and barged in. The man only had one eye and looked as though he awoke recently with a hangover; he clearly had seen better days.

"Please, come in," Walid said.

He scowled at Walid. "You are both to report immediately to the emir."

Nobody knew much about the emir other than his name: Abu Bakr—perhaps the most common and ambiguous name in the region. This lent even more mystery to his identity. *Is it even his real name?* Walid wondered. The men said nothing, struck with incredulity. Nobody in the organization, save his closest advisers, met with the emir.

"Is there some confusion? Should I tell the emir you were too busy to see him?"

"Why can't you call him by name? Who is he? Lord Voldemort?" Walid asked, baffled at everyone's seeming inability to do so.

"Lord who?" the man said.

"No, sir, we're right behind you," Bashir said in a militaristic manner, grabbing Walid by the arm and pulling him toward the door.

Walid was far more excited than Bashir, who looked panicked after being placed in a white Toyota truck and blindfolded with opaque masks. The men tried to maintain their bearings after being driven around in what felt like circles over so many bumps it was a miracle that the tires were still intact. The truck slowed to a stop, and the men were kept blindfolded as they exited the vehicle. They were led by arm up a flight of stairs and through several curvy hallways that reminded Walid of the mosque that ultimately was responsible for his appearance here.

Finally, the blindfolds were removed. The men looked around in shock at marble floors, emerald furnishings, and a golden television with a giant HD screen, which was simultaneously playing several worldwide news stations. The place was beautiful but empty, aside from a large conference table in the middle of the room. Scents of strong Arabic coffee filled the air as the men were directed to the opulent table. Servants brought the coffee and perfectly constructed French pastries, a delicacy here. This area had formerly been controlled by French imperialistic powers, and that influence was still evident, most commonly in the food.

Walid's excitement grew, while Bashir looked as though he was questioning whether this would be his last meal. Walid knew this meeting would perhaps change his life and suspected Bashir knew it too.

Finally, the emir appeared with five bodyguards. He walked toward his extravagant seat. Gemstones had been woven into the arms and the headboard. *Might as well be a throne,* thought

Walid. *What a douchebag.* Walid tried not to laugh at his own insult. The emir was a man in his late sixties but appeared far younger and maintained an excellent physique. Walid had half expected the man to be assisted by a walker and to speak with a low voice similar to Darth Vader. Instead, Abu Bakr smiled as he took his seat at the head of the table.

"It's fine to meet you both. You two received the highest scores on your entry logic and shooting tests. Not to mention, your tactical expertise saved you from imminent death in Tunisia. If the others at the training camp could think for themselves, perhaps they'd be under your tutelage." The emir paused a moment. "Natural selection, I suppose," he calmly quipped as he laughed with a discomfiting look in his eyes.

The emir was far more charismatic than Walid had imagined. Yet there was something almost sinister about his laugh, his apparent disregard for human life.

"How right you are," Bashir said awkwardly.

"Gentlemen," the emir said, a more flattering title than they had ever received before. "I have chosen you to lead an operation that will go down in history. It will require the utmost secrecy and attention to detail. I need to know that you are committed to the cause before we proceed."

"Yes of course!" Bashir said quickly.

"Yes," Walid agreed.

The emir stared at the men for several seconds before proceeding. Walid hated his green, malicious eyes—a paradox to his charisma. They were piercing and almost maniacal. "I'm going to need more than a simple *yes*..."

The men were intrigued. What would prove their commitment to the emir? Would they have to kill someone? Lead another dangerous operation that could result in their premature deaths?

Walid sat forward this time. "What did you have in mind?" he asked with a tinge of conspiracy in his voice.

"Gentlemen..." There it was again. He paused for a moment, as if purposefully building tension. "You're going to be the first men to prove the Bible wrong," he said. Walid's jaw dropped, and Bashir raised an eyebrow as though waiting for the real task. This was not the type of operation that they had in mind. Was the emir playing with them?

"But...we give credence to some of the Bible," Walid said.

"Of course. I am referring to the New Testament. Specifically, the growing belief that Jesus is the son of God. Blasphemous!"

"How are we supposed to do that?" Walid asked skeptically.

"Do I need to tell you everything?" the emir asked. "You've both been published, you're respected Islamic authors, you're capable of writing a treatise—and you will do just that! If you must, then peruse the Bible itself to find its fallacies..."

"You can't be serious!" Walid interrupted before he could censor himself. Walid knew that the consequences of being caught with a New Testament in one's possession involved the worst kinds of death. Bashir punched him under the table and looked down as if to disassociate himself.

The emir's expression softened. He stood and approached the two men. His feigned sympathy was palpable. "I can understand your concern, but you must focus on what this would mean for the caliphate. There is an epidemic occurring amongst our community. Those who claim to see Isa in their dreams and convert on a whim. Disgusting! We must stop it."

Walid felt discomfited with this plan, though he was starting to see the emir's point. How famous would this make them if they succeeded? He imagined epic music playing in the background.

"What if people see us with a New Testament?" Bashir asked.

"Then you deserve to die," the emir said. "I know you two are more than capable of avoiding that disaster."

"Of course," Bashir said unconvincingly.

"Then it's settled."

What? I didn't agree to this, Walid thought.

"Five weeks," the emir continued. "If you've written a convincing piece, you'll be leading an operation from Syria. If not, then I think you know what's coming."

Without leaving time for the men to respond, the emir disappeared with his bodyguards. Both men had many questions but knew that questioning the emir too much could cost their lives.

The one-eyed man returned to put the blindfolds back over their faces. Before they knew it, they were back in their barracks room, sitting in silence.

CHAPTER 4

The Showdown

Several trips to bookstores and Internet cafes had occurred since Walid and Bashir's meeting with the emir. The men had pored over so many verses in the Quran, the Bible, the Hadith, and several scholarly religious books that their heads were starting to spin. Bashir slammed a Matthew Henry commentary on the table in front of Walid.

"I'm starting to think the emir's playing games with us. Who could possibly write such a paper in a month? Two weeks and what've we got to show for it?" Bashir said in a hushed, exasperated tone.

"Well, we can't just give up. If we do this then Syria will invite us to be lead planners. They only choose the best of the best."

"If we do this successfully you mean. I'm not saying we quit, but, Walid, if we don't start writing something—*anything* at this point—we'll probably be dead in a few weeks!"

Walid stared down at the table, troubled that after reading most of the New Testament in two weeks, he had nothing. No major fallacies, no big ideas, certainly nothing that would make the group go down in history.

"Got any ideas? 'Cause I sure as hell don't," Walid said.

"No. I need to walk. Coming?" Walid placed ten dinar on the table and followed Bashir outside.

"I have an idea," Bashir said.

"Already? We should've left hours ago," Walid joked.

"Devil's advocacy. Surely you did some of that at the university."

"All right, I'll try anything at this point." Walid linked his left arm with Bashir's right, signaling to passersby that they were not to be interrupted.

"I'll start," Bashir said. He paused a moment to think.

"Have *you* done this at university?"

"Watch it, I'm about to school you," Bashir said in good-spirited competition. "All right, I'll be the devil, you the advocate. So, I'll argue the Christian perspective, and you'll refute. Ready?"

"Steer the ship, Captain." Walid liked seeing this side of Bashir. A true academic at heart, he was wholly in his element.

"Okay, let's start with a simple point of authenticity. The Bible's many books, authors, and perspectives seemed remarkably reconciled, especially New Testament chapters that act as a fulfillment of the prophecies in the Old. Take Jesus for example. His appearance fulfills the prophecy in Isaiah 9, his death prophesized in Isaiah 53, one example showing the harmony of the Scriptures. How could this be? The authors came from different countries, time periods, and upbringings. The Quran is written by one author. How do you respond to its inconsistencies? For example, should you live at peace with those who don't follow Muhammad's teachings, or should you kill them?"

Walid looked at Bashir as though he had already converted. "Where did that come from? Do you believe this now?" he said in disgust.

"Walid, please. These are common disagreements we're both aware of! Just argue the side we both know is right."

"Fine. First of all, we know the New Testament was corrupted. Muhammad wrote the Quran after the Bible. He was charged with writing it to correct the Bible's fallacies."

"But the Quran declares the Bible to be a true revelation of God and demands faith in the Bible" (Sura 2:40–42, 126, 136, 285; 3:3, 71, 93; 4:47, 136; 5:47–51, 69, 71–72; 6:91; 10:37, 94; 21:7; 29:45, 46; 35:31; 46:11).

"The Bible does not include the New Testament. Like I said, that part was written years later, clearly corrupted."

"But the Quran says nobody can change the word of God. How, then, could it be corrupted?" (Sura 6:34; 10:34)

"Let me respond to your first question. The Bible has inconsistencies too. God killed people in the Old Testament. He commanded the Israelites to kill. And then changes his heart in the New. How is that consistent?"

"His message from old to new never changed. He consistently preached love and acceptance, not to kill. If you read that story in context, God had given the Israelites' enemies many chances to repent, and they had refused. The Canaanites, for example, sacrificed babies and children to demons, had amoral sexual relationships, and worshiped every kind of demon imaginable. They refused to be redeemed despite God's desire to save them. Because of this, God knew that if they were not destroyed, they would be an enticement to the Israelites to engage in the same sort of behavior…which is exactly what happened.

"Allah wouldn't give them a second chance. Not with that kind of behavior," Walid said in disgust.

"Let's move on, I don't wanna park here. Second point. The God of the New Testament is described as a loving God, one who loves everyone, even those who aren't Christian, equally. In fact, His love is so great that he sent his own Son to die for humanity—that's what they claim at least. The New Testament authors even considered Jesus a friend who wanted a great life for His followers. Allah, by contrast, cannot be described that way."

"No," Walid said. "Allah is not a Father, nor does he have son. Jesus was a prophet. To so humanize Allah and call this man his Son is blasphemous."

"But so many faithful Muslims are seeing Jesus in dreams. How could someone who isn't the Son of God appear to them in a dream?" Bashir asked.

"Easily. I've had dreams of the prophet. I've also had dreams of friends, of family—that doesn't mean they're literally existing in my dream."

"Right, but they say it was real when Jesus appeared. That he revealed Himself after they prayed to Allah."

"Sure, they *claim* that."

"Thousands of them? Have so many people lied? So many people with no connections at all described such similar depictions of Jesus?"

Walid thought for a moment. He hadn't considered that before and didn't know how to respond. He felt himself getting angry, yet he couldn't figure out why. Dropping Bashir's arm, he resorted to ad hominem arguments.

"Sounds like you've made up your mind then. Is this your way of telling me you're changing your opinions about God?"

"What? No, Walid, I'm being the devil's advocate. How could you accuse me of that?"

"Well, how would *you* respond to those questions then?"

"I don't know! I've been trying to for days. That's why I'm asking you."

"This was a bad idea. We're not getting anywhere."

"Fine, what do you propose then?"

"I'm going home."

Walid stormed off in the direction of his villa through the dirty, winding streets of northern Tripoli. He felt angry with himself. *What must Allah think of me? I should be able to refute those questions easily and logically!*

Walid lived beyond what most people would consider walking distance, but he welcomed the trek, hoping to clear his mind of all things religion. Soon, his mind was racing more than ever. Walid debated praying, but just as quickly dismissed the thought. *Where has that gotten me so far?*

He tried to make sense of everything. Walid had grown up believing that the Quran and Sunnah contained God's words spoken through his prophet, Muhammad. It was never permissible to question the authenticity of these books; in fact, doing so would bring grave consequences. Walid knew this firsthand. His father had been caught with a Bible under his bed, and his mother reported him. Within a day, he was killed. Walid was never told the full story but knew of honor killings and didn't really want to know the details. It had shamed his family until Walid joined ISD, making things right again.

He focused again on his conversation with Bashir. The emir's "genius" plan had only caused him to question everything. How could the Christian God love everyone equally? The things Walid had done were despicable, and he knew many people far worse than him. Such a concept seemed impossible, though desirable.

Where would he even begin in his writings?

Walid slowed his pace and then stopped in his tracks. He heard a low rumbling that reminded him of the sound he had heard prior to the airstrike in Tunisia. He felt the rumbling in his bones. His heart pounded. Then he heard another larger explosion and the sound of breaking glass from what must have been several blocks away.

Walid ripped his shirt off and put it over his head, expecting embers to pour down from the sky in what he knew was a completely illogical stream of thought. He was thankful nobody was around to see this. What was happening to him? Violence was anything but infrequent in Tripoli since the civil war had begun more than a year ago, but rarely did it bother Walid so much. He began to run the rest of the way home, refusing to look back. He wondered if it was even real, or his mind was playing tricks on him.

Finally, Walid reached his house—a moderate-sized villa near the water, paid for in full by ISD. He ran straight through the gate, his front door, and into a study with nothing but a large, wood-carved desk, a recliner chair, and scores of books, including different versions of the Bible, a Quran, Sunnah, commentaries, and other religious books. Walid threw a notebook filled with his thoughts against the wall. He fell to his knees, and came before God once again.

"God, if you're real, then reveal yourself to me! If not, then I'm done with you. I can't keep praying to someone who refuses to answer me!"

Walid sat there for a few minutes, expecting God to walk through the front door or send a bolt of lightning; perhaps write him a message on the wall, similar to the passage in Daniel he read about a few days earlier. Nothing happened.

"Idiot," Walid muttered to himself. He felt foolish. This God he spent countless hours praying to—a God that so many people in his group had killed themselves, and thousands of innocent people over—wouldn't respond. He wondered if everything he had done on behalf of ISD was all for nothing.

He stood up, wiped a few tears from his face with a torn handkerchief, and grabbed a Corona from the fridge. He went to the porch to gaze on the Mediterranean Sea. The water was extraordinarily blue, glistening against the reflection of a red sunset in what seemed like a temporary moment of calm. He closed his eyes, taking in the scent of the salty ocean waves crashing against the sand. He drank a few more beers, trying to drown his thoughts and think of nothing at all. That night, he slept for only a few hours before receiving an unexpected visitor.

CHAPTER 5

In Living Color

Walid opened his eyes and glanced at his alarm clock: 3:00 a.m. Scarlet hues encompassed his bedroom. *What's going on?* he wondered. It looked as though all of his lightbulbs had been replaced with red lights, but practical jokes weren't exactly commonplace in Libya. He got up, rubbed his eyes, and walked in a calm confusion to the light switch. It wasn't on. He flipped it a few times, but nothing happened. He shook his head, trying to wake from whatever dream he was in. Suddenly, the light became brighter, shining like day even through the cracks in his blackout curtains.

Walid ran to his balcony, throwing the French doors open so drastically the glass nearly shattered. He squinted from the light, looked up, and saw a bloodred moon. He ran across the living room to the front door and threw it open with equal gusto. The sky still appeared red, but this was not the Tripoli he knew. *What happened?* he wondered. *Had invaders dropped some kind of savage bomb on the place? How could I have missed the sound of an incoming bomb?* He wanted to run back inside but couldn't move his feet, or anything else for that matter.

He peered down the street, somehow able to see clearly to the end of the road. It was like he viewed the scene through an eagle's eyes. Soldiers dressed in black armored suits rode on horseback through the streets, patrolling as though looking for anything or anyone out of place. Their faces were unobtrusive, as though shrouded in shadows. They looked more like ghosts than human beings. The creatures carried 9 mm pistols and another device that Walid couldn't identify. Hardly any civilians roamed the streets, and those who did were stopped by the soldiers to have something on their wrists scanned with the strange device. Walid heard a droning sound as one of the devices blasted. Everyone's focus shifted to the man who clearly had failed the scan test. The man had barely started to run from the horseman when he was shot in the back of the head with the horseman's 9 mm. Walid gasped, and all of the soldiers turned simultaneously to face him.

He finally plucked his feet from the entryway and slammed the door behind him. As he turned away from the door, the red lights dissipated and were replaced by a shining white light with myriad colors intertwined. The colors swam and danced through the stream of light shining from a central point in the living room. The light felt warm and comforting, bright but not blinding. Walid felt an indescribable peace consume him. He no longer focused on the images he had just seen outside. Then the figure of a man emerged from within the light.

"Who are you? What's happening?" Walid asked.

"You know who I am," the figure said in an authoritative but comforting voice. "You asked me to reveal myself."

"Jesus..." Could this really be happening? Walid slapped himself in an attempt to wake up from what must be nothing more than a dream.

"The world you just witnessed does not yet exist."

"But it will? I don't understand. How can I stop it?"

"You can't. But you don't have to experience it. Follow me, Walid."

"They'll kill me..."

"Follow me," he repeated. "I love you."

"Don't you know who I am? How could you love someone like me?"

"Easily."

Walid was prepared to ask a barrage of questions, but the figure vanished and took the light with him. Walid ran to the door, unwilling to part with the feeling of peace Jesus's presence provided. It was like nothing he had experienced. He opened the door, and everything was back to normal. But he was gone. Walid walked back to his room and lay down in the darkness.

- - - - - - - - - - - - - - - - - - - -

Despite his early morning visitor, Walid awoke the next morning feeling refreshed. He had not slept so well since he was a child, when his cares consisted of what kind of mischief he might stir up on any given day. He lay in bed for a while, thinking of how much trouble he gave his mother back then. He remembered playing spy games with his friends: sneaking out of their huts before dawn, wandering nearly a quarter of a mile away, and attempting to make their way back home without detection. Walid chuckled at the thought of his mother lecturing him on the importance of security when he failed to conceal himself, though she admired his sense of adventure—something she had longed to experience herself.

It reminded him of the words Jesus used in his dream. "I love you," he had said. The words made him uncomfortable. He had never felt that kind of love before, and a lifetime of training told him to forsake his emotions since they made him weak.

"Follow me," Jesus had said. *How?* Walid thought. He'd have to choose between going on the run or hiding it from the emir. *No, he'd see through any con. And if he finds out...* The emir had cut off men's hands for less. His own hand trembling, Walid misdialed Bashir's number then misdialed it once more. It rang, and he dropped it. When he pressed it to his ear, he barely recognized his friend's quavering voice: "Walid, we need to meet immediately. Use Grey protocol."

Bashir hung up and Walid knew better than to call back. *If there's one thing you must remember in this business, it's emergency protocols.* Walid began to assume the worst: Had they been compromised by some Western intelligence service? Or perhaps...were they going on the run from their own organization? Had the emir tapped their private conversations about their lack of progress?

Walid grabbed his laptop bag, an ISD-issued tactical Beretta knife, and threw on an old pair of tan trousers and a T-shirt. He would need to avoid attention where he was going.

Walid walked to his 2013 Ford Fusion—a gift from ISD for its more prestigious members, something more than most people could afford in this town—and flattened himself on the ground, looking underneath for any signs of tampering. He manually unlocked the door. Walid started the car and began his trip to the Old Town, trying to maintain a normal speed and avoid unwanted attention. He parked at another ISD member's villa and walked half a mile to the bus station. He sat on the lone dusty bench at the terminal—the station was unusually quiet. The skiff of sand on the terminal tile began to writhe, snakelike, just as he had seen it move before sandstorms back home.

He waited there for what seemed like an eternity, staring at the coarse sand as it created a piece of artwork while continuing to spiral around the terminal. He thought of neither the potential danger this natural warning sign created nor the rather clear danger he and his partner faced but just watched the sand. He couldn't shake his dream from his mind; he wanted—and needed—to have that feeling again.

A bus wheezed its way into the terminal, and Walid was so eager to board that he collided with the first exiting passenger.

After a short ride, the bus entered Old Town—an ancient village known for its busy bazaars, corrupt vendors, and criminal activity. Walid zipped his wallet inside his coat pocket before exiting and walked like he belonged there, avoiding eye contact, weaving in and out of crowded streets, until he finally reached the door of an old gray apartment with cracked paint and dark-red stains on the door handle. While instinct told him to examine the door for explosives or look down the extremely narrow alleyways for traps, he pushed the door open and closed it behind him immediately to avoid suspicion.

Walid slouched down and scanned the small apartment. The open-concept living room and kitchen was unkempt. The signs of recent occupation were evident: recently moved furniture and a faint flow of steam rising from water on the stove.

"Bashir!" he whispered loudly into the apartment. No response.

The smell of must and incense wafted down a long hallway leading to what Walid surmised was a bedroom.

"Who's there?" he said louder this time, moving with agonizing slowness through the apartment. A dim glow emanated from the floor toward the end of the hallway. He drew his knife and advanced, sensing a trap.

"Bashir…," he said, nearing the light. Something scurried past his foot, causing him to nearly lose his balance. Then he recognized the light source; it belonged to him! He had given Bashir a glow stick to use in case of emergencies weeks ago. *Is this some kind of signal?* he wondered.

Just beyond the glow stick, Walid made out a small door that blended well the wall clearly meant for disguise. He had seen doors like this in safe houses or training camps that belonged to ISD; members would use them for concealment in case of an attack or as an entrance to an escape tunnel. The musty smells grew stronger.

He picked up the glow stick and pushed the door open just enough to throw it inside. Clearly a tunnel; it appeared to be empty. He pictured Bashir running through the tunnel with suspicious ISD members or even Western forces in hot pursuit. He feared what he might find at the end of this tunnel. Nevertheless, he pushed on. Where else was he to go?

Walid opened the door quietly. The only sound came from the flutter of a flock of doves alighting outside an open window. He approached the glow stick, planning to use it as a light source until he found his way out.

As he leaned over to pick it up, a voice: "Oh, it's you."

Walid seized the dark figure by his neck, pinned him against the wall with one hand, and drove the glow stick into the man's belly with the other.

"Walid, it's me!" Bashir gasped. Walid dropped the glow stick—and Bashir—and held his head in his hands.

"What's wrong with you?!" Walid yelled.

"What's wrong with *me*? You're the one who just tried to kill me!"

"You couldn't hear me screaming your name? You think some stranger just happened to guess your name?" Walid said.

Bashir took a step back. "You were hardly screaming...and how could I be sure that it was you? This place was raided just before I called you!"

"By who?"

"Don't know, but they were looking for something. It's like they wanted to be in and out unseen. I tried to sneak a peek from here, but they were wearing masks."

"Bashir...do you know what this means?"

"No...no, I don't." Walid looked at the exit door quizzically. "Do you?" Bashir asked sarcastically.

"Bashir, this has to be ISD. Why would the enemy skulk around in here trying to find something? If they knew about this place, they'd wait 'til one of us was here to take us out," Walid explained excitedly.

"Sure, that's one theory," Bashir said.

"Think about it. What would ISD be looking for? The only thing we have of any value to them is our nonexistent book."

Bashir's eyes opened wider in both comprehension and concern at Walid's implication. "How could they know about that? This could just as easily have been some stupid criminals looking for valuables. In fact, that's probably far more likely in these parts."

"Sure," Walid surrendered, pausing to look around the room blankly. Should he tell him about the dream? This was hardly the time to appear crazy. "Next time, save the emergency protocols for real emergencies, huh?"

"We're not in the clear, you know," Bashir countered with a look of concern, which accentuated his wrinkles, more defined than most men in their early forties. "We only have three more weeks to produce a work of genius, Walid!"

"And just what are we going to write?"

"Anything! Maybe something sensational. The emir wants notoriety. He never said we had to tell the truth. Besides, how could we? We haven't even found anything…"

Both men paused a minute to think before Walid advanced toward the door. He turned before exiting, shaking his head. "We just need more time. If he believes this is so important, he'll give us that. We'll just exaggerate our progress so far and write up an outline. We have to stall."

"This sounds like a terrible plan…"

"Got anything better?"

Bashir shrugged his shoulders, and Walid walked out.

"Wait!" Bashir said, causing Walid to turn back. "We shouldn't discuss this here, but I had a dream the other night.

I think we need to talk about it before meeting the emir. It's important."

Walid hesitated for a minute and avoided eye contact. He nodded and left.

CHAPTER 6

Damascus Calling

A woman in her mid-thirties wearing a tan business suit and a blue headscarf stood confidently with two nondescript men in a conference building at ISD's Tripoli headquarters. They discussed a matter of clear urgency in hushed tones. Walid surmised they were European, maybe French. The woman was unlike many Walid had seen in North Africa. She carried herself with a boldness that made him uncomfortable, but was quite attractive. Why his religion suppressed female leadership and encouraged timidity was beyond him. He sat there trying to discreetly overhear their conversation while reading the news on his iPhone. He must have read the same sentence twenty times.

There was nothing remarkable about the room they occupied. Clean, bright, and recently constructed, as were most buildings in ISD's headquarters, recently acquired by force from the Libyan military forces. Walid wondered if the emir hated decoration or beauty of any kind, favoring white walls and boring, modest furniture. Anywhere other than his own offices, of course.

"You know why we're here," the younger man whispered.

"Don't be presumptuous. Nobody does," the second man said.

"It's almost certain. No matter, we can't give up now."

"This is not the place to be discussing this," the woman interrupted. "Not now."

Lost in his curiosity, Walid fell off the edge of his seat. He pretended to pick up his phone from the ground, laughing awkwardly. As though on cue, Bashir came bursting through the front door into the small lobby. Walid got up as Bashir walked swiftly toward him, smiling and nodding at the anonymous group of three as though they were long-lost friends.

"You're late," Walid whispered loudly.

"We need to talk."

Before they could move, a man entered the lobby and smiled at them.

"Friends, the emir must take a most important call from Syria. We will convene back here at 1700." And just as quickly as he entered, he left them all alone.

"And now I'm early. Come on, that gives us thirty minutes!" Bashir said excitedly. He held the door open for Walid, who was still planted on the bench. The other three watched the commotion. Walid heard the woman try to stifle her laughter. He lowered his head to avoid eye contact as they all moved toward the door together.

"Smooth," she whispered as they departed.

Bashir led Walid to an Internet cafe three blocks away. ISD's compound was set up like a small village, with everything from a supermarket to a car shop where the group made tactical adjustments to stolen vehicles. The government had designed the village to be self-sustaining; it was a perfect complex for

ISD to commandeer. Although leaders tried to maintain loyalty by touting this place as a reward for elite members, the duo long expected it was more like a prison—a way to keep members from any outside influence, ensuring their propaganda and training inspired maximum impact and loyalty.

The two walked in without a word. The place was sparsely populated and seemed an excellent location for privacy. ISD rarely bugged its own facilities despite the existence of surveillance cameras around nearly every block. Their presence would be known, but at least their conversation would be private.

"Two cappuccinos, please. And then privacy," Bashir said to the waiter, who nodded in acquiescence.

"Walid, we need to talk about my dream," Bashir said. He sipped his cappuccino, burnt his tongue, and placed the cup down quickly.

Walid stared at him quizzically and smiled. He couldn't help but find the humor in such a ridiculous situation. Plus, Bashir looked goofy with how joyful he appeared.

"You dragged me over here to tell me about your dream. You're kidding," Walid said as he waited for the real reason.

"Well, I didn't expect the emir to call us in like this. Just hear me out." Bashir leaned forward and invited Walid to do the same. "In my dream, I had a vision of a time of great turmoil and terror. It seemed like something from the future. And then I saw the most amazing thing I've ever seen in my life: a powerful man in white. He rescued me from the terror!"

Walid gaped, unprepared to tell Bashir about his ostensibly identical dream.

"Walid, I know you think this is crazy, but I wish I could convey how real this was. It was Jesus. And," he leaned in even closer and whispered, "I went to the church in the fourth district."

"Bashir, are you crazy? What if someone saw you!"

"I thought the Christians would kill me once I told them who I was. But I figured I had nothing to lose, thought the emir would kill us anyway."

"Did you tell them who you work for? What'd they do?"

"Yeah, I did. They showed me mercy. Can you believe that? They helped me understand what I saw. It really was Him! Walid, *nothing* has felt more real to me in my life. One guy in particular…" And before he could finish his sentence, three men in uniform walked in, talking boisterously about their adventures in training. New recruits, clearly.

"We need to get back," Bashir said. "We'll finish this after the meeting."

Something seemed too coincidental about this to truly be a coincidence. Had they dreamed the same thing? How was that even possible? And what happened to Bashir? He was like a different person. Same quirks, but with a newfound confidence and almost a peace about him. And he seemed joyful! Walid hardly cared about the meeting anymore; he wanted to find out what had happened at the church.

The men walked down the dirt path that was lit now by fancy Parisian lanterns, illuminating the fake grass on either side of the pathway. It was only 4:50 p.m., but the moon already floodlit the dim gray sky. A cool breeze blew away from the French-style villa, as though warning them to turn back in the opposite direction.

Earlier that day, the men had been called to an exclusive meeting with the emir. There was something peculiar about the emir's cronies' use of emergency protocols to gather them together. This was serious. They weren't scheduled to provide a status update on their failed treatise for another two weeks.

The men reached the conference center doors and moved inside. The two European men were gone, but the same woman was now sitting on the couch.

"Welcome back," she said. The men smiled politely and remained standing. After a few minutes of awkward silence, Walid made his way to the couch and sat as far as possible from the woman.

"Hi," he said. Bashir grunted, feeling like a third wheel despite the fact that she and Walid were complete strangers.

A man dressed in a guard uniform came in to retrieve the three of them.

"Finally." Bashir winked at Walid.

The four walked silently through a winding hallway to a vast opening like a cavern. This room was just as opulent as the last room in which they had met the emir, and yet quite different. A gigantic crystal chandelier hung in the center of the room and a red and gold inlaid carpet spread beautiful designs throughout the room. There was no table in this room, but two chairs and, yet again, what appeared to be a golden throne with the same red patterns mimicking the carpet.

The more Walid saw the wasted wealth of this group, the more he doubted its sincerity and cause. Walid was so enthralled and yet repulsed by the extravagance of this room that he didn't realize only he and the woman remained. He suddenly whipped around to see the guard escorting Bashir to a separate room near the exit.

"Hey!" Walid called to them. "What's going on here? He's with us!"

Before he could finish yelling, the guard slammed the door, which echoed throughout the chamber. He looked at the woman next to him, whose confidence seemed to wane as she scanned the room.

"I'm Walid," he said, abruptly extending his hand.

"Grace. Nice digs, huh?" She rolled her eyes, and he chuckled. At least he wasn't the only one sickened by this display of wealth.

The emir entered the room with his entourage of angry guards. He wore a golden head scarf; they wore black suits with red and gold armor that matched the room. One of them carried a majestic bird on his shield—a falcon, perhaps. Walid and Grace shared a look; amused at the way everything in this room matched, except for them. It looked like something out of *Alice in Wonderland.*

"Sit," the emir said curtly as he took his seat.

The duo sat quickly and tried not to stare at him. He had shadows around his eyes, which looked tired. Walid couldn't get over the disturbing feeling he got every time he looked into the emir's eyes, and yet he couldn't look away.

"Something very fortuitous has arisen," he said. "I expect you may have an idea what I'm referring to."

Neither said a word.

"Do you not watch the news?" the emir said, his frustration rising. ISD members were expected to keep abreast of international news on a daily basis. It was crucial to understand the nature of world politics to be able to exploit the enemy, create propaganda, and take advantage of upcoming world events.

Walid expected this had to do with the latter, but he had not seen the news in at least a week.

"Yes, of course," Grace said. Walid felt relieved by her save. "You mean the UN Assembly."

"I suppose you knew that too," he said to Walid, shooting him a look of condescension. "Anyway, both of you are working on tasks of utmost importance for ISD. However, I have a new task for you. I will need you to delay your current tasks immediately and expend all efforts towards what I am about to say."

"Should we wait until Bashir arrives?" Walid said, immediately regretting his question.

The emir stopped and examined him. Walid felt nothing but pure malice emanating from him.

"I suppose you think you can interrupt whenever your heart so desires. Have you so quickly forgotten the special privileges I gave to you?" he said. Walid looked away. "If your little friend was supposed to be here, he would be. Now if you're done questioning my decisions, we'll move on."

"Of course," Walid said apologetically. He was starting to hate working for this man, but he valued his life far more than showing his true feelings.

"Syria headquarters is planning a very unique operation around the UN event. I cannot reveal any details here. You will receive information on the plan and training requirements when you arrive in Damascus in one week. I expect you to make arrangements to leave within the week. You were both requested by name for this."

Walid and Grace nodded.

"Get ready. Represent ISD-Libya well. Do not disappoint me. Or Allah."

As they rose to face the exit, Walid felt a clammy hand grab his arm and turn him around. The emir fixed his cold gaze on Walid, which made him shudder.

"Don't think I'm unaware of your progress, or lack thereof," the emir said. "I certainly hope you're not keeping all of your research in Old Town."

It was him? Walid felt uneasy knowing the emir was having him followed.

"You will write me my book, and the consequences will be unthinkable if you fail to produce anything."

Walid nodded and avoided eye contact, afraid to see the horror of his eyes once more. He hustled out the door and ran to catch up with Grace.

"Wait!" he said louder than anticipated. She slowed her pace but kept walking. "Grace," he said as though proving he remembered her name. "So…what do you do for ISD?"

"A little of everything I guess." She looked disappointed.

"That's very descriptive."

She smiled. "It's a long story."

"Well, we should talk about what just happened."

"Not here, they'll hear us. I'll contact you before we leave."

"But you don't have my number," Walid said as she reached the gate and stepped outside without another word.

Walid stood there in confusion for a moment. What could Syria possibly want with him? As a member of ISD's Libya branch, Walid never thought he would hear from the group's main headquarters. Perhaps he would be meeting the emir of the entire organization. He felt important in that moment, yet cared less than he imagined he would.

He turned away from the main gate to see Bashir approaching a separate, smaller gate.

"Wait!" He ran right over a row of perfectly planted tulips to reach him. "What happened?"

"It's fine, I think they grew those to be trampled on," Bashir said with a small smile.

"What happened?" he repeated, softer this time.

"I was escorted into a separate room and told I should keep working on our initial task while you're gone. Nothing more. I have a really bad feeling, Walid. I can't place it."

"What do you mean?"

"I don't really know, it's just a bad feeling."

Something seemed wrong with Bashir. Like he had just received the news of a friend's death. "Well... I'm leaving soon for Syria. I don't know much else," Walid said.

"How soon?"

"About a week."

"Hey, man," Bashir said. "I was serious earlier about my dream. There's something really important I heard at the church that you need to hear. You should go there."

Walid nodded. It was reckless to discuss Christians on base. They exited the same gate and strolled in opposite directions. Walid quickly become lost in his thoughts yet again. What did Bashir hear that was so life-changing? *It has to do with the man in living color; it must!* he thought. He couldn't shake that image and longed to feel that peace again. He would do anything for it. Maybe it wouldn't hurt to walk in the general direction of the church...

Walid was jerked out of his thoughts by the sound of an explosion thundering from the opposite direction. He covered an ear with one hand and habitually covered his head with the other. He waited for a moment for the ringing in his ears to stop. It sounded like the explosion happened right down the street around the corner. He began to run as he saw the typical dark, red cloud of a car bomb rise and collapse in a burst of heat. He reached the site and felt the heat singeing his goatee. Children screamed and ran away from the charred vehicle.

"No!" he yelled in horror before even reading the license plate; he recognized this vehicle and knew it was Bashir's car. He ran to the burning vehicle and pried the door open with almost superhuman strength.

"Bashir! Bashir!! Answer me!" he yelled into the car but found nothing but ashes. He pounded what was left of the steering wheel and lowered his face into it. He wanted to race back to ISD's compound and light it up with gunfire. *This had to be them.* He backed away, staring into the wreckage. The world tilted, and he stumbled, his face and arms covered with soot. And then he saw nothing.

CHAPTER 7

Mysterious Gas

New York City

Walid jerked back from the body. He didn't even know the man's name. *Did he have a family?* Walid wondered. When would it be enough for ISD? *Was this even them? It had to be…* Now was hardly the time to think about these things.

The storm clouds had grown larger and more ominous as large raindrops started to fall. Walid had never seen a yellow, sepia-toned sky like this, with clouds so tall and dark it appeared to be dusk. He took a few steps back. Discoloration spread across the man's abdomen rapidly. It looked biological. "Impossible," Walid said aloud. He wondered what had caused the bomb to fail. Unless…*a delay*, he thought.

Walid sprinted and ducked into an alleyway in case his assumptions were correct. ISD typically utilized secondary detonators in case the primary failed. *Maybe it's set to a timer.* He kept running down curving side streets to avoid the blast. And then a thunderous explosion shook the earth. As he looked back, he saw a gray plume cloud rising over the buildings. This wasn't like typical blast clouds he had seen in the past, which would expand and rise quickly. Instead, the cloud slowly grew higher and more expansive in the sky. *What is this?* he wondered.

The cloud blocked the yellow sky, and it was nearly dark now. The rain droplets had transformed into a torrential downpour. Walid tried to see down the long alleyway he had just run down and felt as though his feet were glued to the gravel. There were only a few people in sight who, like him, probably assumed they were beyond the range of the terror.

But for the rain, it was almost silent. Walid squinted to try and see through the heavy wall of rain between him and the people. Then the sound of footsteps and coughing—and a figure appeared: a short man in a white raincoat, running toward Walid down the alley. A billowing cloud from the explosion was about to overtake him.

The man gestured wildly with his hands. His pace slowed. Walid shouted, urging him to run faster, but was too far to be heard. Then he realized the man was telling him to run. He fell to his knees, pulling the coat away from his neck, seeking relief. He appeared to be suffocating. He then collapsed and his movements ceased.

Walid turned and ran as fast as he could. *It has to be biological...It's actually happening.* He looked back; the cloud was slowing, finally settling.

After running a few more blocks, he found a subway tunnel and descended past the same holographic figures he had seen nearly an hour ago. The terminal was a mess. A chaotic sea of people moved quickly to board the subways. Walid passed through the turnstiles and tried to push his way through an impossibly dense crowd of unfamiliar faces. On a TV screen above, CNN was already airing footage of the cloud from a distance and streaming the words "Unidentified Gas Floods Times Square; Casualties Unknown." Well, Walid knew of at least one. *What has gone so terribly wrong?*

Walid bumped into a young woman dressed in a blue-and-black striped runner's outfit who grabbed him firmly by the arm. "Follow me," she said.

She led him downstairs onto a train platform. None of the trains were running due to overcrowding. They pushed their way to the end of a terminal straight into an underground door that appeared to be an electrical room. In the chaos, nobody was paying any attention to them, or so they assumed. They entered the room and hustled down a narrow hallway along a two-foot wide metal platform, watching rats scurry beneath them in the same direction. The walls were dark and damp on both sides; this place reminded him of a sewage tunnel. They came to another metal door, which the woman swung open and walked through. Walid followed, unsure whether he should trust this woman, but fearing that circumstances left him no choice. To his surprise, the door opened into an expansive, crowded mechanical control room. Some turned to greet them warmly. Others remained transfixed on HD screens showing live surveillance footage of the area.

A tall, slightly overweight New Yorker wearing army fatigues stood up from one of the small computers and ran over to Walid. "Brandy, thank the Lord you found him," he said as he hugged her.

"You were looking for me?" Walid asked.

"It's so good to finally meet you! You need to come see this immediately." He shook Walid's hand firmly and dragged him to a computer screen.

"I don't understand…what's going on? Who do you think I am?"

Walid was still reeling from the botched operation. The original plot had involved a suitcase bomb that would explode in Times Square, but a bio bomb had never been part of the mission. On top of that, he couldn't figure out what exactly had been placed in the man's body. It was not uncommon for fighters carrying out operations to have a remote trigger puller standing nearby in case the bomber had a last-minute change of heart. However, this did not seem like one of those situations. Somebody had changed the plan completely and tried to prematurely kill Walid and his partner, and he was almost certain that he knew why: they had figured out what he was doing. That he was there to stop the attack.

"My apologies, I know you must be confused," the military man said. "I'm John. You can trust us. We've been following you and we're here to help you." A room full of people tracking his movements? This was not reassuring.

John pointed at the screen, which showed a massive cloud encompassing several blocks expanding outward from Times Square. "It appears from the footage we saw earlier that something delayed the bomb. I think you were supposed to be among the casualties. We were watching you through the traffic cameras and saw your partner come through that door into the street." He pointed at a building half a block from the detonation. "There's a small medical clinic on the first floor, but anyone who was with your partner prior to the operation is certainly long gone by now."

Walid stared at the screen, trying to make sense of everything. "Who are you people?"

"We're from all over. I'm working with the NYPD. Several of us follow Jesus, Walid, like you."

"How do you know that?"

"Please allow me to explain this all later. I know this is confusing, but we have a small window of opportunity we need to jump on."

"For what?"

"There may be another device in the city."

"Where? How is that possible? I was in charge of this operation. None of this was supposed to happen!" Walid regretted his words instantly. Implicating himself in a room full of policemen was the last thing he needed to do right now.

"I know. Something prevented that bomb from going off when it was supposed to. Maybe an angel for all I know. Whatever it was, it saved far more lives than we'll ever know. Also, there's this…" He zoomed into a street two blocks from Times Square. Three people lay motionless in the street. "Their faces…from what we can tell, they appear to be covered with something like boils. Can't zoom in quite enough to tell."

"So how will we survive out there? Any leads on the next bomb?"

"We have a plan. We don't have much time though. I can read you in quickly if you're in. And, Walid, you're not alone here anymore. We've got your back."

Walid liked this man. He was rather frank but reassuring in chaotic situations. Further, he addressed Walid with respect and treated him like an equal. He had never met any leader like this in North Africa.

Walid sat back in his chair and shook his head. "Okay, I'm in. What's the mission?"

CHAPTER 8

Saved by Grace

Walid awoke to the smell of charred metal and a burning sensation on his legs. He recoiled upon realizing a piece of Bashir's car door was resting on the lower half of his body. He pushed the wreckage off his leg and pushed his body away. *Did I black out? Was there another explosion?*

He stood, tremulously, noticing locals watching through nearby windows as a security patrol began to cordon off the explosion site.

"Sir, you can't be here," a first responder said as he grabbed hold of Walid's arm and pushed him away. He must have looked completely lost, standing there, examining the scene with a blank look in his eyes.

"Wait, he was my friend. Please...tell me what happened."

The man looked back at his crew, who were busily working to contain the site and start the cleanup. He leaned in to avoid being overhead. "We're not sure yet...but there were two separate blasts. At least one was an incendiary device. Whoever's responsible obviously knows how to cover their tracks. Now please, you need to leave." The man hurried back to his crew.

Walid wasn't surprised. This was a fairly common and effective tactic—timing a secondary bomb to explode when first responders arrived at blast sites; a cruel method of maximizing casualties. It also confirmed to Walid what he had initially expected. That it was probably ISD's doing.

He departed, noticing a few curious stragglers trying to hide themselves behind building posts. Bashir was the closest he had come to a real friend in years, though tears would not come. Instead, he felt disillusioned, hatred rising up in his soul. Walid speed-walked down a main street until he lost track of time, and his whereabouts.

He finally stopped to take in his surroundings. The urban area had disappeared. Shanty houses and huts intermittently lined the orange-hued dirt road. *If ISD has several throne rooms for one man, surely they can help their own countrymen struggling to make ends meet.*

And not far ahead, against the backdrop of the Mediterranean Sea, stood a church. "What are the odds?" he said out loud, and in the silence that followed, he could feel something—someone—listening. He shook his head. *I must be imaging things.*

The church looked majestic standing alone against the glistening water, the sun nearly touching the water on the horizon. The church was white with red and gold trimming around its wide stone-bricked arches. It stood tall and strong—resembling a castle in its architecture—with a white cross gracing the pinnacle.

Walid thought of Bashir and the secret he held; the one he received from this very place. *Could it have been worth killing him for?* he wondered. He fixed his eyes on the ground before his feet, striving to make his approach seem accidental. He looked back to ensure nobody had followed him. And so what if they did? He could always say he was looking into Bashir's death or something.

Walid's face was still dark with soot and his shirt partially torn from the blast. He probably looked like exactly the type of person he was: a killer who had been conditioned by ISD to believe Christians were the enemy. Walid was thankful for the mud that had encrusted over much of his outfit; maybe they wouldn't recognize his ISD fatigues. If they did, perhaps they would shoot him on sight to protect themselves.

He reached the door and stopped motionless as he strained to hear the sounds coming from within. It sounded like a party. *What is there to party about in this Godforsaken country?* He pushed the door open and stepped inside. People were singing and dancing, raising their hands to the sky. He averted his eyes, as though watching something inappropriate, and reached for the door when he felt someone's hand on his shoulder. *Here it comes.* He was about to meet his untimely demise at the hands of a dancing churchgoer.

As he turned, however, he was met with a warm handshake. "Welcome, my friend! I am Amin. I've been expecting you."

"Excuse me?" Walid said. "I think you have the wrong guy." He looked at the man like he was crazy. Walid was surprised at his appearance; the man wore casual jeans and a white T-shirt, which revealed several tattoos on his arms. He was taller than Walid by a few inches and somewhat muscular. He looked like a military man but didn't talk like one.

"No, you're him all right. I spoke with your friend not too long ago."

Bashir must have told him he'd bring me back with him. That's the only thing that made sense. Walid looked at the man, angry and aggrieved. "Well, my friend is dead. Murdered!" Walid said louder than planned. He wanted to say something insulting but couldn't find the words.

"I'm so sorry to hear that!" Amin tried to touch his shoulder, and Walid pushed his arm away. "We loved Bashir."

"You barely knew him!"

"Love isn't time-bound."

"I'm leaving."

"Wait. I'm truly sorry that your friend was killed. Thank God he came here first."

"What's that supposed to mean? What did God do for him?" Walid asked.

"I will tell you, but not here. It's too dangerous. Please, come with me, the service will end soon." His voice was calming and loving despite Walid's harsh reactions.

Walid wanted to leave, but he couldn't. His legs were weighted, as though the floor was magnetic. He couldn't leave without knowing why Bashir was killed. Amin ushered him down a hallway and two flights of stairs. He paused for a moment, wondering if this was a trap.

"This way," Amin said.

The men were now underground, and Amin stopped after heading down another corridor that finally opened into a large room softly lit by baroque-style hand-cut lanterns. Walid surveyed several landscape pictures on the wall with biblical memes and verses. He felt mesmerized at one in particular that reminded him of the desert oases in Tunisia. Lions, zebras, and camels had gathered to drink from the clear blue water. Grass and irises flourished around the basin. The caption: *I am doing a new thing! I will even make a way in the wilderness and rivers in the desert.*

"The flowers of hope," Amin said.

"What?"

"The iris. It symbolizes hope. Even when all hope seems lost."

"Flowers would never grow in the desert."

Amin smiled. "*Never* is a strong word. Please, take a seat." He directed Walid to the nicest reclining chair in the room, though he remained standing.

"If you really know who I am, why are you being so nice to me?" Walid felt a pang of guilt at his initial thoughts of this pleasant man as a killer church ninja.

"I told you, I was expecting you, and I believe you're here for an extremely important reason."

"So Bashir told you I was coming?"

"No, but someone else did," Amin said. "Let me get you a coffee."

"Stop!" Walid said abruptly, turning the man around in his tracks. "Stop being so evasive! What did you do to my friend? Is whatever secret you told him the reason he's dead?"

"I don't know who or what killed Bashir. I didn't know him like you did, but I can assure you that he's with Jesus right now in heaven, rejoicing that he made the most important decision in his life the day he came here. He told me about your task and the dream where he saw Jesus. Don't you see? He asked God to reveal himself, and He did just that!"

"This can't be real," Walid said. "I had the same dream, on the same night. Jesus the prophet spoke to me like we were friends. It felt like…"

"Like what?"

"It's just coincidence. God wouldn't just reveal himself for normal people!"

"And why wouldn't he?" Amin asked in a serious tone. "The living God spoke to you, Walid. He answered your prayer, and I know you can feel the truth in that, and that it scares you. You're at a very serious crossroads right now. Let me help you through this."

"I didn't come here to get preached to! And I don't have a choice anyway, not that I'm considering. They'd kill me…and you!"

"Why'd you really come here?"

"I don't know. I should go. My group has eyes everywhere."

"God has eyes everywhere, not your group," Amin said. His voice thundered with boldness, and his countenance changed. It wasn't fear that Walid saw. It wasn't rage. It was awe.

"What's that?" Walid asked, his voice shaking as his eyes locked on to the painting of Tunisia that he saw earlier.

"What's what? The painting?"

"It's moving!" Walid kept staring at the picture.

Amin focused on the painting. "I don't see anything." Walid remained silent. "Walid?" Still no response.

After a minute or two, Walid fell out of his chair. He wept bitterly and lay prostrate on the floor. Amin brought him water and a cool washcloth for his face and prayed alongside him.

"The victory is yours, Walid!"

And just as soon as Amin declared it, Walid stopped crying and stood up. "Okay, I'll follow you."

Amin jumped toward the ceiling, unable to contain his joy. "Drink this." He handed Walid a water bottle. "What did you see?"

"I saw Jesus again, walking toward me from within the picture. Then it was like a vision. Amin, I saw heaven. He really is God's son. He really is."

"Yeah, I know," Amin laughed.

"He showed me many people who died as martyrs. They looked ecstatic. And…there were several who were there because of me. I just couldn't stand it, what I had done." Walid wiped his face again with the washcloth.

Amin grabbed Walid by his shoulders. "Are you familiar with the story of Paul?"

"Sure."

"Well, read it again. Read what came of his ministry after converting, after persecuting Christians for a living."

Walid smiled. Despite what he had just gone through, he felt relieved, like a whale had just been lifted off of his shoulders. "He also told me that he forgives me for sending those people to heaven. Can you believe that?"

"Yeah, I really can!"

"How am I supposed to get over that?"

"Just thank Him for it. Jesus no longer condemns you, but you have to forgive yourself."

"Sure."

"Don't you dare go soft on me now," Amin said, pushing Walid's shoulder playfully. "You have a purpose for being here on this earth. And besides, we have a lot of work to do."

"We do?" Walid stood up from the chair. He was impressed with Amin's boldness. It was as though he had nothing to lose, no fear. And yet Amin had to know just how dangerous it was to have a church in northern Libya.

"Yeah. Why don't you stay here tonight? It's not safe to leave at this hour."

"No, I need some air. I'm pretty good at making myself invisible."

Amin led him to the exit. It was dark outside, which would offer him some cover.

"I am filled with joy today for you, Walid. I knew when God told me you were coming that it would be the start of something exciting!"

The two shook hands, and Walid departed down the dimly lit pathway to the main road. What had just happened? The last thing he had expected to do today was give his heart to Jesus. *What do I do now?* he thought, wondering if he would still be alive this time tomorrow.

He looked up from the dirt path and watched the moon in the sky, softly illuminating the sea to his left. Despite his nagging thoughts, he felt no dread. Just peace. He placed his hands in his pockets and felt a neatly folded piece of paper. He opened it and laughed out loud, shaking his head. Perhaps he underestimated Amin's ability to handle danger after all… "Monday, 5:00 p.m. third district cafe."

CHAPTER 9

The Underground Believers

Walid and Grace stepped out of a small plane onto the tarmac with three strangers. The air was stuffy and sepia-toned from the desert winds, making it difficult to breathe. There were no other planes here.

"Are we in Damascus?" Grace asked.

"I guess," he said. "I'm not sure this is even an airport."

A small terminal that may have once been a warehouse welcomed them unimpressively. Several security guards stood nearby with assault rifles, but nobody checked them for documents or contraband materials. They walked through in what felt like seconds.

"Why are they even here?" Walid whispered.

"I guess in case the wrong people show up," Grace said.

Three lonely cars waited in the vast parking lot. It reminded him of the bus terminals in Libya. He saw the distant outline of a vehicle driving toward them. Walid grabbed the small bags he and Grace had brought and waited with her on the sole bench. Finally, the car—a tan, armored Hummer—screeched to a stop.

He looked at Grace, who shot him a look of confusion as a man exited the Hummer and approached them.

He pointed at him and Grace. "You two, get in."

They got in and noticed another thin man with several missing teeth sitting in the front seat. He shot them an unnerving grin and forced two black masks over their heads. "Welcome to Aleppo," he said.

"Aleppo?" Walid asked. "You have the wrong people!"

Walid fell back in his seat as the driver slammed the accelerator. "We're going to Damascus!" Walid demanded.

"Take it easy, killer. You're in the right place."

Maybe it was a security protocol, he convinced himself. Grace squeezed his hand quickly to reassure him. There was nothing left to do now but wait.

— — — — — — — — — — — — — — — — — — —

Three weeks earlier, Walid had entered a popular café in the third district. Tripoli's District 3 was known for attracting European tourists before the militia infighting started. After that, it was largely abandoned, save for a few brave tourists determined to see historic sites, some of which were beleaguered with bullet holes. It was sporadically patrolled by militias, but since the city's key source of wealth had all but dried up, nobody really cared to protect it anymore.

Walid and Amin had started meeting almost daily in various locations throughout the district, depending on the security situation. Walid enjoyed Amin's company and grew to like and even respect him—something he couldn't say for anyone in his group.

Walid spotted Amin at a table near the back of the café. He felt exhilarated. There was something exciting about the danger inherent in these meetings.

"You know, if we're caught, they'll kill me on the spot," Walid said as he sat down.

Amin took a huge bite of his croissant and shot Walid an exaggerated look of concern. "You know, if we're caught, it'll be ten times worse for me. Here, have some food." Amin pushed a half sandwich over to Walid.

"Thanks."

"Saw that headline in Al Jazeera last week?" Amin asked.

"Yeah, I know. These are terrible times." Walid left the sandwich on his plate. The thought of such things caused him to lose his appetite. He tried to avoid picturing the truly disgusting video broadcast in the news of a local pastor brutally murdered by ISD. "This wasn't a problem before ISD came here."

"Well, we're trying to do something about it at least," Amin said with a full mouth. "And anyways, their time is limited. Don't sound so down about it."

"When did you last eat? Running short on food?" Walid joked as Amin took another bite.

"Military habit, I suppose."

"I knew it! You don't act like a typical pastor."

"Oh? How does a typical pastor act?"

"I don't know. Not like a military officer." Walid grabbed Amin's fork as he placed it down to sip his coffee. "OK, you with me now?"

"I was multitasking. What's on your mind?"

"It hit me today that you know far more about me than I do about you. In fact, aside from your beliefs, you're pretty much a complete mystery. How is that? What's your story?"

Amin put his coffee down and grinned. "All right, I'll bite. Let's see, grew up in a poor neighborhood in southern Algeria. Joined the military at eighteen, like most other men in the country. Most capable military in the region, as you know. I suppose that should have had some draw, but I didn't really care about all that. Just wanted to provide some kind of security for my family. Make a better life for them. We grew up Christian, which meant constantly moving around to survive. We're not exactly welcomed there."

"Or anywhere else in the region for that matter," Walid interjected.

"Welcome to the proud ranks," Amin laughed.

"Okay seriously, Amin, how are you never upset? Everybody wants to kill you."

"Oh please, not everyone! I learned something crucial after resigning from the military. I went to Tamanrasset to hear an evangelist preaching on revival. I've never been to event where I witnessed more power. People were getting healed all over. And I heard about the authority I have as one of God's own. He actually gives me the authority to use His name to overcome fear, heal the sick, make change in this region—all kinds of things! Changed my perspective. I've no reason to be sad knowing that."

"Changed my perspective too. In the back of my mind, I always thought ISD's brutality was just a way to incite fear and maintain control—not that it was God's will like they said. I was reminded every day of the consequences of disloyalty. It's almost like they were afraid of people finding out the truth. Why would God want me live under that kind of dictatorship?"

"He doesn't. He loves you more than you'll ever know." Amin downed some more coffee.

"'Cause you're not already excited enough," Walid said, grabbing his coffee and holding it hostage along with his fork.

"Can't help it! When you get a full revelation of His love, you just want to tell everyone."

"Do you think I'll ever feel that?"

"Of course you will. Just ask Him for it."

"You know, my dad was a lot like you. He was a Christian too, actually."

"Was?"

"Yeah, he's passed. My mom did it. An honor killing, you know? 'Live at peace with the world, Walid,' that's what she would tell me. And yet we're forced to murder our own family members if they convert. At least I know now where he is."

"Yes, and you'll see him again someday. Rest in that knowledge, my friend."

The meetings continued for two weeks. They discussed the nature of God's love and his desire for Walid to forgive ISD members. He was still struggling with that one. Despite the peace he now felt—which was overpowering his hatred—he hadn't brought himself to forgive them, though he didn't care to reveal that to Amin.

One evening, while overlooking the Mediterranean Sea on his balcony, Walid thought of his imminent trip to Syria, which was less than one week away. Since becoming a double agent, he had made no progress at all with his trip preparations. He still hadn't told Amin about the ISD operation, fearful of his reaction. *I'll tell him tomorrow*, he thought.

He sipped a glass of wine and watched the sun paint pink, purple, and orange hues as it bid him farewell. *This could be my last sunset from this place. I wonder who will live here, after they discover my secret. I wonder if I'll live to find out.*

Walid sat in bed that night, restless. He thought about praying but couldn't decide what to say. Walid had prayed countless times in his life, but he felt almost embarrassed praying now to a different God. Still, he had to start someday, and now was as good a time as ever.

"Hey, God, what's up?" Walid felt stupid as soon as he said it. But then he thought of Amin's conversational prayers and thought, *Maybe it's okay. He's a friend now, right?* He decided getting straight to the point was the best method for now. "Look, I need your advice. I don't know what to do about Amin, or Syria, or anything really. Please, speak to me like you did the last time I asked for you. Good night." Walid finished, "I mean, Amen."

Though his prayer felt forced and awkward, he sensed that God heard him and would honor his request, regardless of how it came out. Walid turned over and fell into a deep sleep. That night, Walid received another unexpected visitor.

— — — — — — — — — — — — — — — — — — — —

Walid's phone rang and jerked him out of a deep sleep. He felt somewhat disappointed that Jesus didn't come into his bedroom and give him the exact advice he needed, but brushed those feelings aside. He looked at his alarm clock: *4:00 a.m.? In the middle of curfew? Who could possibly be calling at this time?*

The government had issued a curfew in several cities just last week after an uptick in militia and terrorist attacks. Anybody out between 11:00 p.m. and 6:00 a.m. would be arrested or killed, depending on who found them first.

"What?" he said tersely into the phone.

"Walid? Is this you?" came the unexpected sound of a woman's voice.

"Who's this?"

"It's Grace, of course."

"What?" he said, still half-asleep.

"We met a few weeks ago. You don't remember?" she whispered.

"Yes, of course!" he said, perhaps a little too excitedly. He remembered how nervous she had made him during that first meeting, and yet he hoped she would have called sooner.

"I need to meet with you very soon," she said.

"How soon?"

"Well...how about right now?"

"Are you in some kind of trouble?" Walid asked. "Where would I meet you at this hour?"

"Well, how about your house? Actually...I'm right outside," she said.

"You can't be out there!" Walid hung up and threw some clothes on. He ran to the door and nearly dragged her inside. Grace was dressed in a black runner's outfit, undoubtedly to avoid attention. Her long, brunette hair fell over her face in messy curls. He surmised she hadn't been up too long either.

"Thanks," she said politely.

"I'm not sure that I had much of a choice." Walid smirked. He led her to the living room. "Please, take a seat. Coffee?"

He kept moving into the kitchen, and she followed him, smiling. "What?" he asked.

"I barge in at 4:00 a.m., and you're not mad…"

"Why would I be mad?"

"*And* you're so hospitable…you don't seem like most other ISD guys I've met."

"I'll take that as a compliment."

"Walid…" Her voice was more serious this time. "I know this all seems a little reckless, but I've been ordered not to speak with you before we leave. Coming here tonight is the only thing I could think of that would keep them off our tail."

"Them?"

"ISD, of course."

"They ordered you to avoid me? Well, they didn't tell me to stay away from you, so…" He started the coffee and haphazardly began to chop vegetables with a paring knife, eliciting a look of confusion from Grace.

"They must be afraid of something," she said.

"Yeah, I guess." He put the knife down and looked her in the eyes. "But what's so important that we have to talk now? That you're risking your life—*our* lives?"

"Let me ask you something. You say you're different than other ISD members."

"You said that, technically."

"And you agreed. So how are you different? I need to know I can trust you, because I have something extremely serious to discuss."

"Who says I can trust *you?*" She remained silent for a moment. Walid went back to chopping carrots.

"Do you really think I'd come here at four in the morning if I was messing with you?" He put his knife down again and filled two glasses with water, handing her one. She ignored the offer and headed toward the door. Walid ran after her.

"Wait…" he stepped between Grace and the front door. "Grace, I'm trying to figure out your intentions here, that's all. I have a feeling you know why I'm different from the others, given you seem to be questioning my loyalty. So unless I'm way off base here, I can only surmise that you feel the same way." He watched her intently, fearing a negative response. Instead, she appeared relieved.

"I knew it! This is so great!"

"Well, now that we understand each other, I suggest we celebrate," he said sarcastically, fetching the water glasses from the kitchen. *Women…Do they ever get to the point?*

"I think we do, actually. You're not loyal to ISD!"

"Keep your voice down!" Walid said, pointing a carrot stick at her.

She approached him and looked directly in his eyes. "And neither am I. Which is what brings me here at 4:00 a.m."

Walid wanted to dance in excitement. *That'd probably freak her out.* He never would have imagined someone else in ISD feeling the same way he did. He had grown to love and respect Amin, but it was quite another thing to find someone who knew exactly what he was going through. "Go on…"

"Walid, we have so much to discuss! Don't you see? We both want the same thing."

"A cup of coffee?"

"We want to take down ISD," she whispered. "And that's exactly what we're going to do!"

Walid sat in one of his kitchen stools but could not find his voice. *It's not possible,* he thought. *It would take an army.*

She sat in the stool next to him. "I think I'll take that coffee now."

CHAPTER 10

Holes in the Desert

Padema was only thirteen the day that her father received a rare opportunity. That same morning, she had traveled at least two miles to barter for fresh food and supplies for her family. She found herself skipping, giddy about her father's business success, which would at last deliver their family from this impoverished neighborhood. They made a meager living by selling spices and trading items at a nearby souk in Tataouine—a small desert town in southern Tunisia.

She pushed her way through hordes of people purchasing fabrics, bread, spices, and other supplies in the souk. Fatima held her nose to the resist the urge of stopping at her favorite tent selling treats like baklava, chocolates, and other sweets. The market was swamped, as it usually was on Saturday mornings when locals and travelers from across the largely isolated wastelands of southern Tunisia came to trade, eat, and socialize. Finally, she reached the produce stand.

"Good day to you, sweety," a woman said, taking Padema's empty bag. "What will it be today? The usual? Perhaps we can sneak some sweets in there."

"Please!" She beamed.

"Oh, do we have some news? You're extra chipper today."

"Yes, Baba, I'm in a hurry today. Father was invited to Tunis. We just need a few things before we leave."

"How exciting! Business?"

"Yes. He's sharing his ideas with the ministry."

"Well, don't you forget about us little people when you go out there now," the woman said, brushing Padema's hair out of her face.

"Of course not. He's doing this for people like us."

"I know, sweety," she said as she handed a full bag back to Padema. "This one's on me."

"But I brought money. You can't afford that."

"I sure can, love. The Lord always provides. Especially when we give."

Padema hugged the old woman and took her bag, thinking about Tunis. She had only been there once in her life, but its touristy, lavish ambiance excited her more than any place she had ever been. The city was exotic to her—hosting world heritage sites, museums, and upscale restaurants along the shores of the Mediterranean Sea. In just two days, her whole family would be staying at the Hotel Paris, a luxury hotel known for housing expatriates and named to reflect the rich culture that endured since the days of French colonialism.

She strolled back to her family's village while balancing a bag full of fresh vegetables, spices, and grains on her head, her mind swirling with her future life in Tunis.

Padema stopped in her tracks and dropped her bag. Tomatoes and cucumbers rolled down the hill behind her. Thick black smoke was rising from over the hilltop in front of her. *My village!* She gasped and ran to the top of the hill. Below, her family's tent had become a pillar of fire—three men wielding torches scarred her vision. She screamed into her hands. Padema felt as if she was tearing in two—wanting to run to her family, wanting to flee into hiding. She hesitantly chose to hide behind a nearby tree until the men left.

— — — — — — — — — — — — — — — — — — —

Grace stopped talking, and Walid placed his hand on her shoulder. "I'm sorry, that's terrible," he said.

"My family tried to escape. Mom, Dad, Asma—she was only eight—the men wouldn't let them. I never forgot their faces. Anyway, I slept in the sand that night. Didn't have anywhere else to go. The very next day, the same men returned and found me. Took me to a training camp. They told me some pathetic lie about how robbers had raided and killed my family, and they were too late to save anyone. Probably their way of making me feel indebted to them for 'rescuing' me."

"Did you ever tell them?"

"That I knew they killed my family? They would have killed me too."

"Good point...why was your family going to Tunis?"

"Dad was an exceptional businessman. The nomadic life was never for him. He met a man in the souk one day who invited him to share his ideas in Tunis after he talked for a while about economizing cities in southern Tunisia. Could have created a whole new way of life for the people there."

"Maybe you'll get to share them someday." He squeezed her hand hopefully. "I wonder if ISD found out about his plan.

You know as well as I do that they have a vested interest in keeping that area impoverished."

"Probably," she agreed. "I'm just happy he was saved, though I wasn't at the time." She looked at Walid to gauge his reaction, her voice became more sanguine. "So here's the kicker. When I was twenty-five, ISD sent me on a recon mission in Paris, sent to scope out ISD's next target. Well, I did my recon all right! I marched straight into the target, DGSE headquarters, and turned myself in."

"French intelligence?" Walid was shocked at her bravery.

"What did I have to lose? I expected the worst, but long story short, they wanted to use me as a double agent. So, I started providing them intel. Told me they've never had anyone so entrenched in the group! We've already disrupted several plots directed against European targets. And the best part is that ISD has no idea about any of this!" she chuckled and shook her head, seemingly nonchalant about telling another ISD member that she was a double.

"I knew I couldn't trust you."

Grace looked at him, startled.

He held his fake scowl as long as he could, but when he lost it in a laugh, she snatched up a tomato and threatened to throw it at his head.

"No? Well, what's your story, Mr. Hardened ISD Man?"

"I want to tell you...but curfew's almost over. We can't risk anyone seeing you leave this place. Grace, are you serious about trying to take down ISD? As in the entire group? That's a lot different than stopping a few attacks from happening."

"A few?" she said indignantly. "More than you think! ISD is planning this type of stuff all the time!"

"Okay, but even if you stopped hundreds, how are we going to take down a group that has an army of loyal followers, not to mention hundreds of trained snipers and assassins?"

"Very carefully."

"Oh, now I understand."

"Walid, I've given this a lot of thought. Don't write it off. We should discuss it again soon when we have more time."

"If only time was a commodity."

Grace rolled her eyes. "Don't be a Debbie Downer, Walid!"

Walid laughed. "I didn't know people younger than fifty said that…"

"I'm just saying, open your mind. And besides, you're missing an important key."

"A key to what?"

"To our grand scheme!"

"Oh, it's *our* scheme now?" He shook his head.

"The key is collaboration. So of course we're not going to do this alone, right? Between the two of us, our contacts are pretty amazing, don't cha think?"

He liked her boldness and certainty about all this, though he felt fearful about the inherent danger in such a plan. "My contacts? Who might that be?"

"Your church, of course!"

"What? How did you know about the church? And what are they gonna bring to a fight? Prayer?" he said, quickly regretting his sarcasm. As Amin had been telling him for the last several weeks, he should never underestimate the power of prayer.

"Walid, my guys have people all over the place. And if you don't know what that church of yours is up to, you really need to go back and find out."

A distant siren signaled the end of curfew. Walid and Grace said their good-byes, and she left immediately to avoid being seen. The guards were rarely outside at the early morning siren, but Walid watched from behind his window shades to ensure Grace made it out of sight safely. He felt as though it should be time for bed, and yet the sun was hailing the new day. He made a fresh pot of coffee and dialed Amin's number. He knew he needed sleep but was too excited and confused to do so now. More than anything, he needed answers.

— — — — — — — — — — — — — — — — —

At half past ten, Walid sat near the back of an American restaurant in the fourth district. He and Amin had grown accustomed to staggering their arrival time to avoid being spotted together on the streets, which were monitored far more systematically than any location indoors. Walid gazed out the window and saw the church in the distance, looking as powerful as ever against the backdrop of the shining sea.

Amin walked in, told the waiter to bring them two cappuccinos, and sat with Walid.

"My friend! It's so good to see you," Amin said.

"Amin, if I have any more caffeine today, I'm gonna have a heart attack."

Amin chuckled. "Choose your words wisely, they're powerful!" Walid always felt as though he was talking to a philosopher when he spoke with Amin.

"Okay, fine," Walid said, eager to start asking questions. "Look, I need to talk to you about something. One of my colleagues came and spoke with me last night."

"A colleague?"

"Yeah, her name's Grace."

"Oh, a woman," he said with an awkward insinuation.

"Oh come on, Amin." They paused when the waiter brought cappuccinos. *Fantastic, more caffeine…* Amin matched Walid's apprehensive expression as he spent the next few minutes summarizing his discussion with Grace, focusing chiefly on Grace's role as a double agent.

"And you believe she's telling you the truth," Amin asked.

"Well, yeah, I mean, I guess…"

"Don't take offense, dear friend. I'm merely seeing how you feel about her intentions given your emotional investment."

"I'm not invested!" Walid said. "I believe she's telling the truth. When I was younger, I met my recruiter in a mosque, excited by the intrigue and clandestine nature of the ISD life. He promised many things he could never make good on. After meeting him a few times, I told him I had to stop since my father wouldn't support me. Days later, he was killed by my mother. The only option I had left was to join." He stopped to sip his cappuccino, collecting his thoughts.

"They killed him, didn't they," Amin said sympathetically.

"There was never any proof, but they had to be behind it! I always expected they talked my mom into it. The only impediment to my indoctrination, destroyed merely days before they came to collect me. Too convenient, you know."

"This is what they're programmed to do, Walid. It's going to be very important in the future to forgive them," Amin said.

Walid looked at him for a moment and raised both eyebrows; that was not the response he anticipated. "Why do you say things like that? Like you know some secret about my future."

Amin sat back and finished his drink. "I believe God brought you into my life for a reason. I truly believe we will play a big part in each other's lives in the very near future."

"So what's the secret?" Walid asked.

Amin crossed his arms and laughed. "I don't have some big secret. God speaks to us through the Holy Spirit. And now that you're saved, He will speak to you too. You just need to take the time to listen."

"I'll work on it."

"It doesn't have to be work. Just listen and don't worry, you'll hear from Him."

"All right, Obi-Wan," Walid said. He leaned forward and lowered his voice. "And that's not what I meant when I asked about your secret. Grace told me your church was up to something. Look, we haven't known each other long, and I know you probably don't trust me fully yet, but we talked about"— he leaned over so close that Amin could feel his breath on his face—"destroying ISD."

Amin's countenance grew ten shades more serious. He looked out the window toward the church.

"Listening to God?" Walid said, trying to lighten the conversation he had clearly just killed.

Amin did not return his smile this time. "In fact, I am," he said as he looked over toward the waiter. "Someone's listening. We need to go," Amin said quietly. He wrote on a small piece of paper, passed it to Walid, and exited the cafe.

"What?" Walid said aloud to himself. He looked over at the waiter, who averted his eyes quickly. *Oh no*, he thought. *He's right, we've been made.*

Walid waited until he saw Amin turn down the church road, which blocked him from view due to the high berms on either side of the road. Then he followed, scanning the streets for any possible tails. He looked back once more to see the waiter on his cell phone. He unwrapped the paper Amin gave him. "Look for the hole in the ground, and let go."

— — — — — — — — — — — — — — — — — —

Walid turned onto the narrow path leading to the church. After a short distance, he reached the berms, which were around a hundred meters long and concealed his position from town. He moved slowly, scanning the ground and trying to appear casual even though there was nobody in sight. He didn't see anything that even resembled a hole.

Suddenly, a few feet in front of him, he saw the Earth move as dirt became slightly displaced in a roughly three-by-three square foot area. He stopped in his tracks and shook his head, looking around again to ensure nobody was watching him. Perhaps the caffeine was really getting to him!

He stared at the area and it moved slightly a second time. This time, he could see a more distinct square-shaped outline. He knelt down to clear the sand away from the area. Even with the sediment completely displaced, the panel matched almost perfectly with the ground. Walid felt around the outside of the square and finally reached a small area where his right hand fell below the surface. He felt a button slightly under the square and pushed it, causing it to sink. Walid stepped back quickly and his eyes grew wide. When the movement stopped, he stepped closer and looked down into the hole, seeing nothing but darkness. *Well, I found the hole…Now what? Let go of what?*

"Hello?" he said down into the hole as he kneeled in a defensive position, half expecting some giant snake to jump out of the hole. He knew he could thank all the sci-fi movies he watched for that ludicrous thought. He heard faint noises coming from within the hole. Walid felt around the dirt and reached what felt like a stepladder. *Who goes down into a random hole? This is stupid!* his training was telling him. And yet, he felt a strange peace about it. *This has to be the entrance.*

He lowered one foot into the hole until his shoe found a ladder. He very slowly commenced his descent. The ladder felt wobbly, as though it wasn't touching the ground. He spotted a cross etched into a panel at the top of the ladder. He continued descending. Once his head fell below ground level, he heard the faint rumble of mechanical movement and looked up to see the square panel move back into place. The sunlight faded until it was pitch black. His heart beat quickly as he clung desperately to the cold, metal ladder.

Walid heard the buzz of old lights switch on, illuminating the tunnel just enough to see a meter below him. After moving down a few more steps, he reached a point of no return; he couldn't feel any more steps under him! *Maybe this wasn't Amin after all.* For all he knew, this pit could go down farther than he'd like to imagine; many old, abandoned well shafts were covered up for this very reason. *It has to be Amin. He said, "Let go."*

With no other choice in sight, Walid let go of his feet so he was only hanging on by his hands on the lowest bar, hoping that he would be able to feel something, anything! His feet dangled in the cold air. At least if he died now, he knew where he was going. He said a quick prayer and tried to pull himself back up with no luck. He hung on a while longer until his hands gave out, and he fell into nothingness.

CHAPTER 11

The Rescuers

Walid waved his hands wildly as he fell through cobwebs and small roots jutting out from the sides of the hole. *This is it,* he thought, praying for the Lord to spare his life. *Why would Amin lead me into a trap?*

Finally, he landed in a net that broke his fall but trapped him like an animal stepping into a booby trap. He could see the bottom. He reached for his pocket knife and cut the net, falling to ground just a few feet below. Walid stood up and winced, his ankle complaining. He could barely make out dimly lit wall lights leading down a tunnel.

As he started hobbling down the passageway, he heard the faint sounds once again; only this time he heard something far more disturbing: the sound of footsteps clinking toward him quickly. Walid came to a sharp left turn and flattened himself as much as possible against the wall. The steps became louder as the person grew closer; Walid feared that his heartbeat could actually be heard. The person ran right past Walid and stopped suddenly, reaching for some kind of weapon in his holster.

"Walid?" the person whispered loudly.

"Are you kidding me?" Walid said directly behind Amin. Amin whipped around and instinctively threw a punch, which Walid blocked. "Stop, it's me!"

"Why were you hiding? You scared me!" he said apologetically.

"Hiding? Amin, are you crazy? How should I have known it was you?"

"I figured someone as smart as you would figure it out," Amin joked. "Sorry, I had to be so cloak-and-dagger. I wanted to be extra careful in case that guy grabbed you, or my note."

"And what kind of entrance is that? That has to be a good thirty-meter drop."

"Well, well, I did warn you about the drop. We need to fix the net. Though I suppose on the off chance someone from ISD discovered the entrance before you, they'd never just drop into a dark abyss. Who does that?" he said with a hearty laugh.

How can I be mad at this man?

Amin embraced him. Walid, still unaccustomed to such open shows of physical affection, tried to return the embrace. And failed. Awkwardly. "Come on, I have something to show you." Amin grabbed Walid's arm and pulled him along then paused when he noticed the limp.

"Oh man, casualty of the net, huh? We'll need to find something for that ankle of yours."

"So...what is this place?" Walid asked as the two made their way down the pathway.

"Oh, this one's been here for years, but there are so many more."

"Creepy tunnels?"

"Walid, this 'creepy tunnel' leads to something very unique. The tunnel network in this region is expansive. Most were used for smuggling, weapons storage, some were old government bunkers abandoned after the regime fell. Of course we needed a lot of help to make them useful."

"Useful for what?" Walid asked.

Amin stopped, smiling from ear to ear. The lighting and noises were more distinctive now as they approached a cavernous opening. "For many things…perhaps most importantly, we use them as safe houses for the underground church."

"A safe house for the church?"

"Among other things…"

"What are you hiding from me?" Walid tried to look over his shoulder to see the large room just beyond them.

"Come, my dear friend." Walid never grew tired of hearing someone refer to him that way. "There's so much to discuss! And there's a few people I want you to meet."

Amin led him into the vast cavern, which looked almost futuristic due to the steel reinforcements forming a dome above them. There were several large television and computer screens lining many of the walls and another tunnel leading out the other side. People worked busily in the space and greeted Walid and Amin as they walked by. Amin stopped at a table where a man operated two giant screens; one appeared to be a social media site while the other included some kind of satellite footage.

"Stephen! Greetings, my brother," Amin said.

"And to you." The man gave Amin a fist bump. "Dude, I've got something amazing to show you later. It should save us a lot of time—a little thing I like to call Voltron."

Amin turned to Walid and rolled his eyes, "Stephen likes to name his programs."

"Oh wow, hey there," Stephen said, thrusting his arm out toward Walid, his eyes glazing over as though being starstruck.

"Hey," Walid said. "You okay?"

"Of course, sorry! It's just...I feel like I know you."

"Maybe you do," Walid said sarcatically.

"Well, to some extent. We used to follow you."

Walid turned his eyes away, uncertain how to react to a man telling him he used to hunt him. *First time for everything.*

"I'm afraid I'm too blunt at times."

"At *times?*" Amin said.

"Anyway, how do ya like the place?" Stephen said, desperate for a topic change.

"Very much," Walid said. "Though, I'm a little confused. How did you guys throw this all together?"

"Oh, it's an awesome story," said Stephen. "Allow me."

"Better pull up a seat. This one likes to talk," Amin said.

"Nothing about this place is thrown together. Back in 2007, before I got hooked up with this crew, I found myself in some trouble. Now, this is crazy, right? So I deploy to Libya on a strike mission with SOCOM—that's US Special Forces. Long story short, mission is a bust, and I find myself captured at the mercy of ISD. Come to find out, they don't have much mercy..." Walid looked down as though ashamed at his association with the group. He wondered how Stephen would react when he told him.

"But you'll never guess who I met at the prison camp!" he said, looking directly at Amin.

"I could probably guess..." Walid said.

"This guy!" he pointed at Amin with both hands.

"It's been quite a journey since then, my friend," Amin said.

"So how did you escape? And why were you there, Amin?" Walid said. He had never been part of a kidnapping cell but was intrigued to be talking with former captives.

Stephen held his hands out as though prompting Amin to speak. "It was truly nothing short of a miracle. I had been in the camp for days already. I was with an Algerian convoy that was assisting US forces on a counterterrorism mission. Well, ISD received intel about our mission somehow and set up an ambush for us. We took heavy fire and saw no other choice than to surrender. They captured us and brought us to a makeshift camp in Benghazi. I knew they were keeping us alive for a reason—probably to create a hostage video and make some quick cash. Anyway, I spent that whole time praying, even out loud at times, which only seemed to infuriate my hostage takers."

"Then I showed up!" Stephen said. "I wasn't praying though…"

"Not *yet*," Amin said. "Stephen and eight others from his group, US and Brits, were captured in Darnah and brought to the camp. It wasn't a pretty situation. The place was absolutely squalid, and they were barely feeding us enough to keep us alive. Anyway, the low-level ISD members guarding us were growing tired of our daily discussions about God."

"They were pissed! Amin saved us though. Most of us started following Jesus," Stephen interrupted again.

Amin laughed. "God saved you. He just used me to do His will. Anyway, the guards became complacent. At first they would try to beat us to stop the talking. Eventually they just gave up. Probably realized we weren't gonna stop on their account. But man, God sure gave us strength! He lifted our spirits in the worst of circumstances!"

"How did you escape though?" Walid asked.

"I'm getting there...the Lord brought to memory a passage from 2 Chronicles 20 when God confused and defeated Israel's enemies. I prayed every day for this quietly. Then one day, as a group of twelve ISD members drove to the camp for resupply, one of them walked right over to me and held a gun to my head. He said 'Get on your knees. Who are you to sit here day after day blaspheming Allah?' Well, I refused. I told them I would only bow before my God, who sent his very Son to save me!"

Awestruck by Amin's boldness, Walid could not help but imagine dramatic film music playing behind these scenes. Amin continued, "I knew the danger in this, but I also knew God had made promises to me through the memory of His word! He told me I'd be leaving. I listened to Him as carefully as I could."

"This part is epiiiiic!" Stephen said.

"The ISD men just stood there. I could have easily doubted at that point, but I refused to believe the lie that I misheard. Then after more than a minute of silence, the man lowered his gun slowly. He reached into his pocket and gave me the keys to his vehicle. God did just as he did in the days of old! He confused the enemy. Don't you see what exciting times we live in?" Amin could hardly contain himself.

Walid was speechless. He had never seen anything like this while following Allah. In fact, the emirs would often thank Allah for obvious victories, claiming them to be proof of his power when they overcame weaker, defenseless villages. Some power, Walid thought...

"So…you drove off. How'd you wind up here?"

"Well, before we drove off, I told the ISD guys we'd come back to save them if they desired. It didn't even make sense at the time, but I felt it was part of God's plan."

"After that, we started a new mission," Stephen continued. "One that involved taking down ISD by saving victims of terrorism. And yeah, that includes the terrorists themselves who repent. People like you, Walid."

Guess Amin told him already. Walid knew God had forgiven him but still didn't like others acknowledging his ISD association. He felt ashamed. Stephen noticed and quickly tried to rectify his statement. "Oh, I didn't mean that personally. Amin told me about you already. We're thrilled at how God has turned your life around!"

Walid had never met a more accepting group of people. "I still don't fully understand…how do you do it?"

Walid felt a tap on his shoulder. He whipped around and his eyes grew wide.

"Hey, stranger," said Grace.

"What are you doing here?" He pulled her in for a hug and released her quickly. *Too much,* he thought.

"I work here, part-time of course. Well, triple part-time! When I'm not at the agency or getting ready to end the world for the emir. No big deal."

"When do you sleep?"

"I'd like to say, I'll sleep when I'm dead— but that doesn't seem as funny as it used to, given our present circumstances. I feel like it's only a matter of time before they find out what we're up to."

"I'm not worried about it," Walid said. Grace made a dramatic motion like she was taken aback. "I'm just saying, we have a lot more going for us than they do."

"Guys, we got a hit," Stephen said as he examined his computer screens.

"A hit?" Walid said. "Just what kind of operation are you running?"

"Dude, it's fine," Stephen said, laughing. "A hit on our social media site. This is seriously awesome, get a load of this." He motioned for Walid to come closer. Walid was already starting to like this man. Stephen—like Amin—treated him like a friend, no questions asked. Walid read the screen closely, "'The Rescuers'...oh, like that children's movie!" he said jokingly.

"Yeah, well, we needed a name, and it fits, right?" Stephen said. "It took a while to get this running, but the site is becoming prolific through word of mouth! There are three portals you can enter, see? One if you have knowledge of the location of kidnapped people, the second if you are the person who needs to be saved, and the third to educate the world on these issues. There's training on biblical truths and even discussion groups where Muslims can speak to Christians about the issues."

"This is incredible," Walid said. "But I don't understand the second portal. How would you get to a computer if you need help?"

"This one is my favorite, personally," Amin said. "It's for anyone who needs to be saved, but mainly for members of ISD."

"What?" Walid said. "How so?"

"You know better than I do that lots of ISD members are recruited by force. These guys have no alternatives though," Amin said. "Well, we provide them alternatives through rehabilitation, including employment. This safe house is just one of many existing throughout the region, and our enterprise is growing. We give them incentives for leaving. Not to mention, many former members just like you have had dreams and visions of Jesus Christ and want to learn more or get out!"

Stephen continued, "So they can get all their questions answered in our forums and post coordinates in the second portal where they need evacuation."

Grace touched Walid's arm and smiled, "Why so skeptical?" She could see his face hardening as they spoke and wondered if this was all making Walid uneasy, given he was still technically a member of ISD.

"Grace, it's not that," Walid said. He turned to address the group. "I just can't help but wonder about the practical aspects of this enterprise. If your site is widely known, how do you know one of the emir's cronies won't post a bogus location as a trap?"

"We don't," Amin said. "But we sure have help! You haven't met all of our teams yet. Follow me."

They walked toward a second cavern as red hazard lights started to blink. Walid expected to hear a blaring siren similar to the one he heard the night of the raid, but there was no sound. Nobody seemed to be bothered by the lights but started talking in hushed tones.

"Don't worry about it, it's just the Watchmen," Grace said.

Walid shook his head. "The longer I'm here, the more I feel like I'm in a superhero movie. Who are the Watchmen?" he matched everyone's hushed tone of voice. "And why are we whispering?"

"The Watchmen raise the alert if they see intruders. It's usually nothing—could be someone interested in the church. The lights will turn blue if they suspect malicious intent."

"How does a church pay for all of this?" Walid asked in shock.

"Lots of ways, really. People from all over the globe provide support. And it doesn't hurt to have agencies like mine helping out."

"They openly assist a religious group?"

"Well, it's not the religion they're sponsoring. They've seen the progress we're making, and we all have the same goal. We're partners to them. Partners who aren't bogged down in politics like most. Quicker wins for them, you know?"

Walid nodded as they continued into the next room. He scanned the room, which was slightly smaller than the first and covered with overlaid maps and large flat screens displaying satellite imagery. His eyes met those of another man sitting in a desk chair across the room; a man he recognized. Walid felt his heart sink. His hands almost mechanically formed fists. He did an about-face and planned to leave the room until Amin caught him by the arm.

"Please, we must move forward," Amin said quietly. Walid paused for a moment to collect himself and turned to face the man who recruited him so many years ago.

CHAPTER 12

The Power of Voltron

Walid stared at his former recruiter as though he was only person in the room, shocked to find him in such a place without some kind of restraints. He didn't greet Walid as others had since his arrival in the safe house. In fact, he looked down quickly upon recognizing Walid and started typing on his laptop.

Amin broke the awkward silence. "So…this is the OPS control room. You know how I said we ask the people who need rescuing for coordinates? Well, this is where we plug them in, assess the location, and deploy teams."

Walid nodded. He hadn't anticipated how difficult it would be to see this man—a man he had always assumed was responsible, if not indirectly, for his father's death. He stood there as though waiting for the man to say something, anything.

Walid walked toward the man to provoke some kind of response. "It's been a while." The man said nothing and started typing faster on his laptop. Walid closed the laptop cover.

The man finally looked Walid in the face and sat back in his chair, crossing his arms. "What do you want from me?"

I don't know, Walid thought. His emotions changed from anger to sympathy after noticing the man's dejected countenance. He looked like a different man from the one who recruited him years ago. His hubris had been replaced with despair.

"Nothing."

"Eli is part of the operations team," Amin interjected, leading Walid away from Eli, who went back to typing. "If somebody provides a location—the team assesses it, studies the groups in the area, picks a neutral location, posts the location and date-time-group, and deploys."

"You make it sound so simple," Walid said.

"Never said it was simple. Effective though. If we don't get any hits for a while, we pick the location and deploy a team to visit local tribes in the area. Building these relationships has proven invaluable so far."

"And the tribes are receptive?" Walid asked halfheartedly, his attention torn between Amin and Eli.

"Not always right away. But we bring peace offerings, and Bibles of course, which helps. You'd be amazed at some of the testimonies we've received! Once we gave just one Bible to the Phantom tribal leader, and he ended up saving the whole village." Amin's excitement was becoming more palpable.

"That's brilliant," Walid said. And it really was. He knew that tribal leaders have tremendous influence over hundreds, if not thousands, of people. He had observed tribesmen frequently following the direction and even belief system of their leaders. If the leaders follow God, the rest will follow suit— that's the theory he'd come to accept. Not to mention, tribes control massive amounts of territory in the Near East, and often wield more influence and military strength than official security forces. Walid knew this part firsthand. Oftentimes, ISD would make deals with local tribes, offering them some kind of reward in exchange for their protection. Get these people on your side and you've got power.

"Great, you're on the team then!" Amin said.

"Wait, what?" Walid asked. He looked over at Eli once again, who appeared to be typing gibberish into his laptop. Walid couldn't imagine having to work with this man on a regular basis. He briskly walked out of the room.

"Hey, hold up!" Amin motioned for Walid to follow him into a small, makeshift conference room with a missing door. The room was empty aside from a small table, chairs, and a coffee machine. The essentials.

"Eli mentioned the history between you two when I told him you were coming. I should have warned you he was here. Forgive me, brother… Can you at least try talking with him?"

"I did try."

"You approached him like an interrogator!"

"Okay, fine, so I could soften my approach. But, Amin, can't you see the warning signs he's exhibiting?"

"Of course I can. He's struggling, anyone can see that."

"And you're trusting him to lead a ground team? He's not stable."

"Walid, that's why I need you on the team. Eli reached out to us for help. Just like you, he was visited by Jesus in his dreams not once, but seven times, one night after another!"

"Seven times? He only came to me once."

"It took seven visits before Eli made a move, before he reached out and joined this team. You? Only one."

"So…you think he'll be OK?"

"I believe he will. Self-condemnation is keeping him in chains. He hasn't fully grasped that God has already forgiven and forgotten his sins. Your forgiveness can only help him at this time." Amin grabbed Walid's shoulder and shook it playfully.

Walid rolled his eyes and pushed him off. "All right, all right, I'll talk to him."

As they entered the common area, Amin's smile grew.

"Stop," Walid said. *Is he taking any of this seriously?* Walid wondered. Though he appreciated Amin's optimism, it took some getting used to. Walid's former colleagues were an entirely different breed in the field.

"Stop what?"

"You're always smiling. It's weird. Doesn't anything get you down?"

"Hardly," Amin said. "I was just thinking about Eli. What a story, right? I can almost see it as a headline: 'ISD Recruiter Converts, Starts Working for Former Enemy.'"

Walid nodded. "What a story…" He thought for a moment about Stephen's website, and how powerful this story truly was. "I think I have an idea." He turned around and yelled "Stephen!" only to find Stephen's face a few inches from his own.

"Come on, Walid, I miss you too, but this is just embarrassing." Walid punched him in the shoulder playfully. "By the way, I totally was not listening…nope! Just walking by. Funny timing, right?"

"Sure you were," Walid said, grasping his arm to explain his idea. "So I was just thinking, some of the converts here have amazing stories. High-level ISD members and leaders are reforming, converting, trying to save lives…How powerful would it be to tell these stories online?"

"Oh, man." Stephen clapped Walid's shoulder. "We're on the same wavelength, Walid. I'm devising a little program that I like to call"—he warped his voice to sound like a cartoon villain and growled—"*Voltron!*"

"Oh boy…*here* we go," Amin said.

"Voltron is a bug. It detects when someone tries to hack the system. Hides our IP and sends a bug to their system."

"What's that got to do with telling stories?" Walid asked.

"Well, we can get more creative with this, but for now the bug it sends is what I like to call a 'banner of love.' Literally just a giant banner that goes across their screen with the most basic gospel message: John 3:16, along with a simple prompt: 'If in doubt, ask God to reveal himself.' If they click the link for more information, it brings them to our education page. Anyway, long story short, we can send stories or anything else we want to."

"And they'll have a heck of a time deleting that banner!" Amin said.

Walid tried to imagine the looks on his former coworker's faces. "Won't that just piss them off even more?"

"That's not the goal," Amin said. "We're praying for God to soften their hearts so they'll be inexplicably receptive to the messages they receive."

"That's great and all, but sending stories directly to their site will just paint a target on the storyteller's head," Walid said.

"So we'll make it a separate tab on the page," Stephen suggested. "There's so much we can do with this! Can you even imagine the impact it would have?"

"All right. Who can we get to risk their lives to kick off this project?" Walid asked.

"Grace, come over here and talk some sense into this man!"

Grace walked over, and they caught her up on the conversation.

"I'm not saying I disagree," Walid said. "It's just...they'd be putting their lives in danger. No way ISD wouldn't go after them if they saw the broadcast."

"There's already a hit out on their lives for leaving the group," Grace said.

"Still..."

"Still, it requires bravery. I'm thinking of doing it, actually. You know, after we get back from Syria."

Walid wondered if she was just baiting him. "Well, I've always admired your bravery."

"Um, Syria?" Stephen asked, looking at Amin to see if this registered with him.

"You didn't tell them?" Grace asked, raising her voice in surprise.

"I planned to!" Walid said. "Amin, I should have told you earlier." He felt he owed more to Amin than anyone else. That, in respect for all that Amin had risked, he should exercise complete honesty.

"Go on," Amin said.

Walid started from the beginning, detailing the entire meeting with the emir in Tripoli. "We leave in three days, and we'll be back the very next day."

"You really shouldn't go through with this," Grace urged Walid.

He was surprised by her protest. "Where's this coming from?"

"I have no choice. I still work for French intelligence, and they expect me to go undercover to get the mission details. You're under no obligation though! The emir is already suspicious of you. This could be nothing more than a trap. Just get out while you can."

"No, I need to go. And besides, I can't let you go alone."

"I think I can handle myself." She tried to sound tough, though was clearly touched by Walid's feelings for her.

"No, you can't," Amin said. Everyone turned to him in surprise. "No, I mean, you can't go alone! This is perfect, can't you see?"

"No, not particularly," Walid said. *Here we go, more of Amin's weird excitement over dangerous things...*

"You guys go, play the role, do what you have to do. You're about to hear ISD's strategy for the biggest attack they've ever planned. This puts you in the perfect position."

"I like where you're going with this," Grace said. "So when we get back, we can brainstorm a way to stop them."

"Exactly!" Amin said. "Look how many people we have in this place alone." Walid surmised there were close to a hundred people throughout the entire station. "There are hundreds more in different stations. Not to mention, we have the Lord to guide us." Amin did a premature victory dance.

"Amin, I love your enthusiasm, but this is a really sophisticated group."

"Well, so are we!" said Walid. Grace looked at him and exaggerated her shock, though everyone was surprised by his reaction. "He's right, we can do this! We're the ones on high ground here."

"Wow, this doesn't sound like the ultrarisk averse strategist I know," she said.

"I'm full of surprises."

"Well, what do I have to lose? Actually, don't answer that… I'm in."

CHAPTER 13

Ushering the Mahdi

Walid and Grace groaned as the Humvee trekked over rocky terrain in Syria. They were still blindfolded. Walid's frustration was rising. He raised his hands to his blindfold, only to be met with a swift blow to his head by what felt like the buttstock of a weapon.

"All right, all right!" Walid said, clasping his head in his hands. "Figured you guys were lost."

After another few minutes, the man in the passenger's seat finally removed their blindfolds. "The emir will be pleased to see you," he said impassively.

"Yes, and he's treated us like valuable visitors so far!" Walid said.

"I've been warned about you, Walid," he said. His laugh was sinister as he leaned back in his seat. Walid was a little surprised that he knew his name. *And who warned him?* he wondered. "But who am I to question the emir's decisions?"

"Yes, who *are* you?" Walid said, causing the man to clench his fists. The driver hit the passenger's seat to get his attention.

"Don't talk to them! They are to arrive unharmed." The driver's voice was more compassionate than the other man's, whose scowling stare made Walid turn his face to Grace. She was ignoring the ruckus, looking intently out the window. There was no coast this time, only desert and a few warehouses.

After the vehicle stopped, the two were brusquely pushed out and led into the closest building. There was nothing remarkable about this place except for its stench; it smelled of a hundred camels, and yet there were none in sight. The inside of the warehouse looked like a hangar for small planes. In fact, there were two very small planes, possibly UAVs, in the back of the hangar covered by giant sheets.

A man in military fatigues walked through a door at the opposite end of the hangar and spoke loudly, echoing through the facility.

"Welcome, visitors!" His voice was warm, and his arms opened wide. As he grew closer, he looked younger than they had anticipated. A young man in his early forties, and handsome, except for a mark across his face as if he'd fought a wolverine.

"Walid, Grace." He shook their hands. "I trust you had a pleasant ride?"

"We made it just fine," said Grace.

"Of course," he said kindly. "I am Damon. Please, follow me. We have prepared a feast in your honor, and for those who will be joining you in this most special of missions!" His eyes were almost glowing. Walid and Grace looked at each other and smirked. Walid wanted to like this man but knew he was helping the emir, and as such, this was probably just a façade. Yet his charismatic demeanor put the two at ease, for now.

They exited and crossed a small sandy alcove. Damon made small talk the whole way. Walid and Grace said nothing to each other, knowing they wouldn't be able to discuss anything of value until they boarded the plane home.

They reached a second warehouse, and Damon pressed a button on a metallic contraption on his keychain, causing the doors to slowly open. The inside of the second building appeared nothing like the first. It was well fortified, such that Walid and Grace could hear nothing going on inside until the doors had opened. And yet, everything inside the facility seemed transitory, like it had been set up for this very occasion. The wooden tables were beautifully ornate, with designs that looked like gargoyles carved into the giant legs of each table. The chairs were plush with purple cushions, undoubtedly to signify royalty.

Walid and Grace were led to separate tables where they joined nine men and nine women. Nobody was talking. Some looked around the warehouse to appear occupied, others followed Walid and Grace with their eyes, most appeared anxious to hear the emir speak.

There was a larger, more lavish chair and table in the center of the room. Damon lingered for a moment by the entrance and scanned the group, as though trying to read everyone there. He locked the door and went to the lone chair. The design of this place, the robotic actions of the people, the entire situation seemed so unsettling to Walid.

"Esteemed guests," he started, his voice reverberating throughout the warehouse. "Peace be with you. Do not look so worried! You are all distinguished visitors, and you have all been gathered here for your unique talents."

Walid thought this man seemed quite well-spoken for an assistant, or butler, or whatever he was. The individuals around the room tried to appear calm but couldn't hide their discomfort. Walid noticed one man at his table who nodded his head in agreement about how awesome they were. *Where'd they find this one...*

Damon continued to walk about the room. "Friends, you are all most impressive! And I'm sure you have gathered that you are here today to receive instructions of the utmost importance!"

His voice sounded inspiring, though Walid and Grace knew better than to believe him. Waiters began to bring a delectable array of food as though on cue, serving each guest. The scent of char-grilled lamb, tahini, and spiced baba ganoush made his mouth water.

"Please, eat. We have little time, and must use it wisely." He walked over to the chair in the center of the room. "Oh, and how rude of me," he laughed. "Allow me to introduce myself. My name is Damon al-Sayid. I will be your host for this afternoon."

Walid and Grace looked at each other in surprise but quickly tried to hide their expressions. Al-Sayid himself, the emir of the entire ISD enterprise, had escorted them from their vehicle! *What a clever plan*, Walid thought. Appealing to the group through his false humility, making them feel like royalty.

Despite the instructions to remain calm, nobody spoke. This was one of the most awkward dinners Walid had ever attended. He looked at the emir, who had eaten nothing at all despite a full plate before him. *Is the food poisoned?* Walid wondered, though he knew that was highly improbable. After a few minutes, Damon arose and addressed the group from behind the table.

"Dear friends," he started. Walid was growing tired of this charade; clearly they were not friends. "I have brought you here because we are to change the course of history together. ISD's attacks have been reactive for far too long. Punitive but lackluster. No enterprising group has ever gone down in history for mediocrity. ISD will become a household name, and each of you is going to help me reach my place—*our* place of fame! People will come to know that they must follow Allah or perish."

Grace looked around at the women, all of whom appeared transfixed on this attractive man as he spoke, their eyes fiercely engaged on him. She worried for a moment that her lack of enthusiasm would be too obvious.

"Your mission, if of course you accept it, is to bring the West to its knees, that they should bow before Allah, before this group. This attack, my fierce warriors, will usher in the coming of the very Mahdi himself!" Walid felt his heart beat faster; he knew how grave this statement was. This was more serious than he thought. He knew that many in ISD believe they are living in the end of days—awaiting the coming of el-Mahdi, or the Messiah—who will force nonbelievers to either convert or die. The most concerning aspect of the emir's statement was that most believe the Mahdi will come only when the world is engulfed in chaos and carnage. An operation bringing about the Mahdi's return would be as significant as World War III.

"The plan is threefold," Damon continued. "The first attack will be led by Walid and will hit America in an area bursting with worldliness and tourism. Tens of thousands of people walk there daily. Just think about the scale and ease of this!"

Walid looked up in shock but said nothing; why was he the first to be called out?

"The second will be led by Mokhtar, who will lead the charge in this very country." Walid noticed Mokhtar's face drop from directly across the table, as though he had just received news of a close relative's death. The man maintained this expression for the remainder of Damon's speech. "This is a special, difficult mission, which I am trusting to your capable hands."

"And third, the grand finale, which will be led by Ari, will target a very important meeting of the European Union." Walid saw Ari raise his head proudly—the same man Walid believed to be utterly arrogant. "This, my friends, will be the location of our final base of operations. A grand symphony! I can almost hear the music playing as this beautiful chain reaction leads to the finale, followed by grandiose applause and fanfare." His eyes grew darker. *Oh brother,* Walid thought. *How much more self-indulgent can a man get?*

"As I said before, we will not force compliance. If there are concerns, I implore you to speak now."

"Sir," Mokhtar began cautiously. The entire room stared at him as though warning him to stop. "My family is Syrian."

"Which I don't hold against you," Damon said.

"I…I cannot do this to my home. My tribal line runs deep throughout this country. There will no doubt be collateral damage."

"And so what?" Damon said, sounding heartless in his quest for greatness. "Can you not see how this must happen to achieve a greater goal? We must bring the world to its knees! Are you not able to comprehend?"

Mokhtar looked down. "Sir, allow me to take another operation. Allow me to remove my family before this happens."

"Are you questioning my judgment?" Damon said calmly.

"Never, sir. But…I cannot do this to my family."

"Then your decision is final. I did give you the option, after all," Damon said, smiling at the man with no visible signs of anger. Mokhtar returned his gaze but said nothing in return. "As you wish. Allahu Akbar." He reached into his coat pocket for a gun and shot Mokhtar at his table without hesitation. "Any other concerns?" he asked. Walid barely heard Damon through the ringing in his ears; the sound of the gunshot still echoing throughout the warehouse.

Several people gasped but tried to control their shock. Walid couldn't avert his eyes from Mokhtar, who had fallen face-first into his tomato-basil soup. The blood from the wound in his forehead flowed down into his bowl. The men next to him pushed their soup aside; one tried to suppress his gag reflex. The group became so quiet you could hear the wind whistling through cracks in the warehouse.

"Very well then," he said with a smile. He turned to face a woman at Grace's table. "Fatima, the task is yours," he said. "If, of course, you are up for the task?"

"Yes, yes, of course," she said quickly. Walid hadn't noticed her when he first arrived but realized at that moment that he recognized her. Fatima was from the same branch and base in Libya as he and Grace. They had spoken on a few occasions, usually about her dream of owning her own business after rising through the ranks of ISD. He tried to imagine why she had been kept segregated from them, the only other two ISD members from Libya.

Damon interrupted his thoughts. "You will all receive further instructions, along with your teammates, as you depart. Now, arise."

Everyone stood instantly and walked toward the exit. "By the way," Damon said, "be sure to read your instructions before you board the plane. You will have approximately one hour to memorize the details. And of course, thank you for visiting."

Each person was handed a small tablet and boarded nineteen individual vehicles, which took them to the airport. Walid and Grace memorized their operations, handed the tablets back to their drivers, and boarded the plane. It may have been safe to talk, but they rather stared out the windows in silence.

— – — – — – — – — – — – — – — – — – — –

Back in Libya, the emir of ISD's Libya branch held a closed meeting with two other individuals. One of them was the waiter at the American bar near Amin's church.

"How can you be certain?" the emir asked the waiter.

"Emir, they were sitting together. I am certain of their connection. But it's worse than just that..." He appeared pleased with himself for what he was about to reveal. He took a small voice recorder out of his satchel and handed it to the emir. "Walid has committed the ultimate sin, the ultimate infidelity to not only ISD but to Islam!"

The emir pursed his lips and spoke through his clenched jaw. "What...did...he...do?"

The waiter knew better than to beat around the bush any longer. "He's planning to destroy ISD with the help of the church."

The emir stepped back for a moment and let out a condescending laugh. The waiter returned his laugh though didn't know what was so funny. He was afraid to say anything further.

"The church...is going to help Walid take down my enterprise? And you're raising this to me as a serious concern?"

"Emir, I don't mean to insult you! But we know where that pastor came from and what he's capable of. We've been letting him stay there unharmed, but who knows what he's been up to?" the waiter explained frantically, hoping to convince him of wrongdoing so he didn't get shot on site.

The emir grew gravely serious and paused a few moments. "I'm not convinced. Still...we must take precautions, for preservation's sake. Go, it's time to put some fire under their feet."

"As you wish," the waiter said as he walked out. The second man remained in the room with the emir.

"I have other plans for you," the emir said. "You have been faithful, haven't you? You will ensure that Walid carries out his task from Syria. He trusts you. You know how important this is, Bashir."

CHAPTER 14

Worshipful Warfare, Prayerful Weapons

Walid and Grace walked out of ISD's Tripoli compound after providing the emir with a back brief on Syria. This was the first step in their memorized protocols. The meeting was painful; Walid and Grace tried to match the emir's inflated exuberance as he reminded them how these operations would make ISD infamous. "Part of the history books!" he exclaimed. Walid felt sickened by such enthusiasm for something that would destroy countless innocent lives.

Walid and Grace ran serpentine through the streets to avoid any potential tails after leaving the gate. Once they felt safe, they ducked into an alleyway and embraced quickly.

"Walid, I don't even know what to say or do right now."

"We're going to figure this out, Grace. You must keep faith with me."

"I will. It's just...did you see the look on his face? On Damon's face? If I didn't already believe in angels and demons,

I would now. Nobody could be so peacefully maniacal without a demonic influence."

"I know…which is why we need to figure this out quickly. How are you feeling?" The two had barely slept since the meeting in Syria.

"Tired."

"How tired?"

"Why?" She saw the entreating look in his eyes and pretended to be more tired than she really was. "Let me guess. You want to go see Amin, don't you."

"So you agree!"

"I didn't say that," she laughed.

"Grace," he moved in close to her. "We can sleep when we're dead. Come on, let's go!"

"You know curfew's starting. Don't get reckless."

"I know. The alternate route to the safe house is near Amin's house, right? Let's just see if he's home."

The two made their way quietly down five blocks before entering Amin's neighborhood. They had only been to his house once before. It was moderately sized for the neighborhood, as nice as one could get here. Only ISD leaders and powerful militia members owned the villas that nobody else could afford.

As the duo made a ninety-degree turn onto Amin's street, they both gasped. Grace covered her face in her hands and Walid shook his head. "This isn't happening," he whispered.

He ran to the pile of ruins, and Grace quickly followed suit. Amin's house was nothing more than a giant pile of charred lumber. Walid yelled for him though he knew it was unsafe. If ISD discovered their connection, he would surely be next on their hit list. The two searched the rubble for only a few moments. Nothing in the building could have survived a fire like this. Walid picked up a small brown leather notebook and brushed ash from the cover. It looked like the same notebook Amin typically carried with him everywhere.

"Maybe he wasn't here," Grace said, her hands blackened with soot.

Walid wasn't prepared to deal with more heartache. "Yeah, no doubt," he said unconvincingly.

Grace walked back to the street and saw two uniformed men walking in their direction from several streets away. Whether they were militia men or ISD members, the encounter would likely be unpleasant. She ran to Walid and grabbed him by the arm, whispering loudly, "They're coming!"

Right as they reached the street, they heard one of the uniformed men yelling. "Hey! Hold it right there!" They were out past curfew now and could be arrested if caught.

"Run!" Walid said as they took off in a sprint and turned down the closest side street they could find. After weaving through a few streets, Grace spotted a familiar storefront—an antique store—just a block away.

As they neared the place, another uniformed man walked directly in their path from a perpendicular street. He looked young, probably in his early twenties and inexperienced. He hesitated as though completely caught off guard. Walid, however, kept running and knocked the wind out of him by shoving his shoulder straight into his abdomen. Grace typed in a keypad code to unlock the door, and they dragged the man inside. They pushed their way through a disorganized cluster of antique furniture; the musty, metallic smell made it difficult to inhale. Toward the back of the store, there was a wide bookcase with several old, weathered books and magazines tossed haphazardly on the shelves. *Who runs this place?* Walid wondered. Grace pushed a large, encyclopedic book toward the wall until they heard a click, which caused the shelves to slide open sideways, revealing an entrance to a dark hallway. "Get in!" she whispered loudly. Walid forced the young man through, and Grace shut the door behind them.

"We should be safe now," Grace said.

"Where are we? In a Sherlock Holmes movie?" Walid asked.

"You'll recognize this soon enough. More importantly, what should we do with Joe Bad Guy?"

"Joe? I'm Sayid! And I'm not one of the bad guys! Who are you? I'll have you reported!" the boy said, trying to sound intimidating. He was clearly no match for Walid's strength and had stopped struggling. Walid grabbed his radio and threw it against the brick wall, smashing it.

"Sure you will," Walid said, sounding far more intimidating. Grace shot him a look of disapproval. There was no point in frightening someone already at their mercy. "Look, we're not going to harm you," he said in a calmer tone.

"Yeah, I bet you'll treat me as good as that radio!"

"Come on, we don't have time for this," Grace said. Walid grabbed the boy by the arm and followed Grace to a small cavern, which opened into a room that Walid recognized. This was the same underground safe haven that he had fallen into several days earlier.

Stephen spotted them and ran over to hug them both simultaneously. The young man's collar was still in Walid's right hand, causing him to choke. "Oh, uh, hey there," Stephen said to him. "Guys? We'd kind of appreciate advance notice of guests."

"He's not a guest. It's a long story. Stephen, we just passed Amin's house..." Walid blurted out.

"So you know then," he said somberly.

Walid and Grace looked at each other as though about to break out in tears, if not for their unwelcome visitor. "Oh geez, he's not dead or anything," Stephen said.

"Come on, man! What are we supposed to think? So where is he?" Walid said.

"He's in a prayer meeting. I'll show you. Just...bring him for now, I guess."

"A prayer meeting...Now?" The more he grew in his walk with God, the more there was to learn. Why anybody would be in a prayer meeting at such a time was beyond him. Stephen led them to a moderately sized room that was completely filled with people. Walid scanned the room and saw Amin toward the front of the room worshipping. He had never seen anything quite like it before. Amin wasn't just content, he was joyous—despite the fact that his house had just been burned to the ground.

Others around the room worshipped in song and dance. Some people sat in groups and prayed together, while others walked around the place, completely enthralled in their prayers or worship. One thing Walid couldn't question is the feeling of joy and peace that overcame him as he merely approached the room.

"Somebody help!" Sayid yelled, hoping someone in the room would have sympathy on him. A woman came over to the boy and handed him a bottle of water. "I don't want water,

I want help!" he screamed, struggling to escape Walid's death grip.

Walid dragged him to Stephen's desk, grabbed a pair of handcuffs from his drawer, and fastened one cuff around his wrist.

"Okay, okay, no need for restraints," Sayid said.

"Clearly. Come on." Walid led him back to the room, looking for Grace. She had already made it to the front of the room.

"Amin! We need to talk!" she said loudly over the noise.

"No, we need to worship!" he said, his laughter contagious.

"Follow me!" she led Amin to the back of the room.

"What the hell is going on?" Sayid asked, looking terrified.

"Nothing to be afraid of," Amin said. "We're praising God for his goodness. Don't you feel his presence?"

The boy said nothing, but Walid felt it. Despite their precarious circumstances, he could feel the presence of God. It filled him with an inexplicable peace. *How could I have ever lived without this?*

"We saw your house, Amin," Walid said.

"It's just a house," Amin said. "Actually, God gave me a dream last night, in which I was encompassed with fire, lying in my bed with no escape. I saw a red light shooting out like fireworks from my house. It landed on this safe house. I woke up from that dream with a very bad feeling that I needed to get out. So I packed a bag and escaped minutes before the intruders arrived at my house. Isn't God amazing? I was supposed to be home last night, but God saved my life!"

"That's amazing. Wow..." Walid was nearly speechless.

"He's good," Amin beamed. "And besides, there's no point in being upset when I'm doing warfare."

"Warfare?" Grace asked.

"Sure. Worship is our warfare. It always precedes a victory, and I believe we're going to see one real soon!"

"Yeah, I was just reading about that!" Grace agreed. "When Jehoshaphat put worshippers in front of his army. Most people would think it's suicide, but he clearly heard God's voice, so there must have been no doubt in his mind they would lead his army to victory."

"Yes! People greatly underestimate the power of worship," Amin said.

"Hey, guys?" Stephen interrupted, pointing at Sayid. Walid had loosened his grip on him, and he was staring vacantly into the prayer room as though incapable of looking away. Amin placed his hand on the boy's shoulder, which caused him to start crying. *Where did that come from*, Walid wondered. He let go of him completely.

"We're not going to hurt you," Amin said. "I'll let you go."

Walid wanted to protest. The boy's knowledge of the safe house was extremely dangerous; he could lead his forces straight here! Not to mention, the boy had already threatened to do that. Despite this, Walid felt prompted by the Lord to let him go. He reached for the boy again, causing him to flinch, likely expecting violence. But Walid's hand rested lightly on his shoulder, with the reassurance of a coach.

"You can't release me now," Sayid said. "They'll kill me!"

"Who's they?" Walid asked.

"The Martyrs."

Everyone in the room knew of the Martyrs' Brigade—a powerful militia that emerged in 2011 after the fall of Qadhafi. The group paled in comparison to ISD's brutality, yet they still sporadically attacked Christians and others they deemed as nonbelievers, including the government.

"Where are you from?" Walid asked.

"I come from Darnah." This revealed more to Walid than anyone else understood. Many men from Darnah in eastern Libya had been taken from their families at very young ages, forced to work with local militias or extremist groups. They became child soldiers. Many families had willingly given up their children while the minority moderate population stood powerless to rise up and fight the corruption. Walid always thought of it as a lawless town of thieves and gangs. He avoided it whenever possible.

"Brother," Amin began.

"I'm not your brother, quit calling me that!" Sayid said. "Can you just let me go? Please?"

"I said I would, didn't I?" Amin said. "And we're all brothers in Christ Jesus."

Stephen called a security guard over, who escorted Sayid toward the exit.

Walid and Grace had nearly forgotten the entire purpose of their visit after all the commotion. They sat with Stephen and Amin and described their trip to Syria, and most importantly, their attack plans.

Walid had just finished his description of the Times Square attack. "It's really quite easy to carry out...which is why this is so concerning. I'm the point guy for the mission. I won't even meet my accomplice until I'm on site, but I'll have to get him to safety after he places the bomb and handle any unexpected challenges." Although he didn't elaborate, Walid knew this meant he would be expected to kill anyone who got in their way.

Amin and Stephen said nothing but listened intently, taking everything in. Grace went on to briefly describe her assignment: the final attack in Europe. "There weren't many details," she admitted. "I know the target but not even the timing or process. A smaller group of us will meet in a month. I guess they didn't want to take any chances. The secrecy of this whole operation is unusual even for ISD. It must be something huge."

"All right, so what are we doing about this?" Amin said.

"Well, I guess we'll just have to go stop them," Walid said sarcastically.

"Walid, you see this team?" He pointed to several people who were still praying and interceding. "These warriors are just as powerful as the operations team. In fact, this is probably our most effective team."

"Hey, look, I wasn't trying to—"

"I know, Walid," Amin interrupted. "But you must realize how important this is. These people pray and seek guidance from the Lord before, during, and after every operation we run from here."

Stephen started to smile the way he did when first discussing Voltron. "Nerding out," as Walid came to call it. "Guys... let's do this. Let's take down ISD!"

"Take it easy, killer," Walid said. "One plan at a time."

"Amin!" the security guard came running toward the group from the direction of the exit.

"What's wrong?"

"The boy. He threatened to bring the Martyrs back here."

CHAPTER 15

The Snare Is Broken

New York City

John brought a water bottle and protein bar to Walid and sat him next to the computer screen where they viewed the smoke from the bomb. "Sorry, man, it's all we have right now."

"Thank you, sir," Walid said.

"Please, John is fine. Look, I hate to cut out all the small talk, but we don't have a lot of time. We might be able to find some clues at the medical clinic before the police ever connect the place to the attack. Is there anything you remember about the man you were supposed to meet?"

"I never met him before. I was only given his description."

"You were doing this with a stranger?" John asked.

"It's not that uncommon, especially for an attack like this. Takes away any possible emotional attachments that could get in the way of work."

"Well, we never saw him enter the clinic. We only saw him exit a few minutes before the bomb went off. What else do you know? Any details might help."

Walid looked back at the screen and ran his hands through his greasy black hair as he tried to analyze the situation. Hardly anything could be seen through the smoke. He felt his frustration growing. Frustration over his confusion, and even more so over his failure to stop the attack from happening. He couldn't shake the feeling that he was somewhat responsible for the lives that were taken today.

"None of this makes sense!" Walid said. "Nobody was supposed to die! My accomplice was supposed to pick up a suitcase bomb from a locker rental place nearby, leave it under a table in the square, and join me at the Italian café where I would help him escape. Thing is, it was my job to place the bomb in the locker, and I made sure it was a dud!"

"Slow down, it's all right," John said. Walid was becoming more distressed by the second.

"It's clearly not all right! ISD must have changed the plan at the last minute. So if I had to guess...they forced him into the clinic through a private entrance to avoid attention. Doubt the guy even realized what was happening until he was inside. ISD probably brought several people to force his compliance. Maybe that's why he tried to warn everyone: saw ISD for what they really are. It's all speculation."

"Hey," John said, placing his hand on Walid's back. "We'll get to the bottom of this. I can't imagine what you went through today, but you must look to God right now to keep you strong and alert. We need to focus."

"I don't know if I can do this."

"I know you can, Walid! The Lord will give you strength. And you're not alone anymore. We're here to help you."

Walid appreciated his candor. John was authoritative yet calming, and more importantly, Walid knew that he was right; they needed to be lucid right now. He said a quick prayer and tried to match John's demeanor. There would be time to grieve later. "Okay…what can I do?"

"Take this," John said, handing him a wireless headset. "Put it on now, see if you can hear me."

"You're not going out there?" Walid asked as though John had a death wish. Walid put the headset over his ears and listened, giving him the thumbs-up.

"You're right, I'm not. Me and two other guys are going out there!"

"It's suicide! The gas out there will kill you long before you reach the clinic."

As though on cue, John picked up a bag from his desk. "That's why we'll be wearing these," he said as he pulled out military-grade gas masks.

"How do you even have those?" Walid asked, impressed by this man's determination.

"Emergency response. They were already in storage here. All right, man, we're out. Stay on comms."

He walked away to join his two-man team before Walid could protest further. *This man is all business*, Walid thought, though he admired his ability to stay alert and authoritative in such chaos. Not many people can do that. He would have been proud to serve with such a man back in Tunisia.

The woman in the blue runner's outfit hustled over to Walid as soon as John left. "Sorry for my abruptness earlier. I'm Lucy," she said with a thick British accent. "Quickly now, follow me, we have a few people who will be thrilled to see you."

Walid followed her to a large screen displaying a zoomed-in view of the medical clinic. Directly beside that screen was another showing a video teleconferencing application, which started ringing. Within a few seconds, Walid was looking at Amin and Stephen. For the first time all day, he genuinely smiled.

"Aw, Walid, I miss you too!" Stephen said facetiously.

"Oh shut up. How did you guys even get this number?"

"Hacked the global VTC networks," Stephen said.

Amin flippantly slapped him on the back of the head. "John and Lucy started working on this makeshift post the moment you told us about the operation. Longtime friends."

Walid couldn't help but feeling like Amin was friends with everyone. "But why did you call? I mean, I'm glad you did… but I have to go."

"Good save," Stephen said. "We're here to help, dude. You've seen my space station here. You guys don't exactly have those capabilities in your subterranean rat hole. No offense, guys!" he added to anyone who might have overheard him.

"Walid!" John said loudly into the headphones.

"What? What happened?" Walid asked nervously.

"Nothing yet, we're about to leave. Just seeing if you're awake."

The two other men on comms introduced themselves as Mike and Collins, both fresh out of the military in NYPD's counterterrorism ranks. Collins sounded particularly young.

"Let's do this," Mike said.

"This. Is. Spartaaaa!" Collins yelled, causing Walid to recoil.

"What is going on?" Walid asked.

"Come on, man, we haven't even left yet," John said to Collins.

"Just trying to pump us up!" Collins said exuberantly. "Better than focusing on what just happened. We've gotta keep our heads clear."

"I like this one," Walid said.

The trio tightly fastened chemical masks to their faces and adorned their chemical suits before opening the door to the subway terminal. The area, which was recently flooded with hordes of people, was nearly deserted. Some were still trying to run through the subway tunnel to nearby terminals.

"Where is everyone?" Mike asked.

"Dunno," John said. He assumed everyone else had either made their way through the tunnels already or run upstairs to the street.

The group remained quiet to preserve oxygen; it was difficult to breathe in the masks. They stepped onto the escalators and watched the advertisements floating on the wall to their right as they started rising. The same ones they saw every single day. Though this time, something had changed. A bright red banner suddenly appeared over the ads. It read, "The Snare Is Broken." The three looked at each other in confusion. John gave a thumbs-up to encourage them.

As they reached the surface, it looked like they had entered an alternate universe; a postapocalyptic New York City. A thick layer of smoke encompassed the atmosphere. They could only see around twenty meters in front of them. As they moved in the direction of the clinic, it became clear what had happened to some of the people. Several bodies lay motionless on the ground. John passed by a woman close enough to notice the boils on her skin. "Just keep moving," he said to the guys.

The smoke was thicker as they neared the blast point of origin. Collins tripped over something, causing him to gasp and fall to the ground. He stood and didn't look back, afraid to see the corpse.

"It's fine, just tripped," he said to reassure everyone on comms.

"It's worse than we thought," Mike said to Walid, his breathing labored.

"Mike, please, you have to focus right now," Walid said. "Don't think about it."

"Yeah, sure, sure. I'm fine."

John took out a bright-yellow rope and placed a section in Mike's and Collins's hands to form a train as they continued along the street. As they neared the complex housing the clinic, Collins felt a burning sensation in his leg. In a matter of seconds, he fell to the ground and cried out in pain.

"Update!" Walid ordered.

John ran to Collins and examined his suit. "Oh God…it's torn."

John and Mike lifted Collins to his feet. Sores were developing on his leg at the site of the tear. "Torn suit," John blurted out.

He hoisted Collins over his shoulder in a fit of adrenaline and yelled for Mike to run. Mike tore past John and threw open the door with such ferocity that the glass window on the door nearly shattered. John ran past him, and Mike slammed the door behind them as they continued down the hallway to the clinic entrance. As they entered, John carefully placed Collins on the floor. Mike ran to what looked like an operating table and grabbed a scalpel, which he used to cut the pant leg of Collins's suit to observe the wound.

"How bad is it?" Collins asked, carefully observing the faces of John and Mike as he rested his head on the floor.

"You'll be fine," John said.

"Oh man, it must be bad!"

Mike had filled a bucket with water and brought it over to Collins. "Come on, tough guy!" Mike said, trying to lighten the situation. "You're fine. The leg's still there." Mike poured water over the chemical burns, which caused Collins to cry out in pain. Mike and John tried to hide their concern. The burns went deep. Mike started to cover the wound with clean dressings, thankful that their target was a medical clinic, of all places!

"Guys, I'm coming in," Walid said.

"Oh no, you're not!" John said. "We're okay. Investigating the premises."

"Man, this is like a thriller book on tape," Stephen said over the line, forgetting everyone in New York could still hear him. Amin slapped the back of his head once again and scowled at him. Walid shot him the same look.

"Insensitive much?" Amin said.

Mike tossed papers and tools chaotically aside as he searched the clinic for something, *anything* the terrorists may have left behind. The clinic was modern but small, with only one operating table and a chair with arm straps, likely for taking blood. The sight was disturbing; the operating tools on the table were clearly left there in a hurry, unwashed and unkempt. There were bloodstains on the chair, the straps, and the floor.

"This is sick, Walid," John said. "The operation was obviously quick…Doubt he even went under when it happened…"

"John, I know I keep saying this, but please focus. What else do you see?"

John turned from the scene and scanned the room. He searched through cabinets and drawers, pulling things out and tossing them aside. He saw a covered trash can and dumped the contents on the floor. "Oh man…," John said dramatically.

"What?"

"There are two wallet-sized pictures here, partially burned. Fire must have gone out when they threw them in the trashcan."

"Pictures of what?" Walid asked.

"You and the accomplice. Walid, these look like hits."

Walid held his face in his hands. For the first time, things started making sense. This ran a lot deeper than ISD trying to ensure his accomplice didn't get cold feet. "How could I have been so blind?"

"What just happened?" Amin asked impatiently.

"They know," Walid said gravely.

"Know what?"

"I don't know how, Amin, but they figured out our plan. They tried to kill me…same people I've worked with for the last ten years and this is how they thank me!"

"How do you know?" Stephen asked.

"They changed the plan on us. They wouldn't do that unless they wanted both of us dead. And they had both of our pictures, not just his. So not only did they want us to die, they wanted as many people as possible to die along with us. I don't know what delayed that bomb, but they had to have known I'd run over to him to see what happened."

"Hey, guys? Still trapped in a lab surrounded by deadly chemical gas," Mike said sarcastically. "Maybe we can analyze later."

"There's nothing else here, man," John said. "Just a torched data stick. It's probably shot, but we'll bring it. Need to patch Collins's suit, and we're heading back."

John and Mike searched every drawer and cabinet for a chemical suit. Nothing. Mike grabbed a hospital gown and duct tape and tried to cover every possible crack he could find in Collins's suit.

Collins grabbed Mike's arm. "Okay, man, I'm a mummy now, I think we're good."

"All right, get ready," John said, trying to sound far more spirited than he felt. "I'm gonna open the door, and you two run through. I'll be right behind you. No matter what happens, don't stop running 'til you reach the station."

Mike and Collins nodded as they stood to their feet. Collins looked down at his mummified leg and tried to walk but could only limp. "Forget about it," he said reassuringly. "You must be crazy if you think adrenaline won't get me far ahead of both y'all."

"Just be careful, bro," Mike said, patting him on the back.

The three stood close to the door and gazed out the window. The haze of smoke remained but had diminished. Without further hesitation, John threw open the door and yelled "Go!"

Before the three were even ten feet out the main door into the street, they were thrown to the ground by an explosion coming from the clinic. Walid removed his headphones at the sound of the blast and knew exactly how deafening it must have been to the three men.

"John!" Walid waited a few moments but heard nothing. Nobody responded, but he heard one of them groaning as though in pain. "Guys!" he screamed into the headphones. Still no response. Mike and Collins struggled to stand up. John made no sounds and lay completely motionless. Walid could hear Mike and Collins in panic as they tried to figure out if John was still alive.

Suddenly, Walid's voice came thundering over the mic, sounding more authoritative and confident than anyone had ever heard him. "In Jesus's name, get up and run!" He didn't know what came over him and had certainly never used that name before.

Amin shouted in a brief outburst of excitement over the air. Stephen fist-bumped Amin. "This is epic," he said, continuing to intensely follow the action.

The moment Walid said "Run," John came to, and the three pushed themselves up from the ground almost in unison. Collins's duct-taped suit had held up, but John, who was closest to the blast, felt piercing pain over his entre back. He started breathing heavily but pushed aside any thoughts of how bad it might be. John motioned to the guys to run ahead as he followed. His pace quickly slowed and, after taking a few more steps, collapsed on the ground. He cried out in pain, but the blast had temporarily prevented Collins and Mike from hearing.

"Save me, Jesus," he prayed as his breathing became labored. Suddenly out of the fog, he saw a tall, strong man walking toward him, wearing jeans and a white T-shirt. He couldn't imagine how this man survived with no protection. Perhaps he was starting to pass away and this man would take him to heaven, he thought. The man leaned over and picked him up with ease. "It's time to go," he said right before John passed out.

The tall man carrying John caught up to Collins and Mike as they reached the station. They ran down the escalator to the control room. John woke up as the tall man tapped his head. Just as quickly, the man disappeared and left John resting on their shoulders. Walid heard the commotion and opened the door.

"What was that?" Walid asked. "You guys stopped answering!"

Collins and Mike led John to a small military mattress and laid him on his side.

"Medic!" Mike yelled. Three people came running to attend to their wounds.

"Take care of him first, I can wait," Collins said to the medics.

"Where'd he go?" John said, looking around in confusion.

"Where'd who go? You okay?" Walid asked.

"There was a man with us. He carried John here," Mike explained.

"You must have seen him," Collins said. "He was with us when we got to the door."

"Guys, there was nobody there," Walid said.

John cringed in pain as the medics put something on his back. He looked as though he was about to pass out again. "He was my angel," John said weakly.

The group looked at each other in amazement for a few moments after that. Finally, Stephen's voice echoed through the computer screen. "That's...awesome."

"I thought you guys hung up," Walid said.

"Nah, man, this is way too cool," Stephen said. "And besides, we need to know what you guys found out 'bout the next attack. We can start workin' it from here."

"Well, you might be disappointed," Walid said, turning to face Collins and Mike. "Did you guys bring the data stick? Maybe we can find something on there."

"Nah," Collins said. "Too busy getting blown up. Lost it after that final blast."

"Okay, well, there's gotta be something else we can do!" Walid said emphatically.

"Like what?" Mike said. "We lost your only chance of figuring it out."

"No, you didn't," Amin said from the screen. "The thing was burned anyway, probably useless. Walid, I have an idea... didn't you say you knew the woman in charge of the second attack?"

"Well, yeah, but we're not exactly best friends."

"Doesn't matter. You know where she is right now?"

"Um, yeah, probably at the Tripoli camp. What are we going to do? Walk right in and ask for the plans?"

"Something like that," Amin smiled. "With a little more strategy. Walid, you know that place like the back of your hand. I'm sure we can figure something out!"

Walid shook his head. "I don't have any ideas...but why not. I'm in."

"Yes! We'll start planning before you get here."

Walid turned to face the other guys. "Will you be all right?"

John was passed out under the power of sedatives, and Collins was now being attended to. "Yeah, we'll be okay," he said. "We'll see each other again soon." He smiled up at Walid and shook his hand from the floor.

"I only wish we could have helped you," Mike added.

"Are you kidding me?" Walid said. "Because of you guys, we have a huge piece of intelligence we didn't have before. We know that ISD is on to our plan. We know they're coming after us. And because of that, we can be prepared. We have the upper hand again. Mike, those next two attacks are not going to end up like New York. You've got to believe that with me."

"I do, brother."

Walid pulled Collins and Mike in for an embrace. He felt such a close connection with them despite only having known them for a day. He was starting to feel this connection with most believers he met, viewing them as brothers and sisters in Christ. God was fulfilling his longing for family in the most unique of ways.

"Walid, can you get to Newark tonight?" Amin asked. "You can't risk leaving from New York, and we haven't got much time."

"How will I get a ticket at this time?"

"Leave that to me," Stephen said. "Just get yourself to the airport and you'll have one by the time you get there. I'll call you with details."

"Okay, deal." Walid was getting excited about the next phase of their plan. He felt more prepared, more strategically aware of what he should do. Thanks to his team and the leading of the Holy Spirit.

Mike hooked him up with a chemical mask and suit, and Walid left the terminal. Despite everything that had happened today, he smiled and thanked the Lord for his goodness. In that moment, he heard the Lord speak to him in his spirit, "I broke the snare." Walid didn't have to ask to know exactly what He meant, because it made perfect sense. He truly believed that God had delayed the bomb, and probably delayed the booby trap in the medical clinic as well, saving countless lives. "Why, God?" Walid said aloud. He heard the Lord in his spirit just as clearly as before. "Because I heard your prayers, and I love you. And I love them."

Walid started crying, not in sadness but in being overwhelmed by God's love for him. He thought about what John told him hours earlier, and he knew it to be resoundingly true. He was truly no longer alone.

CHAPTER 16

White Phoenix

Walid looked out an oval-shaped window of a small Cessna 172 from ten thousand feet. Libya looked so serene from this vantage point. He tried to imagine how the country would look if anarchy and terrorism had not emerged from the revolution of 2011. If, perhaps, a unifying government that prioritized development and security had emerged in the aftermath. And what if a Christian leader had emerged? Would the land be more prosperous or fertile? It was hard to imagine as he gazed on the brown landscape below in this desert wasteland.

He had recently read in the Old Testament about dramatic transformations that occurred in the topography of North Africa and the Middle East over time. Many of the once-fertile lands had become desert wastelands due to the rampant sin that covered the Earth at the time. He wondered if this could be reversed in a period of great awakening. He prayed and hoped to see this during his lifetime, but the likelihood seemed bleak.

The Cessna passed Tripoli and was nearing Sebha in the central part of Libya. Walid remained pensive as he watched the bird's-eye shape of the city become less exotic and more sepia-toned from the desert winds as he grew closer to the ground. He had only been to Sebha once in his lifetime—a voluntary business trip with his family many years ago. This time, it had become necessary.

The day before Walid boarded a flight in Newark, local militias in Tripoli started another revolution against the secular government. For now, he only knew what he had read in the newspapers. One particularly powerful and previously marginalized militia saw an opening to seize power when the fledgling government's leadership traveled to Europe for a conference. After hurling mortars at several government buildings in Tripoli, the militia destroyed part of the international airport's runway with several rocket propelled grenades (RPGs) and surface-to-surface missiles. Control of the airport, to Walid's knowledge, was contested, and even locals were being advised to avoid the city altogether.

The previous regime led by Muammar al-Qadhafi had long instilled resentment amongst the numerous militias he marginalized during his decades-long rule. Since his ouster, the race for power had never really ended despite a de-facto government attempting to rule the country. Walid remembered when he first heard of the revolution in 2011. He was devising a strategy for ISD's Tunisia branch, which was struggling for survival against the Tunisian military's counterterrorism operations. In fact, Walid was the first to bring the idea of moving most of the Tunisia branch to Libya due to the country's nascent security gap. He tried not to think about it but felt partially responsible for the entire situation.

And now, the militias were fomenting another revolution. Walid wasn't surprised. The source of the violence and discontent had never truly been addressed after all. He prayed for the country as the plane touched down. He observed a small, single-tracked runway with only one other plane on the ground. Walid immediately recognized Amin's vehicle in the parking lot, accompanied by only a handful of other cars.

As he entered the terminal, which was essentially a large, open bay, he saw Amin making his way toward him with a big smile on his face. The two embraced.

"Finally!" Amin said. "We're so happy you're home!"

"We?" Walid asked, looking around inquisitively.

"You didn't think I'd come without a reception, did you?"

Amin looked to the terminal entrance. Walid's heart felt full as he watched Grace enter the bay. He ran to meet her. "Miss me?" he asked.

"Maybe a little," she said.

"Just a little?" He pulled her in for a hug before she had a chance to respond.

"Guys!" Stephen said, entering behind Grace. "I feel like such a third wheel!"

"What are you guys doing here?" Walid asked.

"Uh, it's good to see you too, Walid," Stephen said sarcastically, and they too embraced. "We'll tell you about it soon. We've also got a few guys from Eli's team, and Eli himself of course. I'm sure he misses you as well."

"Sorry to break up the love fest, but we need to go," Amin interjected. "It's not safe to linger here."

The group rode in two Toyota trucks to a house in Sebha near the airport. The house was unimpressive—off-white, dirty, and constructed in haste, or so it appeared. Amin knocked, and a short, elderly Arabic woman answered the door.

"Welcome!" she said, motioning for the group to enter. The living space was quaint and homely, decorated modestly with African artwork and ceramic pottery.

Walid leaned over to Stephen and whispered, "Why are we at some old lady's house?"

"I may be old, but I'm not deaf, dear," she said to Walid, making him blush.

Grace chuckled. "Safe house, remember?"

Amin led them down a winding staircase to what looked like a closet door. They entered a moderately sized room that could fit around a hundred people. Two men greeted them and invited them to sit.

"I trust you weren't followed," one man said.

"No, we weren't," Grace said.

The two men introduced themselves to Walid as Cyrus and Abdul; they appeared to know everyone else. Cyrus looked stressed and concerned while Abdul treated Walid as a war hero.

"It's so nice to meet someone of your caliber," Abdul said as he shook Walid's hand furiously. "You're well-known in our channels, you know!"

"Your channels?" Walid asked.

"Yeah, you know—the underground world."

"Oh...I'm sorry, I don't understand. Why am I well-known?"

"For your boldness! Standing up to the most powerful extremist group in the world when most others would run. That takes some gall."

"Oh, well, I've got a lot of good help, Abdul."

"So do we. Isn't it great to see how God's growing the underground church? Something big is happening. I can feel it!"

"It is, brother," Walid said. He felt that he could become quick friends with Abdul.

Meanwhile, he noticed that Cyrus looked tense and dejected, the wrinkles on his face prominent for a man in his forties. "I'm afraid we don't have a lot of time," Cyrus said. "We need a strategy. We have no idea exactly where the second attack will take place, so how are we to stop it?"

"Dude, we'll figure something out. That's why we're here," Stephen said.

"You don't know that," Cyrus said. "I just feel like they're always one step ahead of us. We can't fall behind again." Walid had seen men like this in ISD, troubled by something in their past that caused proliferated anxieties. He wondered what was causing this man such pain.

"Like Stephen said, that's why we're here," Amin said. "To get us one step ahead. Let's start with prayer."

"Prayer…" Cyrus said in perplexity.

"You want strategies, don't you? Let's get them," Amin said. He didn't wait for a response to start his brief prayer: "Lord, your Word says that you will reveal your mysteries to us. So, reveal to us what currently seems mysterious. Give us strategies and ideas. Thank you for giving us favor in this time!" He looked up before anyone realized he was done. "All right, let's do this."

"All right, sorry—I'm a little on edge," Cyrus said. "I just wish we had a starting point. Like knowing anything at all about the next attack."

"We do," Stephen said. "Walid and Grace know the chick leading the op."

"How does that help us?" Cyrus asked.

"Why don't we start with what we know," Grace said. "So her name's Fatima. I went through training with her. She's a little crazy, honestly…total badass, more anger than I've witnessed in most people."

"I've seen her too," Walid said. "Talked with her a few times in Tripoli, but nothing deep. And I'd say the same thing about her anger."

"Can't believe ISD put a woman in charge of an operation like that," Stephen said.

Grace punched his arm, causing him to recoil in exaggerated shock. "And why wouldn't a woman be capable of such a thing? Not that it's something to be proud of…"

"I'm just saying I thought ISD had men in all of its leadership positions—not that they should be. Why do you think they picked her?"

"Probably because she's not a typical woman," Grace said. "More capable than most of the men in ISD. She's university trained, extremely cunning, and she's certainly proven her brutality to ISD several times…the things I've heard through word of mouth are just…disgusting."

"So what good does any of this do us?" Cyrus asked impatiently.

"Actually, I think I've got an idea," Stephen said. "Grace, you lived with her in Tripoli for a while, so you know that compound pretty well, right?"

"Yeah, Walid and I both do. A lot of members live there."

"Well then, you should know where the guards are located, what times they roam, what to hide behind…"

"We're going to break in?" Walid asked.

"Yes!" Stephen exclaimed. "We're going to bug her!"

"Of course you'd come up with that," Grace smirked.

"Makes sense," Amin said. "Best way to find out the next location. Can't very well fly to Syria and just figure it out from there."

"So, how well guarded is this place?" Cyrus asked.

Walid and Grace looked at each other knowingly. "Well, it might take an intervention from God," Walid said.

"It's impossible?" Sayid said.

"Of course not. Just might take an intervention…" Walid said. "Security is much lighter than the main headquarters. Women in ISD's higher ranks have villas like mine, but they live at the guarded compound when preparing for important missions. She'll be there."

"Not to mention the housing compound has never been breached," Grace said. "So their guard will be down. They won't be expecting us at all."

"I love this idea," Stephen said. "Seriously, I need to go with you. Bugs are my life! You're gonna need a techno-geek."

"All right, come then," Walid said.

"Wait, really? Oh man…you think this will be dangerous? I mean, of course it will, we're goin' into the enemy's camp. We're like Joshua's spies!" he said with excited and nervous laughter.

"You can't seriously take this guy with you," Cyrus urged, looking at Stephen like he was crazy.

"And why not?" Walid asked. "We may need technical help. He can stay in the car and run ops from there."

"Guys, I'm right here," Stephen said.

"This is a joke," Cyrus said.

"No!" Walid said authoritatively. Everyone paused for a moment and looked at him. "Stephen may be our techie, but he was special ops, and I'd trust my life with him on the battlefield. And I haven't met many Christians as negative as you. I can't imagine it'd help in the field."

Stephen looked genuinely touched. Cyrus said nothing and looked away.

"I'm sorry," Walid continued. "But if we could at least pretend to be optimistic, that'd be great."

"No, I get it," Cyrus said.

Walid placed his hand on his shoulder. "Just want to see some of His joy in you!" he smiled.

"All right gents, and lady," Amin said. "We need to get back to Tripoli soon. This will be interesting, you know, given the second revolution and all. On a positive note, I know a guy who can get you militia uniforms."

"Of course you do," Walid laughed.

"It won't help you once you're in ISD's territory, but at least it should make your way through Tripoli less…burdensome," Amin said.

"How quickly can he get them?" Grace asked.

"He's in Sebha today, so probably ASAP. He's a militia member himself, actually. Not saved yet, but we go way back. He'll do this for me."

"Okay, Grace and Stephen will be support. Cyrus, you and me will go in and place the bug," Walid said.

"Not so fast," Amin said. "I'm going with you. You haven't seen me in action, Walid. May learn a thing or two."

"Okay, Cyrus, if you could communicate this whole thing back to Tripoli, that'd help tremendously." He nodded in acquiescence. "Wait, what are we going to use for a bug?"

"Walid," Stephen said with intentional smugness. "I've got you covered. My team will hook you up, but we'll need to pick it up at the Tripoli office."

"Okay, you guys should leave now," Amin said. "I'll come soon as I get the uniforms. Cyrus, you'll join me?"

"You bet."

"All right, God be with you all," Walid said.

"Guys?" Stephen said. "This is epic. Our group needs a superhero name." Everyone looked away, some rolling their eyes at his nerdy exuberance. "Nobody, really?" Silence. Everyone started up the stairs. "White Phoenix," he said to himself with a nod of approval and followed the group.

———————————————————————

Walid awoke the next day in a dark underground bunker, longing for a day where he might again hear birds chirping or awaken to blinding sunlight. He stretched loudly and spoke to God, asking him to guide his steps and give him supernatural strength.

After a grueling eleven-hour drive, Walid and his team had arrived in Tripoli the previous evening around midnight. Entry into the Tripoli safe house proved relatively easy due to the late hour. Ever since the militia fighting began a few days earlier, even ISD had decreased its patrols after 10:00 p.m. due to the increased danger.

Walid lay in his bunk for an uncharacteristically short time before walking out to the common area. Today was going to be a busy day. He immediately spotted Grace and Stephen sitting with coffee next to Stephen's computer. The two were talking and laughing, which brought a smile to his face. True companionship was probably commonplace to anyone else in the Western world, but it was a completely new joy for him. As he walked over, the two greeted him with a newspaper.

"Thought you'd never wake up!" Stephen said excitedly.

"Walid, look!" Grace said, handing him the paper and pointing at one of the headlines. "We're famous!"

"How about that!" Walid said.

The headline read, "ISD Fracturing from Within? Former Members Speak Out." Walid knew journalists liked to exaggerate, but perhaps it would do them some good if people thought project Voltron was truly fracturing ISD. "Where's Amin? He'll love this!"

"We assumed he was with you," Grace said, raising an eyebrow.

"I haven't seen him since we left Sebha," Walid said.

Suddenly, the red hazard lights started blinking. Walid thought back to his conversation with Amin. Red was good, blue was bad—a reversal from his usual preconception of those colors. Within a few seconds, the lights became blue. People in the safe house started to take positions as though expecting a battle. Several picked up semiautomatic pistols from their desks and took cover behind anything they could use as a makeshift shield.

"What are they expecting?" Walid asked.

"It might be nothing still," Grace tried to reassure him. "We just expect the best and prepare for the worst."

"Do *you* think it's anything?" he asked.

"One way to find out…" She moved toward the entrance.

"Wait!" Walid ran to catch up with her. As they took a sharp turn into the dimly lit dirt tunnel, they spotted someone in a militia uniform walking quickly toward them. *Jesus, protect us,* Walid prayed quietly as they stopped moving and drew their weapons. There was no cover in the tunnel.

"Stop!" Walid yelled into the darkness at the figure, who complied.

"Walid?!"

They recognized the voice immediately. "Come on, man! Are you crazy?" Walid said.

"My friends!" Amin said happily, ignoring his comment. "Have I got a story for you! Come on." Amin walked right past them and yelled, "All clear," to avoid being maimed by friendly fire. Walid was intrigued given Amin's sense of urgency.

As they walked into the conference room, Amin tossed three uniforms on the table and opened his camouflaged trench coat, revealing four pistols. He took them out of his chest holster and placed them neatly on the table. The group looked around at each other in confusion.

"Dang! Was your contact a warlord or something?" Stephen said.

"I got us some guns!" Amin said proudly.

"Uh, yeah I can see that," Stephen said. "Why do we need them?"

"Guys, you know I believe God will protect us, but I doubt He wants us to be reckless. We're going into an ISD compound! You gotta be prepared."

"Where did you get these?" Grace asked, picking up a .40 caliber semiautomatic pistol and examining the chamber.

"You'll never believe this…" Walid chuckled as this seemed to be Amin's favorite way to begin a sentence. "So my contact in Sebha gave me a location in Tripoli where I was supposed to get these uniforms. When I got there, there were two men waiting for me with all this loot. One of them was Sayid! You remember him, Walid, right? The boy you almost knocked out!" Walid shook his head, amused this was the one reason Amin thought Walid would remember him. "He's a believer now, by the way! Not sure if Sayid's buddy is a believer, but regardless he's Martyrs' Brigade and hates ISD. The enemy of my enemy, right?"

"They must have a lot of confidence in us. Do they even know what we're doing?" Walid asked.

"No, and they don't need to. They know we're trying to take them down."

"So what's the plan?" Stephen asked.

"We wait 'til sundown," Amin said. "Then we move. Your bug ready?"

"Of course!"

"Guys, we don't even know when the patrols are anymore."

"No matter," Amin said. "Nobody will stop you in uniform. Besides, Sayid was telling me patrols are pretty much a thing of the past since the uprising. Too much chaos…" The smile on Amin's face was dissipating. To witness the destruction of their country firsthand was truly disheartening.

Walid grabbed a map from the operations room and laid it out on the conference table. "Well, that'll just make things easier on us. What about this…Stephen, you're the getaway driver. Grace, you can run comms from the vehicle, and Amin can take it from the rear. We'll drive to this location." He drew a line and circled the map around eight blocks from the compound. Walid loved strategizing; he had done it for ISD for years and could finally use his skills for good.

"Hold on," Amin said. "I wasn't planning to take this uniform off, you know. Walid, must I remind you that I'm a SOF guy? I'll be helping you from the front!" Walid smiled at his tenacity. He kept forgetting that Amin really would be useful in the field.

"OK, come," Walid said. "I can lead us to her house, but how will we bug her?"

"Leave it to me," Amin said confidently. "In the meantime, we need to prep." The team discussed a few additional logistics and spent time alone to get ready and use the prayer room.

On his way back to the common area, Walid walked past a room conducting a live recording with the door slightly ajar. He didn't recognize the man giving his testimony but assumed he was a former ISD member. He smiled, truly excited at the impact these recordings might have on the world. Then he noticed someone he did recognize: it was Eli, standing in the back of the room with his distinctive poker face. Walid caught his eye and summoned him into the hallway. If he was going to die tonight, he wanted to set things straight. *How morbid*, he thought. *I really need to stop thinking this way.* Eli quietly opened the door and shut it behind him.

"Hey," Walid said.

"Hey," Eli said. *Off to a great start,* Walid thought.

"Look, I just wanna set things straight. I want you to know I forgive you, and I hold nothing against you." Eli said nothing but kept looking at Walid, as though waiting for more. "I mean, I've done some pretty awful things too, so who am I to hold you accountable for anything?" *Too much.*

"You blame me for your path in life?" he asked with apparent sorrow. His voice had changed drastically since Walid first talked with the indignant recruiter in the mosque.

"I mean, well no, of course not," Walid said. He hadn't thought about it until that very moment, but part of him did blame Eli for everything—his decision to join ISD, his father's death…And yet God had given both of them grace, and provided peace for Walid where every human emotion desired hatred.

Eli paused again and took a deep breath. "I know I haven't been easy to speak to. The truth?"

"Of course."

"I don't know how to speak to you, or anyone I've recruited for that matter. I don't know how to face what I've done. How could you possibly forgive me? I ruined your life!"

Walid was suddenly filled with compassion for this man. "Eli, you can't think that way! I did my fair share of that, and it ate me up inside…but when God forgives, he forgets, and so should you! This isn't the vengeful God we'd always been taught to fear. The true God doesn't promote violence, hatred, or even unforgiveness!"

"I get it, I know. Amin said the same thing. It's just hard to come to terms with the past."

"Well, read up on Paul then. That helped me more than anything. If someone who dedicated his life to killing and persecuting Christians could go on to become one of the greatest Christian apostles of all times, I don't think it's too late for any of us."

Eli smiled; it was the first time Walid had seem him smile.

"Walid…you should know, the prayer team spent some good time in there for you guys earlier. You have a lot of supporters here."

"I'm glad to hear that."

"And I'm supposed to help you with the next leg of the operation, so you better find out where it is!" he said, smiling awkwardly, as though he was a kid practicing a new skill.

"I'm on it, man," Walid said. They shook hands, and Eli turned back toward the recording room.

"By the way," Walid said. "That should be you in there. You want to make amends? Can't think of a better way…seriously, man, you've got a pretty amazing story." Eli nodded and walked back into the room.

After a few hours, Walid returned to the large computer-filled cavern and met with his team.

"What's up with you? You're pretty happy for this operation," Grace said.

"Long story, I'll tell you later," he said.

"I feel legit!" Stephen said as the group stood there in militia fatigues. "You guys ready? I'm about to drive this baby like I stole it!"

"Oh great," Walid said.

"All right, here's the swag," Stephen said, handing a tiny mic on a clear adhesive to Amin. "Couldn't be simpler: put this anywhere her conversations can be heard. And don't get this on your skin…this is not tape! This will stick to just about anything."

Amin took the bug and zipped it into his pocket. "Got it."

The group joined hands, and Amin began to pray. "God, when Elisha prayed that you blind the enemy marching toward him, you blinded their eyes. So, Father, we ask that you do the same for us. Blind their eyes as we go into the enemy camp!" He squeezed their hands and opened his eyes.

"Well, what are we waiting for?" Walid said.

CHAPTER 17

Storming the Compound

Stephen parked the Humvee next to an abandoned coffeehouse and turned off the engine. The street was deserted save for a lone Toyota truck in the middle of the road, covered with ash that masked its white façade. One of the doors was ajar and one was ripped clean off. *What happened here?* Walid wondered.

Nobody moved. Flickering lights from business signs dimly lit the bullet holes enveloping them. Walid recognized this street, but just barely. He used to frequent the popular coffeehouse across the street when he lived at the very complex they were about to breach. The effects of war were brutal; the relatively new café looked timeworn and all the windows had been shot out. *Is there any hope left for this city? There has to be...* He prayed for strength as he and Amin fastened their chest holsters.

"Earpieces in?" Amin asked quietly. The group nodded. The earpieces were more for emergencies than anything. Neither Amin nor Walid planned to make any noise.

Martyrs Brigade soldiers, who were responsible for the uprising, had always been somewhat indifferent to ISD despite

155

their differing ideologies. Both groups sought first and foremost to oust the Western-backed government seated in Tripoli. They enjoyed tacit solidarity with ISD in their hatred for the West, whom they blamed for Libya's problems. It was more convenient than blaming the violence on the root causes: decades of authoritarian regime brutality and marginalization, which led to factionalized tribal disputes, pervasive distrust and corruption, and economic repression.

Despite these allegiances of convenience, the Martyrs disagreed vehemently with ISD's violent and apocalyptic ideology. It was only a matter of time before the two would fight each other. Walid and Amin knew that if ISD thought militiamen had infiltrated their compound, it would certainly accelerate that timeline.

After a few minutes of idling to ensure the coast was clear, they opened the back doors and dismounted. Walid and Amin jogged down the street and came within a block of the entrance to the ISD compound.

The compound was used solely for housing, and as such, security was inferior to the group's headquarters. Walid tried to visualize the interior layout as they observed the compound entrance from behind a building on the street corner. There were two security guards holding assault rifles pacing at the entrance. They appeared to be distracted and bored.

Walid looked at Amin with a cunning smile and motioned for him to follow. They retreated one block and took a sharp left-hand turn toward the side of the complex, using the neighboring buildings for cover. They were now positioned behind the guards. There was a fifteen-meter gap to the perimeter fence, which was around eight feet tall. Walid peeked around the corner of a building and observed the guards facing sideways. Any movement would undoubtedly draw their attention.

Walid pulled Amin close and whispered, "We'll run on my signal. They can't see us if we're flat against the fence."

Amin nodded. Walid waited for the guards to face the street again. One of the guards nearly nodded off and slapped himself in the face to stay awake. *God, this could take all night…help us, Lord*, he prayed. After a few minutes, he saw the two mutter something to each other before one of them took off down the street toward Stephen and Grace. *There's no way they could possibly know…* The lone guard now focused his attention on the street leading to the compound. Walid motioned to Amin to run and they took off, flattening themselves against the wall. The guard continued to face the street. *So far, so good.*

The fence was made of wood, and there were very few crevices allowing for grip. Amin hoisted Walid just high enough to see inside the compound. Several small houses littered the compound in parallel lines similar to a military barracks. A large, open, arena-style space centered the compound. Walid knew this was used for a variety of activities, including formations, training exercises, and public punishments for violators of their strict Sharia law.

"Everyone's gone," he whispered.

Amin shrugged and pushed him higher until Walid could pull himself over. Then Amin jumped up and pulled himself over. Walid raised an incredulous brow, unaware of Amin's herculean upper-body strength. The two landed around ten meters from a large building and swiftly ran to flatten themselves against it. Walid nodded to Amin to follow him. This was easy; in fact, it seemed too easy.

They walked stealthily to a building around twenty meters away. Still nobody in sight. Finally, they reached Fatima's building, and Walid pointed at the entrance. Were they to simply walk into her room and place the bug? How could it be so easy? There were no sounds coming from inside. Walid cupped his hands to hoist Amin through the open window. Many of these buildings lacked air conditioning, and ISD members kept the windows open to allow the desert winds to circulate.

"Wait here," he whispered to Walid.

Amin stood in the common area. The lights were off, but his night-vision glasses allowed him to see the world in shades of red. *Is anyone even here?* he wondered. He walked quietly into the adjacent room and finally saw his mark. Fatima appeared to be sound asleep, her phone charging on a stand next to her bed. *Perfect.* He crawled to the phone. *God, protect us.* He removed the phone cover, placed the flat mic inside her phone, and replaced the cover. *Too easy…*

Just as he crawled back to the door, he heard a single gunshot coming from the direction of the compound entrance. He dove out of the room and crawled under a table covered by a long tablecloth in the common area.

Right outside, Walid heard the rumblings of ISD members coming to life as some hollered obscenities from inside their buildings and others started making audible movements. With nowhere to run, Walid pulled himself into Fatima's window and landed clumsily and somewhat loudly inside the common area. As he stood to his feet, he saw Fatima standing mere paces in front of him, her eyes wide.

"Fatima, hear me out," he said. *God, what do I do?* he prayed desperately.

"Hear you out? You broke into my house!"

"The gunfire..." he started awkwardly, though he didn't know where to go with that.

"And...you're supposed to be dead!"

"What? Why would I be dead?" He knew precisely why.

"The emir issued a message to the compound...we all saw what happened in New York on the news. He said you were killed by the bomb."

"Well, clearly I wasn't. Fatima, the emir tried to kill me. He lost trust in me somehow and tampered with the operation."

"Blasphemy!" she yelled. "How dare you insult the emir like that?"

"It's the truth! He's not the man he claims to be! You must know this to be true, Fatima." A barrage of gunshots were now echoing outside.

"What has happened to you, Walid? You've lost your way."

"I haven't lost anything, in fact, I've gained everything since I left!"

"You willingly left..." she repeated. This was grounds for murder in ISD.

"You have to let me go," Walid pleaded. "Come with me, I can save you!"

"Never!" She lunged for a knife on her kitchen counter. At that moment, Amin pushed up on the table with great force, hurling it straight onto Fatima. She screamed as she fell to the floor under the table.

"Run!" Amin hollered as they left her house and slammed the door behind them.

They headed toward the entrance but stopped after seeing the flashing lights and explosions of gunfire coming from that direction. They pivoted 180 degrees and once again stopped dead in their tracks. Walid and Amin felt the hair on their body standing at attention as they stared into the eyes of dozens of ISD members. All of them were dressed for battle, grimacing ominously and pointing weapons in their direction.

"Follow my lead," Amin said quietly. Walid continued staring at the ISD hoard; he could hear Amin praying quietly in tongues next to him.

Amin took a deep breath and opened his mouth to speak. Before a single word emerged, a man standing front and center of the group yelled, "Get them!" The ISD members started running directly toward them. Gunfire was now coming from every direction. With nowhere to run, they knelt to the ground and braced for a heavy blow.

To their astonishment, the group ran right past them toward the compound entrance. They looked at each other in shock for a moment as the ISD members continued to run around them as though they weren't even there. *This is surreal,* Walid thought. After they passed, Walid ran to the fence and hoisted Amin over the wall. As he bent his knees to jump over the fence, he felt a blow to the back of his shoulders, hurling his body forcefully into the fence. It was Fatima.

She limped on one leg, clearly the result of Amin's epic table throw. Walid hated the idea of fighting a woman, but she was clearly not in the mood to exchange civil words. She ran at him again, and Walid grabbed her arm and threw her over his leg, a move he learned through years of krav maga training. As she struggled to her feet, Walid jumped up and grabbed the top of the fence. He had one leg over the top when Fatima grabbed his pant leg, which he shook to get free.

"Fatima! I would have saved you!"

"This isn't over!" she yelled.

Walid dropped to the ground, and Amin helped him up. They ran toward the Humvee.

"Where are they?" Walid yelled, wondering if the earpieces had malfunctioned or if something worse happened. They hadn't heard anything from Grace or Stephen.

"No idea!"

They sprinted four blocks until they reached the coffee-house. There was no car. Only militia members running frenziedly toward ISD's compound.

"What's happening?" Amin asked.

The militia uniforms were different from their own. Walid recognized them as Zintani militia uniforms and grabbed Amin's arm to pull him down a side street. The Zintanis worked for Libya's fledgling government but were only loyal to the highest bidder. Walid could only imagine that the government was conducting a raid for some reason. They must have received intelligence about a threat or something. As they looked back, it was now clear why ISD ran past them as explosions lit up the entrance like fireworks.

"Come on," Walid said. They ran down smaller parallel alleyways hidden from sight until they passed the worst of the commotion.

"We've gotta get back to the safe house," Amin said.

"What about Grace and Stephen?" Walid asked.

"Walid, we don't know where they are! If they saw this coming, they probably drove back there anyway." Walid imagined he was right; it was far too dangerous for them to wait.

Walid followed Amin down several blocks in the direction of the church. Finally, the alleyways ended, and they had no choice but to follow the main road back. There was hardly anyone on the road, but they could still hear the commotion.

Suddenly, they heard the screeching tires of a vehicle and Amin stopped abruptly, causing Walid to run straight into him.

"Get in!" Stephen yelled.

They jumped in the backseat, and Stephen sped off toward the safe house.

"I'm so glad you're okay!" Grace said from the passenger's seat.

"Where's the car we came in?" Amin asked.

"Did I ever mention I adopted a little skill called hotwiring in my military days?" Stephen said. "We had to bail on the Humvee when the militia approached."

"Did you place the bug?" Grace asked.

"Yeah," Amin said. "She won't find it."

"But she knows I'm alive now," Walid said.

"It's all right. We did what we went there to do. Ears?" Amin asked, referring to the faulty earpieces.

"No idea! They just stopped working. Amazing how God got us through this," Grace said.

Stephen stopped several blocks short of the safe house and parked the car. "Hey, guys, remember when I said I'd drive it like I stole it? How ironic is this!"

CHAPTER 18

Enemy Trackers

Walid stood on a massive hilltop overlooking a vast, lush valley below. Emerald-green trees moved melodically with the wind. The beauty of this place was deceptive, for he knew what lurked below the canopy. The pink-and-yellow sun had nearly disappeared below the tree line, which meant he was running out of time. He looked to the heavens and said a prayer as he began to descend into the unknown. If everything went as planned, this would all be over soon. Walid's target was just beyond the forest. There was no other path than to walk straight through it. As he prepared to enter the thick woodland, a powerful tiger sprinted out as though running from something. *What could cause a tiger to flee?* he wondered. It was nearly dark now. He stepped into the woods, and everything went dark.

"Walid!" he heard someone yell from a distance. He shook his head and looked around, trying to figure out where he was. He felt thankful that it was just a dream but felt strongly that God was trying to tell him something. Where was he going that was so dangerous? He felt that simply living in Tripoli was dangerous enough on its own. Was it about to get worse?

"Walid!" there it was again.

"What!" he yelled back. He couldn't remember the last time he received a good-night's sleep. Two days had passed since the group returned to the safe house. They rejoiced when they realized the bug actually worked, but impatience was setting in; Fatima was clearly away from her phone during any important discussions. Most of the conversations they overheard involved small talk and gossip, to which Walid would swiftly leave the room. He was starting to wonder if their mission was all for nothing.

Stephen barged into his room unannounced. "A little privacy here!" Walid said, irritable from sleep deprivation.

"No can do, Wally! She's finally saying something of value. You gotta come hear this."

"Wally? No…that's not gonna happen." With a glimmer of hope, he hopped out of bed and threw on a sweatshirt.

"Just tryin something new, Walidsky."

"Stop." Walid pushed him as they joined Amin and Grace in the common area. They were already listening attentively to Fatima's live feed. Grace walked over to Walid and sat next to him.

Fatima's voice sounded muffled but audible nonetheless. She spoke to a man with a familiar voice, though Walid couldn't quite place it. The group surmised they were speaking from her new quarters, probably on ISD's main headquarters compound. Walid and Amin knew from conducting recent recon missions that ISD's housing complex had been largely abandoned as it underwent reconstruction. The compound was severely damaged by the militia attack a few nights ago.

"This new timeline's a little ambitious, don't you think?" she asked the man indignantly.

"The emir wouldn't have tasked it on such a timeline if he thought it was impossible," he said.

"Yes, I understand that, thanks," Fatima quipped in a patronizing tone. "But you saw what happened in New York! The emir tried to rush things, and the operation was sloppy! We didn't even kill that filthy traitor!" Walid smiled proudly as Stephen high-fived him.

"Sloppy?" the man said. "What are you talking about? It was successful! Or have you not been watching the news?" There was something about this man that bothered Walid. He knew this voice, but the transmission made it so difficult to distinguish. It was almost as though Walid didn't believe what he was saying. There was no real passion behind the anger in his voice.

"Enough!" she yelled. Her voice sounded chilling. There was silence for a moment, and she continued, "Look, I would never question the emir's decisions…"

"Well, you had me fooled!" he interrupted. The group heard what sounded like a slap and a gasp. "Have you gone completely mad, woman?"

She seemingly ignored the entire exchange and moved on. "Either way, now I have to book a flight to Damascus immediately." She sounded terribly inconvenienced.

"We all do, Fatima," he said. "And stop worrying about Walid. I don't know why you've been talking about him so much the last few days. As long as he's being tracked, we don't have to worry about him."

Walid's face turned white. "Tracked?"

"Why does his voice sound so familiar?" Grace asked.

Walid thought for a moment as the conversation between Fatima and the man came to an abrupt end. Finally, it hit him. "Because you've heard it before."

"As have I," said Amin. "It's Bashir."

"But how?" Walid asked. "I saw him killed!"

"Did you?" Amin asked.

Walid thought back to that terrible day as he walked up to the crime scene. He tried to picture himself sitting in Bashir's vehicle before it exploded. It seemed so obvious to him now! He would have seen some evidence of human remains if Bashir had died in the car bomb; it wouldn't have turned him to ashes. His face became red with offense. He felt abandoned, stabbed in the back.

"I just don't understand…his conversion seemed so genuine! I saw a change in him. In fact, he even led me to the church, knowing I would meet you."

"I felt it was real too," Amin added. "And I'm not convinced that it wasn't, Walid."

"He's still with ISD! Why else would he abandon me like that?"

"Maybe he didn't! Think about it," Amin said. "He knew we'd meet. He left you in able hands. There may be far more to this than we can understand right now. I dunno, maybe he had no other choice."

Walid prayed for peace to overcome the bitterness he felt. He had grown to love Bashir. Hating him would accomplish nothing; in fact, it would choke the blessing of the Lord.

"Yeah, I guess," Walid said. "That has to be true…"

"What do you suppose he meant by saying you're being tracked?" Grace asked.

"There's no way," Stephen said. "We've been so careful. If they knew where this place was, they would have raided it by now."

"Not necessarily," Walid said. "They could be waiting for something."

"Let's ask the Lord for wisdom," Amin said. "In the meantime, we have something to be thankful for! We know where the next operation is taking place."

"Sort of," Grace said. "It could be anywhere in the city!"

"Well, we have, what, a day or two to figure this out?" Amin rationalized. "I want everyone to pray about it. Let's reconvene tonight at 1800." Walid would have balked at the idea of using valuable strategizing time to pray, but not anymore. Not after experiencing the power of prayer, after getting ideas and strategies in the midst of prayer.

The group parted ways. Amin and Stephen left for the prayer room, and Grace to her quarters. Walid paced back and forth in the common area as he prayed to himself. Ten minutes later, he continued to pace. All he could think about was going outside. He tried to shake the feeling; it seemed absurd to roam around the streets where he was a wanted man. Still, he couldn't shake it. He grabbed his pistol and a hoodie from his tiny room and left through the storefront entrance, telling nobody.

"OK, God, what now?" he asked the Lord as he started walking down a small street parallel to the main road. Walid threw his head back and breathed in the crisp, musty air. Despite the air quality, he felt thankful to be out of the safe house. To avoid praying iteratively for strategies, he started praying for

Libya. That God would place it in the hands of leaders who truly longed for things like development, economic prosperity, uprooting corruption, equality, love, one nation under God!

Walid continued his prayer walk, paying little attention to his surroundings. Suddenly, he heard the pitter-patter of footsteps running quickly toward him. In a matter of seconds, the person was nearly upon him; there was no time to hide. Then they stopped. Walid's heart started beating faster, and yet he felt a strange peace. Why would God lead him out here only to be killed? Walid jogged to a four-way intersection. As soon as he reached it, he nearly collided with the man he heard moments ago. The man wore an ISD uniform and covered his face with a headscarf. Walid reached for his weapon.

"Wait!" the man implored him. "It's not safe here. Please… follow me."

He walked in the opposite direction, waiting for no response. Walid had seen stranger things happen in the last several weeks. *Why not? Just follow the hooded ISD man*, he joked to himself, trying to build his courage. The man walked into an abandoned building that looked as though it was recently shelled. *Is this a trap?* he wondered. *No…it wouldn't be this easy…*

As Walid entered the building, he saw the man standing down a small hallway, motioning for him to follow. They walked into a private room and the man finally removed his headscarf. Walid wanted to gasp and yet felt wholly unsurprised. "Thought so…," he said with little emotion.

"Walid, I can explain everything," Bashir said.

"Is this the point where you turn me in? Get your bounty?" Walid asked. He tried to be reasonable but felt so wounded.

"Of course not, brother," Bashir said.

"We are not brothers!"

"Would you give me five minutes at least? That's all I ask," he pleaded. Walid sat on a cement block and motioned for him to continue.

"The emir was on to us. He had us bugged, knew we had found nothing to disprove the Bible, which I'm sure you figured out by now." Walid nodded his head in obvious agreement. "When he pulled me aside that day, he forced me to fake my own death. He told me they had placed explosives in my car and told me to run to that ISD café across the street."

"Were you watching me? Bashir, I had grown to love you like a brother!"

"I had too! The emir said he'd kill you and Grace if I didn't follow orders!"

Walid's head dropped. He believed him, and knew he would have done the same thing. He felt a strange sense of sorrow for the emir rather than anger. The man was deranged and yet completely oblivious that everything he did for Allah was truly for nothing.

"I tried to direct you to the church at least! And I see that you've met Amin."

"You see?" Walid asked. "When did you see us?"

"The same night you were bugged by Fatima. You need to get rid of that militia jacket you stole, by the way. She placed one on you before you jumped the fence."

"Why should I trust anything you say?"

"You don't have to, Walid. I'm sorry for hurting you. I didn't know what else to do."

"I guess…I probably would've done the same thing."

"I'm trying to defeat ISD too. And now they fully trust me. I'm better placed than ever before."

"Yeah, I get it," Walid said.

"I need to get back, but please listen. I don't know the timing of this next attack, but I imagine it will happen within the next week. I figure you've got at least forty-eight hours to get out of the country, but you should move quicker if possible. Here, take this, don't talk about it out loud," Bashir said as he handed him a small envelope. He started to walk away, and Walid grabbed his arm.

"I just need to know one thing," Walid said. "Was it all a lie? Your change?"

Bashir touched his shoulder and smiled. "Of course not, brother. It's the best thing that's ever happened to me. I'll be in touch when it's safe. I hope to catch up soon when this is all behind us."

Walid started walking back to the safe house, excited to tell everyone about his encounter with Bashir. He stuffed the envelope into his coat pocket and started running as he recalled what Bashir said about the bug. He had to get back to warn the others. If they were being tracked, that would lead ISD directly to the safe house...

He slowed his pace as he neared the safe house, hearing voices close by. Walid flattened himself against a building and peered around the corner. Three armed men dressed in black stood near the safe house entrance, looking intently for something. One man unsuccessfully attempted to pick the lock on the building next to the safe house entrance.

"We don't have time for this," one of them grumbled as he broke the window with the buttstock of his weapon.

"Idiot!" another man said. "So much for being inconspicuous."

Walid smiled upon realizing the coordinates they received from his tracker would naturally lead them to the wrong building, given his jacket was underground. He turned to run toward the church entryway, which remained well out of sight from the secondary entrance. When he reached the area, he began searching for the square, the displaced sand, or anything else that might cause it to open.

He heard voices again, this time coming from the street. Just then, the square moved on its own and revealed the entrance. He quickly descended into the hole and experienced the same landing as before. *So much for fixing the landing gear.* The lights didn't turn on this time, so he made his way slowly down the pitch-black tunnel, hoping to see a flicker of light. Instead, he heard someone else making their way toward him.

"Hello?" he called into the darkness.

"Walid!" he heard Amin call quietly in return.

"What happened to the lights?" Walid asked.

"Generator issue, nothing to worry about. We can't fix it until the pests outside leave, so until then…" He took out a flashlight and turned it on. "Had to make sure it was you!"

"And how do I find that stupid square door quicker next time?" Walid asked. "It opened like it had a mind of its own."

"It does!" Amin said. "It can sense when a person is in need. Pretty cool, right?"

"Oh, shut up," Walid laughed. "How did it open?"

"The security guards can open it from the inside. And"— he pulled out a small device that looked like a car door opener—"I've got my own, in case of emergencies. But never mind that, why did you go out anyway?"

"I just couldn't get it off my mind. I felt like God wanted me to go."

"So what'd you find?"

"Boy have I got news for you...but first, I need to take care of something." Walid took Amin's flashlight and ran to his room. Amin and Stephen followed him. He searched his jacket until he found the tiny bug and pounded it beyond recognition with the backside of his flashlight.

"He wasn't lying..." Walid said to himself.

"Well done!" Stephen said.

"Well, that explains the pests outside," Amin said.

"I'm getting so careless," Walid exclaimed. "I should have checked before bringing it back here! I put you all in danger."

"It's fine! They'll dig around the building above us for a while and go home empty-handed," Amin said.

"Yeah, my compliments to the architect of this place."

"That would be the French! Speaking of, where's Grace anyway?" Stephen asked.

"She's not here?" Walid asked in shock. "Why would she leave in this chaos?"

"Yeah, Walid, that'd be downright crazy!" Stephen said.

Suddenly, the lights turned on again, and the screens powered on.

"Did someone go outside?" Walid asked. Stephen and Amin shrugged and walked into the common area. The television screen had defaulted to the Al Arabiya news channel. One man yelled in excitement from the back of the room, while others tried to drag everyone into the room. "You gotta see this!" another man said. Walid strained to read the headline: "Reformed terrorists speak out."

"Turn on the subtitles!" Stephen yelled to the man controlling the screen. They couldn't hear anything over the whoops and hollers throughout the room.

The anchorwoman briefly described Stephen's website to provide context. Walid stared in shock at the screen after recognizing the man on the screen. It was the same man Eli was filming several days earlier, and he was giving his testimony!

"What type of impact could this be having on ISD?" the coanchor asked.

"Jim, I think this may be the beginning of something big," the anchorwoman responded. "This is a significant psychological blow to the group, and something that nobody else, certainly not the West, could accomplish. Their own people, changing before their eyes!"

"Well, this may be coming at just the right time, after the operation in New York." They discussed the story for another minute before changing topics.

"How about that!" Amin said.

"Praise the Lord!" Stephen exclaimed. "The news is advertising our site for us!"

Walid was speechless. He was simply astonished at how God was truly working on their behalf. He had never experienced such love, such power in all his life.

Walid's thoughts quickly shifted back to his meeting with Bashir and Grace's whereabouts. He pulled the guys close and spoke softly. "Hey, guys, I saw Bashir."

"Conference room," Amin said. He grabbed Eli and two other people before joining them. "They should hear this too since they'll be helping with the next operation."

"Hey," Eli smiled in his social awkwardness and shook everyone's hands. *Well, it's progress!* Walid thought and smiled back. "This is Sydney and Justin," Eli said.

"You guys don't look Libyan," Walid said. "Where you from?"

"Paris," Sydney said. "Grace and I go way back, so I guess you know who I work for." Another reminder. Walid couldn't stop wondering where she was.

"I'm from Damascus," Justin said. "I was a mercenary before the regime killed my family in an 'accidental airstrike.' Long story. I'm here 'cause of your website."

Walid introduced himself and briefly described what they had been doing for the last several weeks. When he described the attacks, Eli became visibly uncomfortable. The guilt of his former role clearly still plagued him. "When I left Bashir, he told me the next attack would happen soon and gave me this." He pulled out the piece of paper from the envelope and placed it on the table. Nothing was written on it. "I dunno, maybe it's all crap."

"Why would he give you a blank paper?" Justin asked.

"I dunno!" Walid sounded more frustrated than he meant to, mainly due to his preoccupation with the mission, Grace, and Bashir's possible betrayal, though he knew the latter was an irrational thought. "Like I said, maybe it's nothing."

Stephen was staring intently at the paper as though words would appear on it any minute. "or," he said and paused for a moment. "It's not really blank."

Walid knew what he was getting at and started feeling more hopeful. "What do you mean?"

"I'll be right back," Stephen said and hastily left the room.

Walid turned to Sydney. "Have you seen Grace?"

"No, I think she went to look for you," she said. "She's not back yet?"

"No, we have to find her." Sydney nodded in agreement.

Stephen ran back into the room haphazardly with two metal objects. "Hang on, guys, just watch the magic happen!" Stephen turned out the lights and waved the first wand over the paper, flooding it with red light. Nothing happened.

"Wow, man, you should take this show on the road," Walid said.

"Everyone's a critic." He took out his second wand, which appeared to be a black light. As he waved it across the paper, Walid again saw nothing.

"Seriously though, what are we supposed to see?" he asked.

"Wait!" Stephen said; his face grew more serious as he strained to read the paper. "There's something here."

Amin looked over his shoulder and smiled in enlightenment, seeing two simple words appear. "Oh Lord…" he said.

"A little help here," Walid said impatiently. Stephen showed Walid, and his eyes grew wide as well. Nobody said the words out loud, as though uttering them would make it more real. But each person in that room knew that it was all too real and that this operation would be more difficult to stop than the bomb in New York.

The paper read, "Damascus Tower."

CHAPTER 19

Descending into the Unknown

Paris, France

"This is getting out of hand," General Durand said to a room full of military officers.

The general paced around the front of a massive operations room, several officers staring intently at him as though waiting for words of genius. Other senior officers around the room spoke frantically into their phones while others engaged in private conversations while poring over maps and computer screens.

His deputy's countenance was grave, and he addressed the general colloquially. "Paul, we stood up this task force for a reason. We knew there would be kinks to work out…"

"Kinks?" Paul said, raising his voice. "One of our finest agents is off the grid!"

"We'll find her," his deputy said. "In the meantime, we must do everything in our power to help her by helping her team. They're the best chance we have right now."

"Jorden," Paul placed his hand on his deputy's shoulder, pausing several seconds for impact as he often did. "You're right!" he said loudly, causing others in the room to stop what they were doing and watch him for direction.

He looked across the expansive room and addressed the crowd, "All right, everyone, listen up! Contact our agents in Rome. They're about to move south. I want every available agent to start preop planning. It's about to get busy, team!" Before he finished speaking, two officers started making phone calls from the room. "And get Agent Grace Carter's team on a secure line!"

— — — — — — — — — — — — — — — — — — — —

Walid found himself standing at the entrance to the same lush forest he saw several nights ago. The tiger was long gone by now. He looked back to the top of the hill where he stood moments ago. Somehow, the hill had been destroyed by fire. There was nowhere left to go but straight into the thick brush. He stepped into the forest. Though he expected to move slowly through the briers and wayward tree branches, they became an illusion and melted before him, allowing him to cut through them swiftly like a hot knife through butter. He shook his head, confused, reaching out to the branches on either side of him. They felt so real. *How is this possible?*

As he moved, he heard the chilling, ominous sounds of a rhythmic drumbeat from deep within the forest. It grew louder with each step that he took. Somehow, from what he could only imagine was a word of knowledge from the Lord, he knew it was an enemy camp. What he didn't yet realize is the form that it would take.

He continued walking, turning to the right or the left as he felt the Lord leading. Then he saw a bright, shining light on the path in front of him. It became illuminated as bright as the sun, such that Walid worried the enemy would be able to see him.

"They can't see you," a voice from within the light spoke thunderously. "Only you can see this path, as long as you keep listening to Me." Walid felt more love than he had ever experienced up to this point. He fell to the ground in awe of the peace and joy he felt. Despite this, he still heard the beating of the drums, louder and closer than ever. Just as he prepared to get up and move forward, he felt someone push his shoulder.

"Walid, get up!" Stephen said. He narrowly dodged Walid's arm swinging at him as he awoke from a deep sleep. "I was just getting to the good part," Walid said groggily.

"Okay, well, we need you up, like now!" he repeated with urgency and excitement in his voice.

"What, what happened?" Walid said, hopping out of bed. He followed Stephen into the common area of the safe house and saw several people gathered around a speaker phone. *This can't be good*, he thought.

"It's some general," Stephen whispered. "How cool is this!"

Walid felt self-conscious by his disheveled appearance despite being on speakerphone.

"We're all here, sir," Amin said into the phone.

"Thank you for coming so quickly," the general said. Walid couldn't tell if he was being serious or facetious as his tone was low and grave. "For those of you just arriving, my name is General Paul Durand, Director of DGSE's counterterrorism division. We have a few brief but important matters to discuss before I hand you to my deputy."

Walid observed the expressions of those around the table. Amin listened intently, Stephen smiled like a fool, and Eli,

Sydney, and Justin looked more serious, none more so than Sydney. Walid felt most connected to her, worried that the director of Grace's intelligence division was urgently calling them.

"Sir, pardon me, but can you tell us where Grace is?" Walid asked as Stephen hit him on the shoulder and motioned for him to shut up.

"Well, that's one of the matters we need to discuss. I was prepared to ask the same question of you." Walid's heart sank, but he held himself together. "She hasn't used protocol for the last two days."

"We haven't seen her since yesterday morning," Walid said. "She never returned after leaving the safe house to come find me."

"We'll get her back, soldier," the general said. "Which brings me to my next point. I need to figure out what you know about the next operation so we can help each other out."

Walid went on to discuss his meeting with Bashir and the two words Stephen uncovered on the paper.

"Ah, we suspected Syria would be targeted for at least one of the three attacks."

"Why's that?" Amin asked.

"It's all about ideology. Your guys there know all about that."

"Yeah, unfortunately," Eli added solemnly. "Ideology rooted in end-time prophecies. ISD believes that the last battle of the ages will happen in Syria. It will be so significant that it'll involve major world powers and catastrophic casualties. This, they believe, will usher in the coming of el Mahdi, their Messiah."

It sounded as though he was reciting from a book. Walid imagined he must be more familiar with ISD's theology than nearly anyone else given his former role as a recruiter.

"Which means there must be more to this than blowing up Damascus Tower," Sydney postulated.

"Right, Ms. Durand," the general's deputy said. *Sydney's the general's daughter?* Walid thought. That explained a lot about her military demeanor and professionalism. "But we may not figure that part out 'til we get there."

A third man spoke over the line. "We need to start planning," he said. "I'm Raul, Grace's handler. My team knows that area of Damascus well. There's a significant extremist influence there, so we've been researching it for years. And…we think they might be taking Grace there."

"Why?" Walid asked.

"We've been monitoring some of their comms. Don't know why or how, but it seems they wanna make her part of the plan."

"Well, let's book the flights," Walid said.

"We need a plan!" Raul insisted. "The place is heavily guarded by a rebel group called the Ares Brigade."

"Ares, like the god of war?" Stephen asked.

"Whatever they're named after, most of these guys really are warriors, trained from childhood to fight. The group is comprised of loyalists to ISD, but they have a vulnerability. They're not ideologically aligned with the group. ISD is paying them off, and they'll support the highest bidder. Which means they're easier to turn."

"I bet we can turn them," Amin smiled. Walid loved his optimism but knew this wasn't going to be a walk in the park.

"We've tried," Raul said. "It's not so easy. If you have a plan, then let's get you out there. But we need to discuss it first."

"All right, we'll keep the conversation flowing this afternoon," the general said. "Amin, Walid, you and your team need to get yourselves to the Mitiga Airstrip by 1800 tonight."

As soon as the call ended, Eli pulled Walid aside from the group. Although he was growing on him, Walid thought he could certainly use some work on his social cues.

"Walid, you remember the advice you gave me about telling my story?"

"Of course," Walid said.

"Well, I did it! It's on the website."

"That's amazing, Eli!"

"Reason I ask is that I really think you should do the same thing. Especially since we don't know how this operation is gonna turn out." He patted Walid on the back.

"Come on, man, you can't think that way."

"I just don't see any point in waiting," Eli said before walking away.

"Wait!" Walid called to Eli. "Come on…show me how to use that techno-geek equipment."

— — — — — — — — — — — — — — — — — — — —

After hours of site study and war-gaming the infiltration strategy, the group was ready to depart for the airstrip. Mitiga, a smaller airfield on the northern Tripoli coastline, would be safer to use than the international airport. The place was controlled by Islamist militants serving ostensibly under the Tripoli-based government, yet several flights and passenger manifests remained off the books. Walid had long heard rumors that this port was used for black market trade and human smuggling, though, like the manifests, the proof was covered up.

There was only one problem. Well, perhaps two. Walid was now a wanted man, thanks to ISD. His face would likely be recognized if any ISD cronies were at the airport. And second, the Islamist officials at the airport would not be friendly to a Christian group. They would need to conceal their religion and activities to gain passage.

Justin drove a black SUV with tinted windows while everyone created cover stories from the back. Justin was excited about seeing his hometown again, though he had trepidations about seeing what Damascus had become after months of heavy fighting. Things had changed drastically since he was a child living under the regime's authoritarian rule. The regime had always ruled by fear, but it was no longer effective at quelling violence. Nowadays, people feared violence itself as a societal norm. Despite this, he considered himself blessed to be returning. Blessed to be part of the Lord's army.

Amin sat with an uncharacteristically straight face, staring out the window. Walid and Stephen inquired about his well-being, but he insisted he was fine. "Something just feels…off," he explained. Justin pulled into a gravel parking area, and they exited the vehicle.

"Guys, look!" Justin pointed to dark-gray smoke rising from beyond the single-building terminal.

"This can't be good," Stephen said. People started pouring out of the airport doors like floodwaters, which revealed the sound of terror from within.

"Come on," Walid said, heading toward the building.

"Yeah, I mean why wouldn't we?" Stephen said.

They entered the terminal, fighting a sea of utter chaos in the form of panicked passengers fleeing from the opposite direction. It appeared that the airfield's staple lackluster security team was missing from the building entirely. People ran to find loved ones or grab suitcases, while others left their belongings altogether.

One man made a beeline to the group and introduced himself in a frenzy, "The general sent me for you, come quickly!"

They ran after him and followed suit as he hopped a turnstile. People continued to flee. The source of terror seemed to emanate from the airstrip outside. They ran through an unmanned metal detector, which beeped in one resounding blast. The Frenchman slowed his pace and stopped in a waiting area just short of the tarmac. They looked through the glass door—the only thing separating them from the fighting outside. It appeared that someone had hurled what they only imagined was a mortar or RPG at one of the planes, which was now on fire.

"Militia fighting, don't think it's ISD, but who can tell really?" the man said.

"How has it spread so quickly? I thought they only had the international airport," Walid asked.

"Later. See that plane with the blue streak on its tail? That's our plane."

"Oh, good, so we're still going," Stephen said sarcastically. "How are we gonna take off in this firefight?"

"Well, you guys pray, right?" he asked. "Now would be a good time to start…"

"He's right," Amin said. "This could only get worse. We need to move fast. Don't stop praying!"

"Get back!" Justin yelled. The group jumped back from the glass door and flattened themselves against the wall as they saw three militia men running toward the door. The men threw the door open ferociously and ran into the terminal, brandishing assault rifles. Two of them ran directly into the main bay while the third turned to look back out the door and spotted the group.

Nobody moved. The man was young, maybe in his late teens. He hesitated, looking toward his two partners and then back at the group. Gunfire and screaming now echoed chillingly from the main terminal. "Uh, don't go anywhere!" he demanded as he ran into the terminal.

"Yeah, okay, we'll be right here," Stephen said.

"All right, when I start running, follow me," the Frenchman said. "Use anything you can find for cover if you need it."

Walid peered out the glass door; he couldn't see any cover at all. Barring several planes on the tarmac and one abandoned food cart, there was nothing but open space. Suddenly, the Frenchmen yelled "Go!"

He pushed the door open, and the group sprinted toward the plane, which was around one hundred meters away. Once they made it ten meters from the building, they had an entirely new vantage point. Men in uniforms from the Libyan Army, Martyrs Brigade, ISD, and other unknowns fired .223 rounds indiscriminately at each other. It was nearly impossible to tell who was who, although Walid imagined most of the uniforms were probably stolen anyway, so it was anybody's best guess. They also noticed the mounting casualties; three bodies lay motionless around twenty meters to the group's right. Beyond that, closer to the fighting, it was more difficult to tell.

Amin noticed three men loading a surface-to-surface missile launcher and yelled "Faster!" as he pointed at them. He couldn't imagine where they would hide at this point. Walid looked over; the men were pointing the missile directly at them. "Jesus!" Walid could think of nothing else to yell.

The group was around forty meters from the plane when a bright flash of light whirled past their eyes, missing them by merely a few feet. The missile hit a plane fifty meters to their left, resulting in a powerful burst of fire that launched them to the ground.

After a few seconds, Eli stood up like a beast, clearly moved by adrenaline, and pulled two other men to their feet. "Get up!" he yelled.

They started running again. They heard the sounds of machine gun fire bursting behind them, though they clearly weren't the targets this time. They ran up the stairs of the plane, seemingly in the clear as another plane was now shielding them from the missile launchers.

Stephen was the last to board. As he reached the final steps, he cried out in pain and collapsed onto the floor. Stephen looked to the rear and spotted the same teenager who warned them to stay put earlier lowering his pistol. He touched his arm, and it felt wet with blood.

"Move!" Walid yelled to the pilot.

"How do you expect me to take off in this?" the pilot yelled back.

"If we don't try, we're dead anyway!" Eli said.

"Just go!" Amin said. He began to pray out loud, and everyone joined in, whether in faith or sheer panic.

The group felt an abrupt jerk as the pilot accelerated. Walid looked out at the runway, thankful that the takeoff strip ran in the opposite direction of the fighting. The pilot expertly maneuvered between two planes, one which burned with a black smoke pouring out from the tail. The sounds of gunfire could still be heard from the rear of the plane. Stephen remained on the floor in case of stray bullets, and others joined him.

Just as the pilot had straightened the plane for a clean take-off, it shook with a jarring blow that threw everyone off balance. "What's going on?" the copilot yelled.

Walid pushed himself just high enough to see out the window. "I don't see anyone!"

The pilot accelerated, planning to steady and straighten the plane as they started moving. There was no time to recalibrate. The plane reached 60 mph when the group felt another strong hit from the rear. Hazard sirens rang loudly from the cockpit. Walid looked once again to the rear and this time saw a man aiming a rifle at them. *He must have been standing right under the plane*, he thought.

"We might not make it!" the pilot yelled.

"We're going to make it!" Amin yelled back, despite hearing a clanking sound coming from underneath the plane, as though it was straining to accelerate.

The front wheels lifted off the ground and just as quickly came crashing down. "Here we go!" the pilot screamed as the plane reached the end of the runway. It powerfully broke through a chain-link fence and started to rise after a few seconds of off-roading. Finally, they were airborne.

"Told you we'd make it!" the pilot yelled. Everyone hollered in excitement as they watched the ground move farther from sight. "Just one problem," he said. "Landing gear might be shot…literally."

"Great," Eli said with frustration.

"We'll figure it out," the Frenchman said. "By the way, I'm Gilles. Sorry, I didn't introduce myself earlier." Gilles was young; Walid estimated around thirty years of age, though he probably appeared younger due to his wild, childlike exuberance. Walid liked him—reminded him a lot of himself before he became jaded by ISD.

"Yeah, should've been more cordial when we were dodging missiles back there!" Stephen said.

Gilles laughed more than most people would have, which made the others laugh as well. "I think I'm gonna like you," Stephen said, patting him on the back.

The rest of the group introduced themselves briefly as they tended to Stephen's wounds. "How bad is it?" Gilles asked.

"Just skimmed my arm. I'll be all right."

"That was quite the dramatic fall for a skim!" Walid said.

"Hey, man, I could've died back there!" Stephen said. Walid rolled his eyes.

"So…what's the plan for when we land?" Gilles asked. Nobody responded. "Okay…so we'll wing it!"

"Amin's always got an idea," Sydney said.

"Maybe we could just listen and think for a few minutes," Amin said. He sounded fatigued and bothered by something, but nobody pushed the matter.

Sydney, Justin, and Gilles discussed ideas quietly while the others prayed. Walid was impressed by their intellect and eagerness but tried to tune them out as he looked out the window. They were nearing the Lebanese coastline of the Mediterranean Sea. It looked colorful, vibrant, and metropolitan—almost like it was part of a different planet than the desert areas of North Africa. Walid tried to listen to the Lord but could only think of the two-part dream he had. He got Amin's attention and pulled him to the back of the plane. After explaining the dream, Amin pursed his lips and looked down, as though deep in thought.

"Did you hear me?" Walid asked. "You've been really different today."

"I know, sorry I've made it so obvious. I believe we're on the right track, I really do. It's just…I have a bad feeling that I can't quite place. It's about someone on this plane, and their safety."

"Who?"

"I don't wanna get anyone worked up just yet. Pray with me, would you?"

"Of course."

"Anyway, about your dream, I believe you'll have another one soon. The final part is missing, and it seems to be necessary for our full understanding."

"Seems like a lot is missing."

"Not a lot necessarily, just the glue. God clearly has you on a critical mission, and it's dangerous, but He's given you safe passageway even when it looks impossible. The sounds of drums represent something evil. Perhaps you'll have a close encounter with ISD soon."

"Oh, great," Walid said sarcastically.

"It is, really," Amin smiled. "The Lord is trying to tell you something exciting. The situation is dangerous by the world's standards, but He will protect you. He is giving you advance notice of a future encounter. He must want you to be prepared."

"Yeah, you're right. I don't feel afraid, it's just hard not knowing the particulars. You know I'm a strategist, right?"

"He'll pull everything together for you. Don't stop trusting in that."

Just then, the copilot yelled to the group. "Guys, we have a problem!" Everyone moved to the front of the plane to listen. "There's been a change of plans. We're goin' to Beirut."

"What? Why?" Gilles asked.

"Damascus isn't responding. The airfield seems to have closed unexpectedly. We can't risk flying in blind, it's suicide!"

"Maybe ISD had the same problem!" Gilles said enthusiastically.

"Let's hope so," Walid said.

"Or they caused it…" Eli said. "We might be too late to stop anything at this point."

"And what if we're not?" Amin asked.

"Come on, man, be positive for once in your life!" Stephen said, frustrated with his doggedly negative attitude.

"Yeah, it's just another adventure!" Gilles said. "What should we do now?"

"Turn around," Eli said before moving to the back of the plane.

"We're not turning around!" the pilot said. "You wanna land in that hellfire we just passed through?"

"Guys, we'll figure it out," Sydney said. "What choice do we have right now?"

Everybody looked out the windows in silent acquiescence. They could debate all they wanted to, but Sydney was right. Where else would they go right now?

Amin walked over to Eli and placed his hand on his shoulder. "What's going on with you?"

"I don't know…I'm scared. Not just about this flight, but…well, I can't really place it." Amin knew he was hiding something but didn't know what was truly frightening him.

"Dear friend," Amin said. "Have you ever felt the joy of the Lord?"

"What?" Eli asked. "What's that gotta do with anything?"

"Everything," Amin said. His voice was sad and impassioned. He ferociously wanted Eli to heal and fully experience God's great love. "You're still angry about the past, aren't you."

"I can't just make that go away," he said.

"God already has, though," Amin said. "He's forgotten your sins, and he wants you to feel His joy. That's what's going to fully heal you. Don't you see? You'll never change what you've done, but you can change the future."

"Yeah," Eli said unconvincingly.

They looked out the windows once again. They had finally descended below the clouds and were drawing close to the airport.

"Hey, team!" the pilot yelled. "Better buckle in, this might be a messy landing!"

CHAPTER 20

The Narrow Pass

"Anyone need this?" Stephen asked, holding the crash landing instructions in the air. Nobody responded. "Too soon?"

Walid could see the airport clearly now. He prayed for Jesus's blood covering over the team. He had only recently learned about the covenant God had made with him through Jesus when he accepted Him as Lord and Savior. There was power in this covenant! And if he called on the blood covenant he had in Jesus, nothing could possibly break through. He tried to focus on this as they descended.

"Here we go!" the pilot yelled as they neared the ground.

The pilot had been conversing with Beirut International's control tower for the last ten minutes. Walid didn't understand the language but recognized the swear word the pilot used before hanging up the phone. He yelled one final warning to the group. "Brace yourselves!"

Everyone braced against whatever they could. Finally, the wait was over. As the plane touched down, the impact jarred their bodies in what felt to Walid like falling from one hundred feet into water at an awkward angle. The plane started to slow down, but not quickly enough. Sparks were flying everywhere. Sydney yelled from the rear of the plane, where she sat with Justin and Gilles, pleading with God to save them. The plane started to turn, moving forward from a diagonal position.

"We're gonna hit!" the pilot screamed from the cockpit. The plane had veered off the landing strip and hit a metal pole with such force that the plane ripped in two. After another few seconds, both sections of the plane came to a complete stop. Amin, Stephen, Walid, and Eli were in the front half of the plane with the pilots. They only suffered minor injuries, which Walid imagined had to be God's doing. Such a landing should have killed them.

As they tried to unbuckle themselves, due to the angle in which the plane landed, they nearly fell out the back of the plane onto the tarmac when their seatbelts were released. Amin's continued to hold him in place; his seatbelt had nearly fused with the metal wall due to the heat.

While Stephen helped him escape, Walid and Eli spotted the tail end of the plane. Their jaws dropped in horror as they observed thick black smoke pouring out from the fuselage in a steady stream. They started running toward the plane. When they came within twenty meters of the plane, a minor explosion knocked them both to the ground.

"Oh, come on! Could anything else happen?" Eli screamed in exasperation. Walid got up and put his hand out for Eli. "Don't…" He punched the ground with his fist and stared at the tarmac.

"Take it easy," Walid said, pulling his hand back. He looked at the plane, squinted, and rubbed his eyes, thinking he was hallucinating. "Do you see that?"

"Oh my God," Eli said as he saw Gilles and Sydney making their way slowly over to them. Sydney was holding Gilles up; he was limping on his right foot. Walid and Eli ran to meet them.

"Where's Justin?" Eli asked. Sydney and Gilles looked as though they were in shock, blank expressions marking their faces. As Eli reached them, he grabbed Sydney by the shoulders firmly, trying to snap her out of it. "Sydney, please, where's Justin?" he repeated. Her eyes welled with tears.

"He's stuck," is all she could manage to say between gasps.

Eli let her go and ran toward the plane. Walid followed suit; he had never seen Eli so concerned about someone in his life. There had to be more to their connection than he realized. As they reached the plane, they tied their shirts over their mouths; the black smoke made it difficult to see or breathe. Finally, they spotted him. Justin was attached to his seat but separated from the plane, and he wasn't moving. Eli ran over to him and unbuckled him from the seat, part of which had lodged into his arm. Forty percent of his body appeared to be covered with third-degree burns. After suppressing a heavy sob that he felt rising to the surface, he started doing CPR.

Walid snapped out of his shock after hearing the sounds of an ambulance. Seconds later, Lebanese first responders arrived and ran over to Justin. Eli refused to stop CPR despite their arrival. Then after his third attempt, Justin gasped for air and opened his left eye; his right was swollen shut. Two medics pushed Eli aside and moved Justin to the ambulance, still attached to his seat.

Amin, Stephen, and both pilots were now standing by and speaking with the first responders and policemen. Eli and Walid stood at the back of the ambulance and tried to speak with Justin.

"Justin, you're gonna be OK," Walid said calmly.

"I know," Justin said with a weak smile. "He told me."

"Who did?" Eli asked, though Walid knew exactly who he meant.

"He was so beautiful, like a rainbow-colored lightning bolt."

"He's delirious," Eli said to Walid.

"No, he's not," Walid said. "Justin, you saw Jesus, didn't you! I saw him once too, in a dream."

"Yes, brother!" Justin said. "Now I need to tell you something. You guys must go quickly and leave me here. There isn't much time left, I saw it. And don't try to convince me otherwise. I'll be fine here, trust me!"

The conviction with which Justin spoke made Walid wonder if he had received some kind of insight from Jesus. "I know you will. God is with you, my friend!"

"So we're just gonna leave him alone in foreign country. Good plan, guys," Eli said.

"Not alone," Sydney said. "I'm staying with him. He'll need someone after surgery." She stepped into the ambulance with Justin and grabbed his hand before they could protest. "We'll be praying for you every day…probably every hour until we hear from you again!"

As the ambulance drove away, Amin and Stephen finally made their way over to them. "Where are they going?" Amin asked.

"We'll tell you on the way to the border," Walid said. "We don't have much time."

_ _ _ _ _ _ _ _ _ _ _ _ _ _ _ _ _ _ _ _

Two snipers lay in the prone position on both sides of a narrow dirt road, waiting for their orders. The bushes concealed their positions from anyone traveling the road. "Hold your fire," a deep voice said into their earpieces as they continued to stare vigilantly into their sights, following a black SUV with their crosshairs. "Stay at the ready," the voice said.

The SUV raced through the narrow pass. It had just entered contested territory, though it was chiefly controlled by the Ares Militia. Stephen drove erratically, trying to avoid any potential stray bullets or pressure plates that may come in their path. Walid, however, believed he was simply living out some dormant desire to be a NASCAR driver.

"Getting there alive would be preferable!" Eli yelled to Stephen from the backseat. Stephen failed to slow his pace but simply gave a thumbs-up. They had passed a bullet-ridden border crossing sign around ten miles back, precisely at the same time their air-conditioning system blew out. The temperature had risen to over 105 degrees Fahrenheit, and nobody had the energy to chitchat, especially after their ordeal in Beirut. Except for Gilles, that is.

"Guys!" Gilles yelled over the sound of wind screaming through their windows. Eli sighed in annoyance. If they had learned one thing about Gilles on this trip, it's that he loved the sound of his own voice.

"I've read about this area! We just passed Jdaidit Yabws!"

"Gesundheit!" Stephen said.

"We're heading into the Ares Brigade's territory. Those guys are savages, from what I've read."

"Yeah…we got briefed on them back in Libya," Walid said.

"So you know they mean business then!" Gilles said. "Supposedly they're supporting ISD's next attack."

"Maybe so," Walid said. "But they're not loyal. The second ISD challenges their authority, they'll fight them."

"They're not loyal to us either," Eli said. "And right now, ISD has a lot more to offer them than we do."

"Ever the optimist," Walid said. He nudged Amin, who was once again strangely quiet. "You okay?"

Amin nodded but looked concerned. "I still have a bad feeling, about him," he said, nodding in Eli's direction. "Pray for him?" Walid nodded in agreement.

Suddenly, the group heard a loud pop, and the SUV rapidly slowed and swerved all over the road. Stephen focused on controlling the vehicle and successfully brought it to a stop. "I didn't see anything in the road," he said. "What did we hit?"

They got out and looked at the tires; one of them was nearly shredded. They looked around but didn't notice anything out of place. The landscape was relatively sparse save a few housing units and shrubs along the dirt road. Amin leaned over and picked a fragment of a bullet casing out of the rubber. "Oh…we didn't hit anything," he said.

"Get back in the car," Walid said.

"Halt!" they heard someone yell before they could move. They looked around but saw nobody. The voice came from beyond the hill they had been driving up.

"We're not moving," Stephen said.

"Shut up, Stephen," Eli whispered.

A man wearing a sand-colored military uniform walked to the hilltop from behind the berm. He carried a .249 machine gun that looked far too large for his gangly frame. Walid knew better than to be overconfident by his appearance; he wouldn't have come alone. The man waved his arm to summon them.

"Go…" Amin said quietly. As the group walked up the hill, he walked down in the opposite direction. When they reached the hilltop, they could see down into the valley.

"Woah," Stephen said. He looked at the others, eyes wide all around.

The valley sprawled for miles. The terrain itself was nearly undetectable as a blanket of people as far as they could see kept it concealed. But they weren't just people. They were armed warriors.

"Guess this would be a bad time to run," Walid said.

He took a step forward, prepared to begin discussions with the man leading the charge. The gangly man who summoned them had stopped moving. He gazed into the valley at the warriors, his right arm still shaking in the air.

"Guys?" Amin said. "Something's not right."

"They don't wanna talk," Walid said.

The man lowered his arm quickly, and all hell broke loose. Thousands of men from the valley released a terrifying shout, and scores of men from their right and left flank ran toward them.

"Don't run!" Amin shouted.

"Where would we go anyway?" Stephen said.

The warriors surrounded them and chanted something they couldn't understand. They had elaborate black markings all over their arms and some on their necks and faces. The gangly leader cut through the crowd, most of whom were twice his size, and they became silent.

"We come as friends," Amin said.

"Of course you do," the man spat.

"It's true, we mean you no harm, brother. We're just on our way through, traveling to Damascus."

"You are not my brother," the man laughed. It reminded Walid of the emir's laugh. "Yes, much urgency I'm sure." He nodded toward one of the warriors and walked away. The warriors tightened their circle again.

"Wait! You must believe us!" Walid yelled.

"Oh, I do," the man said with his back to them still. "You're not going anywhere."

The warriors chanted again and dragged them down into the valley.

CHAPTER 21

The Gate Between Life and Death

The drumbeat grew louder, such that Walid felt compelled to cover his ears with both hands. Despite this, he couldn't stop himself from walking toward it. It was now completely dark. The light that was illuminating his path shone solely on him alone. The faint glow of a multitude of red lights that looked like fireflies peppered the darkness. As he moved into the heart of the forest, Walid realized red lights were torches held by people standing around a massive circular granite panel.

"Wake up!" Walid heard a voice yell thunderously from behind him. He observed his six but saw nothing. He turned his head back to the masses, and the drumbeat ceased. Everyone stared at him with blank expressions.

Walid felt compelled to walk toward the circular panel in the middle of the woods. A woman lay fast asleep in the center. Upon closer inspection, he realized it was her deathbed. She looked familiar, but Walid couldn't quite place her. The same thunderous voice with great authority spoke to the woman. "I said, wake up. In Jesus's name, be healed!"

A bright blue lightning bolt came down from the sky and hit the granite circle, shattering it into thousands of pieces. Walid looked around, and the people were gone. Light filled the bright blue sky and the woman opened her eyes and smiled excitedly at Walid.

"Your voice…," Walid said, nearly speechless. "I want that boldness, Lord! Where'd everyone go?"

Jesus did not appear this time but responded in the same thunderous voice. "That was you speaking, Walid."

– – – – – – – – – – – – – – – – – – – –

Walid heard the eerie drumbeat yet again. *I thought this was over*, he thought. His head throbbed and his vision blurry. *Am I still sleeping?*

"Walid?" he heard Amin's voice and shook his head, trying to focus. Amin and Stephen stood over him in a small dirt cavern cut out of a rock formation with a metal fence blocking the entrance. The place felt chillingly like a tomb.

"Where are we?" Walid said, feeling dry blood on the back of his head. "What happened?"

"Buttstock to the head," Amin said. "You okay?"

"I think so."

"And no idea where we are, they blindfolded us. We didn't go far though. They brought us somewhere in the valley."

Stephen walked over to Gilles, who was huddled in a corner of the small cave. "Hey, man, you all right?"

"Yeah, just another adventure," he said, trying to feign his exuberance.

"We're gonna get out of here, you know."

"Yeah, I know. I've just been thinking, and praying. Wouldn't it be awesome to get out of here miraculously? You know, like how Peter escaped from prison in the book of Acts."

"Epic, man."

"Why shouldn't it happen?" Amin interrupted. "Remember how we escaped ISD when we were captives?" he asked Stephen.

"Of course!" Stephen said.

Amin nudged Walid and nodded toward Eli, who leaned against the cave wall and stared at the ground. Walid shrugged.

"Can we pray for wisdom?" Gilles suggested.

Before they could start, they heard footsteps approaching. "Do it quietly," Amin said. The footsteps came to a halt directly in front of the metal gate. Everyone stood up as it swung open.

"Welcome to the village," a young twentysomething Arabic man said in a strangely welcoming tone. He was accompanied by five warriors who stared menacingly at them. "We're supposed to bring you to the boss. Please, follow me."

"This just got weirder," Stephen said quietly.

"Who's the boss?" Walid asked.

"Oh, he doesn't like to be named," the man said. "Come along."

Walid smirked at the guys and somehow found the whole situation to be ridiculous. It seemed like something he could have read about in a book on cults.

It was dark outside, and the men could see little aside from the torches surrounding them. The torches proliferated as they continued to walk. Walid thought of his dream and wondered if God was giving him some kind of sign. Finally, they reached a large opening in the terrain. The warriors presumably were standing in a large circular formation due to the shape of the torches. *It couldn't be a sign, could it?* It was far too similar to be coincidence. Walid felt fearful over what the Lord might tell him to do. *I'm not strong enough yet, Lord,* he told the Lord. *Have Amin do it.*

The gangly leader walked into the circle to meet them. "What did you think would happen, exactly?"

"What?" Amin asked.

"Barreling through our territory! *What do you mean,*" he mocked Amin. "Thought we wouldn't be expecting you?"

"Who told you?"

"That's no matter to you! I have strict orders to detain you for as long as necessary."

"From who? You have no idea what you're doing!"

"How dare you!" He punched Amin in the face, causing him to recoil. Amin was thankful this man wasn't nearly the size of anyone else in his army. "What do you know of me or what I'm capable of?"

"I know you're not a terrorist," Amin said. The boss raised an eyebrow, clearly not expecting this response. "I know you're better than the people you're supporting. You're not like them. But you do it anyway, probably 'cause they're paying you handsomely. You're not the only one who knows things."

The boss hit Amin again, causing him to fall to his knees. "You know nothing!" he screamed.

"I know that you need the money, which is why you accept it, blind to what you're allowing to happen. And…I know you need the Lord, and that He loves you despite everything."

"Amin, stop!" Eli pleaded.

The boss didn't hit him this time but just stood there boiling in his fury.

"It's not your fault. ISD did this to you! I know they pay you off in return for their safe passage through your land, without which they wouldn't stand a chance against your capable warriors. They're taking advantage of you!" The passion and confidence in Amin's voice grew steadily, which made the boss visibly uncomfortable.

"Stop talking!" the boss demanded.

"No! You must hear what I have to say," Amin said. The boss's bodyguards raised their weapons, dumbfounded. Clearly, nobody had stood up to the boss before.

Suddenly, Walid understood what God was trying to tell him in his dream. Adrenaline pumped into his heart as though being hit with a defibrillator. He had been pleased that Amin was doing all the talking, but now God was prompting him through a still, small voice, telling him to speak. *No, please, I'm not ready.*

"Lower your weapons," the boss said.

Amin continued without invitation. "ISD gives you money, and for what? They either bomb or commandeer any business you create. They're responsible for the impoverished state of this region and claim it's the Western powers, yet they refuse to allow Western nations to bring you aid and training. Don't you see? They need you to remain in this dire third world condition to ensure they remain in power. They rule through fear and yet demand your loyalty because they're doing the will of God. What kind of God wants you to be poor, sick, and hurting? Certainly not my God!"

"God doesn't care about us mortals," the boss said.

"God loves you! And so do we. We want to help you."

"God couldn't possibly love us. You know nothing about us!" he said resolutely, though his tone was softening.

The prompting grew stronger in Walid's spirit until he couldn't hold back any longer. *Okay, God, you wouldn't be doing this if you didn't have my back. Here goes...*

"You have a daughter, don't you," Walid asked the boss.

"What?" the boss said. "What are you trying to prove? Anyone could have guessed such a thing!"

"She's dying."

The boss paused for a moment, trying to suppress his emotions. "Who told you that?" he asked.

"Jesus told me," Walid explained. "And He wants to heal her. Bring her here."

The boss stared at Walid, trying to read him. Nobody said a word for at least a minute; the quiet was deafening. Walid spoke to God in the silence. *Lord, I'm counting on you right now to show your power. Please, Father, show yourself in a mighty way. 'Cause I don't feel very powerful.*

The boss finally spoke. "If you're lying, I'll make sure you never leave this place." He walked away and left the men standing in the circle, still surrounded by warriors. It would be futile to attempt an escape, though Walid debated it in a moment of weakness. Amin smiled at Walid like a proud father.

"Walid," Gilles whispered. "This is so God. How exciting!"

Everyone was truly excited except for Eli. "Man, they're gonna kill us if you can't do this."

"Nice pep talk," Stephen said. "Walid, don't listen to that junk. It's not you doing this, it's the Lord doing this through you. You know that." Walid nodded.

Ten minutes later, the boss returned with four men carrying a makeshift stretcher. There was a woman lying motionless on it. Walid felt more confident than ever. He recognized her from his dream!

"All right, do your magic," the boss said.

"It's not magic," Walid said. "It's our God working through me. He wants to prove his love for you."

The boss simply motioned to his daughter, trying to rush him along. The warriors laid the stretcher on the ground, and Walid knelt beside her. He realized in that moment that he had no idea what to do. *What now?* he asked God. Walid place his hand on her, and she began to shake violently and foam at the mouth. It appeared she was having a seizure.

"What are you doing?" the boss screamed. Walid closed his eyes and remained focused on the Lord. Finally, he spoke. "Lord, show your love for this woman. Heal her and remove the spirit of death trying to take her life."

At that moment, the woman stopped seizing and lay motionless on the ground.

"What have you done!" the boss screamed.

"Guys, come here!" Walid called his group over and had everyone lay hands on her. There was no breath left in the girl. She had died. Walid focused with all his might on the Lord, refusing to be led by fear of the circumstances, which were looking pretty bleak at the moment. Gilles smiled to reassure him. "Jesus is here, Walid. I feel it."

In fact, everyone could feel His presence. Miraculously, as though on cue, Amin and Walid shouted passionately and simultaneously, "In the name of Jesus, get up!"

The woman immediately started coughing and rolled over onto her side, spitting out some kind of growth from her mouth. The boss looked on in amazement, his jaw floored by what he just witnessed. He stared at his daughter, and she tried to get her bearings. "Where am I? And what is *that*?" she said, referencing whatever had come out of her.

"It's whatever was causing you to be sick, but praise God, it's not part of you anymore!" Walid said.

"Bella, you're not well. We need to get you home," the boss said.

"What are you talking about? I feel fine! Better than ever!" she said excitedly and stood to her feet. "You did this, didn't you," she said to Walid.

"No, God did this."

"I know, I saw it! Please, tell me how to get your God in my life. He saved me when I don't even know him."

'You saw what? God?" the boss asked dubiously.

"Yes, Daddy. You need Him too. Please, don't waste any more time."

At this, the boss started crying uncontrollably. His warriors didn't know how to react and looked around uncomfortably. The boss had never shown this kind of emotion publicly. His daughter put her hand on his shoulder. "Father, what's wrong?"

"You are completely well! It's impossible!"

"Obviously not," she said.

"This is real."

"It is," Walid said.

Amin, Walid, Stephen, and Gilles prayed over the two to receive the Lord. When they opened their eyes, there was a line of warriors waiting to say the same prayer! When some accepted

Jesus into their hearts, they would pray over others in the tribe. Many were filled with joy and started dancing. Walid heard the drumbeat start again, but this time it was melodic and rhythmic. One man grabbed Gilles by the arm and brought him into their circle to dance. They laughed as Gilles tried to copy their steps unsuccessfully.

Amin got Walid's attention and pointed in the direction of a few tribesmen who were whispering to each other before fleeing the scene. Clearly some in the tribe were still skeptical.

"Forget about it." "Look how many people *did* get saved. God has given us the victory tonight!"

"Lord knows tomorrow will have enough troubles of its own," Amin agreed.

—————————————————

"I don't understand," the boss said. He had finally revealed his name to be Tarek. "Just what are you planning to do?"

"We don't really know yet," Walid said. "ISD has kept this operation extremely close hold."

Tarek poured more tea for each of the men in preparation for their sendoff. They sat on large, handwoven pillows surrounding a short table in the middle of a tent. Two of the warriors who converted the previous night sat with them as well.

"You'll have the element of surprise if nothing else," Tarek said. He turned to one of his warriors. "Has it been done?"

"Of course," the man said. Tarek smiled deviously.

"What did we miss?" Stephen asked.

"We spoke with our ISD contact this morning. They knew you were coming. We've kindly informed them that you will remain in our custody."

"Perfect!" Gilles said.

"I only wish we could do more for you. What you have done for this tribe is beyond our gratitude. Though some of our fine warriors don't feel the same way. Pray for us, and them, if you would, and return when it's safer."

"We will return," Amin promised. "And we'll bring Bibles and anything else you need. Take this, if you need us." He handed Tarek a paper with a phone number.

"And consider our offer," Walid urged. "We could really use people with this tribe's skills."

Tarek embraced each of them. "I'll be in touch."

CHAPTER 22

Damascus Tower

Stephen drove the guys down a narrow, bumpy road through the Syrian countryside in a cramped, white Toyota given to them by Tarek's tribe. They expected to see destruction after more than three years of intense fighting, but nothing could have prepared them for how bad it would be. The sights were horrendous to behold.

For the last several years, groups who disapproved of the government's authoritarian rule and violent suppression of dissention, among other things, had been fighting for change. Dissatisfaction grew to a boiling point after the government started quelling opposition fighters with bombings and airstrikes.

Close to a year ago, ISD decided to get involved. Walid and Eli were intimately familiar with ISD's Syria strategy. ISD spent much the last year capitalizing on the country's insecurity by carving out a safe haven and building loyalties by helping the opposition fight the regime. The group could then leverage its influence to establish a true caliphate.

Merely two weeks ago, ISD grew closer to realizing its dream. A permanent ceasefire was declared after the opposition killed the country's leader. The militia responsible claimed it to be an accident, unwittingly bombing a location where he was meeting with his closest confidantes. Walid knew better. He suspected they were trying to save face, afraid of an impending violent backlash. He also knew this "permanent ceasefire" would quickly end when the race for power continued.

The event was all over the news. Some protested and rioted while others rejoiced in the streets, ostensibly safe for the first time in years. Most locals didn't even live there anymore; it had become too dangerous to stay put, especially when they had families to provide for.

Nobody spoke as they stared out their windows at the rubble where key infrastructure once stood. News outlets had posted rumors of regime escalation several months ago: bombings of schools, hospitals, farms, and any other form of livelihood to force loyalty and dependence from anyone opposed to the regime. Clearly they were more than rumors.

"Where is everyone?" Stephen asked. "I knew it would be desolate, but this is like something out of a postapocalyptic movie."

"Who knows…Refugee and IDP camps, probably surrounding countries, Europe, anywhere they can migrate safely," Amin said.

"This is sick," Gilles said as they drove past piles of concrete waste resembling the Roman ruins. "Hope whoever lived here made it out before all this…"

As they drove down the dirt highway, they were forced to a stop sporadically due to the debris. "This is insane," Eli said as they removed cinder blocks out of the road to clear a path. "We'll never make it at this rate. How did ISD even get people in here?"

"They probably used the airport," Walid said. "I dunno, maybe that's why Damascus didn't respond."

"I'm starting to think you don't even want to arrive," Stephen said, allowing a rare teardrop to fall from his face. Though humor typically masked his pain, it had been the result of overflowing joy since he came to know the Lord. Today though, after seeing the results of the airstrikes, there was nothing amusing to think about. He prayed for strength, for joy in the midst of this carnage, and for the very people he was about to face.

Once they got back into the vehicle, Stephen accelerated faster than anyone anticipated, launching them back into their seats. "Sorry, guys, like Eli said, time's a wastin'!"

Stephen sped over a sharp hilltop, nearly causing the tires to lose traction.

"Take it easy! Are you trying to get us killed?" Eli said.

"Come on, live a little!"

Damascus was now in sight. Amin checked his map app to make sure they were really in Damascus. It looked nothing like the pictures. While several buildings continued to stand strong, even more sat in piles of rubble. Some had large chunks that had been blown out. Hardly any color remained; the city was a mess of sepia tones as desert winds had covered the rubble with a thin layer of dust.

"Woah," Stephen said, decelerating to a slow roll.

"We have to keep moving, Stephen," Amin urged.

"The place is already destroyed," Gilles said. "Why would ISD want to attack anything here?"

"What if this was just a decoy?" Walid asked.

"It can't be," Amin said. "Every clue pointed us here."

"This is all a waste of time," Eli said.

The tires squealed as Stephen pulled maniacally into the parking lot of an Internet café just off the road.

"Take it easy!" Amin said, hitting Stephen's arm.

"Restroom break," Stephen said. "And sanity break. Sorry, Eli, man, but your negativity is driving me insane."

Everyone followed Stephen into the café, which was open, much to everyone's surprise. The place was modern and exotic. Global cityscapes were painted on the light-green walls like murals. Colorful accent chairs and contemporary metal tables filled the space. More impressively, the place made it through months of intense airstrikes unscathed. Amin asked the waiter for a coffee, and the group made small talk with him, trying to ascertain more about the city as Al-Arabiya news played on the big screen behind the bar.

"I have to stay open," the waiter explained. "It's the only way I can provide for my family anymore. The fighting is over, yes, but there are no customers. I pray for more business as the exiles begin to return."

"Pray to who?" Gilles asked. Stephen pushed him as though he was being rude.

"It's all right," he smiled. "You know, religious debates are unwelcome these days, but I feel that I can trust you. Just between us, Jesus is the only one keeping this shop from going under. Look at the state of this city! Most shops you will find are no longer open. But He has provided for me and my family miraculously."

"Praise the Lord!" Amin said. "We follow Jesus too."

"Guys, look!" Gilles interrupted; his eyes glued to the television screen.

"Turn it up!" Walid said.

An Arabic man spoke in front of a green screen showing various parts of Syria, seemingly the worst parts. "Today is a historic day in Damascus. Our sources have revealed a secret meeting that has been planned since the fall of the president, scheduled to occur this very evening. Representatives from several nations, including the Quartet, will meet with Syrian political and military leaders to strategize the way forward for this battered country. The location remains a secret. More to come on this historic event this evening at six."

"Nope, not a decoy," Stephen said.

'How does Al Arabiya know about this?" Walid asked. "They must have somebody on the inside."

"Or it's a leak, who knows," Amin said. "But we've got an insider too. Thank God Bashir gave you the location!"

"I hope I get to thank him someday," Walid said.

"I dunno what this is all about, and I'm not sure I want to," the waiter said. "But we are brothers in Christ, and I'd honored to cover you in prayer."

Each of them promised to pray for the waiter as well and embraced before making the final trek into downtown Damascus.

— — — — — — — — — — — — — — — — — — —

Stephen drove within four blocks of Damascus Tower and parked on a side street.

"So much for being inconspicuous," Eli said. Their car was the only one on the entire street.

Stephen felt energized by their encounter with the waiter. Amin had started praying aloud from the time the group left the café. Gilles and Walid joined in sporadically, and Stephen kept his eyes fixed on the road. Everyone save Eli was growing more excited about their impending mission despite the inherent danger. There was something exhilarating about the mystery of this operation and their need to completely rely on God.

The men started walking toward the hotel. It was close to 3:00 p.m. As they approached the building from the rear, it was clear that none of the leaders had arrived yet due to the absence of security and vehicles. They didn't know when the meeting would occur or what ISD had in store, but they assumed this meant they had at least an hour or so.

"This doesn't look right," Gilles said. "Seems too easy."

"Let's not walk into a trap then," Walid said.

They had removed their phone batteries and left them in the car for security reasons and decided to use hand signals from that point on. Despite the place looking like a ghost town, they moved with military precision to conceal their positions. As they reached the entrance, Amin signaled for the group to wait as he peered inside one of the many opulent windows adorning this five-star hotel. He looked back and shrugged to indicate that everything appeared normal. He motioned for them to follow as he opened a door and walked into the lobby.

The men were greeted by massive golden pillars, dim lights sprinkling the ceiling like stars, and a huge crystal chandelier shaped like a hawk in the center of the room. Walid shook his head as he walked past a golden statue of the now-deceased president with the colors of the Syrian flag intertwined throughout. Nobody was in sight, but they kept their bodies pressed against the walls. Then out of the silence, a voice.

"Gentlemen! We've been expecting you."

They stopped and observed their surroundings. "Who said that?" Walid whispered.

Then a woman appeared from a door behind the front desk. Her smile gave them chills.

Amin was the only one to return her smile. "No, ma'am, I think you have the wrong party."

"I don't see how that's possible," she said. Her high-pitched voice was extremely sweet but equally as transparent. "Is there a Walid among you?"

Walid's heart dropped into his stomach. *So much for the element of surprise!* he thought. How on earth did they know he was coming? Lost in confusion, he said nothing while the others stared at him. "Thanks, guys," Walid whispered sarcastically.

"You dear," she said to Walid. "Wonderful. Your party is expecting you plus one Amin on the twelfth floor."

"Our party?" Walid asked. "What are you talking about? Who is our party?"

"Shouldn't you know your own party?" she giggled. "Run along now. Unfortunately, the rest of you will have to stay in the lobby as you are not on the VIP list."

"Go, it's okay," Stephen said. What other choice did they have, after all?

Stephen, Gilles, and Eli sat on a plush green-and-white paisley couch while Amin and Walid walked to the stairwell.

"How did they know?" Walid whispered as they started ascending the marble staircase.

"I have a theory," Amin said, "but it's not important right now. We're gonna have to rely on God for this one."

They started praying as they walked up eight flights of stairs. Walid tried to focus on hearing from the Lord, but his mind wandered to Grace and what ISD could have in store for her. "Wait," he said. "What if Grace…"

"Stop," Amin said. "Walid, we need to listen to Him right now. You can't start thinking that way! That's exactly what the enemy wants you to do."

Walid appreciated Amin's bluntness and snapped back into focus. He felt his training kicking in again, just like in New York.

As they reached the twelfth floor, they took their 9 mms out of their chest holsters, flipped the safety off, and cocked the hammer. Walid gently opened the door, though it probably didn't matter. ISD almost certainly had received a call by now from the receptionist. He and Amin remained close to the walls with their weapons at the low ready. Nobody was in sight.

The walked to the end of the hallway, which led to two large double doors with a posh emerald green lighted "VIP Lounge" sign. Walid was reminded of his days in the Tunisian army, clearing rooms left and right while searching for suspected terrorists or violent regime oppositionists. He had done most of those operations robotically; emotion was a crutch for any good soldier. This time, however, there was far more at stake, and Walid couldn't separate the two.

He looked at Amin as he prepared to open the door. Amin nodded his approval and took aim at whatever he might see behind those doors.

Walid opened the door abruptly and barged in with Amin on his heels. Nothing could have prepared them for what they saw. The panicked eyes of close to a dozen gagged people looked straight at them. They sat in a tight circle near the center of the living room. Walid scanned the crowd quickly, but Grace was nowhere to be found. As Walid and Amin drew closer, the people shook their heads as though warning them to turn back.

Then a click, which both recognized as the sound of a gun cocking. They knew better than to take another step.

A voice emerged from the direction of the click. Neither men moved, but Walid noticed a fireplace and a barstool in his peripheral vision. A woman sat on the stool casually. "We've been expecting you," she said. Walid recognized the voice immediately. It was Fatima.

— — — — — — — — — — — — — — — — —

Back in the lobby, Stephen, Gilles, and Eli sat in the waiting area, glancing occasionally at the receptionist who failed to conceal the fact that she was watching them.

"We need to do something," Stephen whispered. "She's obviously ISD."

"Must be," Gilles agreed. "I have an idea." He started to stand, but Eli grabbed his arm and pulled him back down.

"Don't do anything stupid!" he snapped.

"So what, we just sit here and do nothing? Is that your plan?" Gilles asked.

"No. Watch and learn," he said. Gilles threw his arms up in frustration.

Eli walked over to the receptionist and started making conversation, though Stephen and Gilles couldn't hear him. After two or three minutes, a muscular Arab man in a busboy uniform emerged from a back room and escorted Eli to the elevator. Eli winked back at the men as they stared at him in confusion. "No freakin' way," Stephen said.

"Something feels wrong about him," Gilles said. "And not just this one instance. I don't think we can trust him."

"I agree. We need to make a move."

"Let's go talk to her."

"Stop!" the receptionist screeched before they had taken more than a few steps. Two men and a woman in the same busboy uniforms emerged from the back room. "We have very important guests arriving at any moment," she said in the same sweet voice she used before. "We can't have you just lollygagging about in our esteemed lobby!" She turned to the three 'busboys.' "Please, escort them to their private quarters."

"Why'd you let Eli go?" Stephen protested.

"We're not going anywhere with you!" Gilles yelled, causing Stephen to scrunch his face. He felt like he was in a bad spy movie.

"I wasn't asking you, dear," the woman said. Gilles bolted toward the exit and Stephen followed suit. The automatic doors, however, failed to open and their pursuers quickly caught them. The woman dropped Gilles onto his back in a single move, after which Stephen threw his arms up in surrender. "Woah, take it easy, ninja lady."

"You're making this more difficult than it needs to be," the woman said while placing opaque masks over their heads. They led Stephen and Gilles into an elevator and started rising.

— — — — — — — — — — — — — — — — — — —

Walid looked at Fatima. Her face was filled with anger; her twisted smile made Walid uncomfortable, as though he was staring at a lion about to pounce on him. Walid felt sorry for her.

"Put the guns down," she said. They complied. Fatima held no weapon. It was unclear where the click originated from, though they assumed bodyguards or snipers were close by.

A multitude of thoughts whirled through Walid's head. *Where's Grace? What kind of leverage did Fatima have over these people? How did she know they were coming? And what on earth was their plan of attack?*

"I can practically hear you thinking!" Fatima sneered. "Let me guess: you expected to see your girlfriend here. Disappointed to find me instead?"

They said nothing. Walid looked around the room casually, trying to find anything at all he could use to their advantage. Amin was still observing the people on the floor. One woman was trying to tell him something, but he couldn't make it out.

"Stop! Are you seriously testing me?" she said to the woman. "Don't think for a second I won't release it!"

Something didn't sit right with Amin. What were these people so afraid of? There's no way ISD could have rigged something up so quickly, and even if they did, they wouldn't dare risking an explosion before the meeting of nations. She had to be bluffing.

"Where is she?" Walid asked.

"She's having a rooftop party. A big thanks for so many years of loyal service."

"I bet you're nothing but grateful," Walid said.

"You can go see for yourself."

"You're just gonna let us walk up there? Don't think I'm so foolish, Fatima. Nothing's that easy with ISD."

"Nobody said it would be easy. And did I mention? You're going alone." She motioned for one of her bodyguards to secure Amin's arms with a zip tie.

"Walid, go," Amin said.

"Yes, go," Fatima agreed. "You're just in time. Other esteemed guests should be arriving downstairs as we speak. I just love big parties, don't you?"

Neither Walid nor Amin planned to indulge Fatima in a war of words. Not only was it a waste of time, but they refused to respond out of hatred. And at the moment, that meant saying nothing at all. They tried to remind themselves that God still loved her despite everything she had done and planned to do.

Walid went back to the stairwell. They previously decided to avoid the elevators, given it was unclear how ISD had tampered with the place. Walid felt powerless without his gun and started to pray out loud in the stairwell as he ascended. "Lord, I'm out of ideas on this one. Please...I feel completely helpless right now. I need you to help me." Walid felt a surge of peace flow throughout his body. Then he heard a man descending the staircase one level up from him. He heart raced. *Well, they know*

I'm coming, he told himself. *It won't do any good to run back down now.*

As the man reached his level, Walid was speechless. He was massive! Nearly eight feet tall, muscular like a body builder, and wearing body armor like a modern-day knight. There was something otherworldly about this one. He didn't even look Arabic; what was he doing in Syria? The man stared back at Walid, which made him uncomfortable.

"Yes?" Walid said.

The man smiled and walked behind Walid. "Go now, and don't fear," he said. Then he disappeared. Walid felt overcome with joy in that moment—in knowing that this angel, *his* angel, would help him. Despite this, he had no idea what he would do when he arrived.

Walid reached the top floor and walked out onto an expansive rooftop area. He quickly scanned his surroundings, finding an empty helipad, a small structure that he imagined was an electrical unit, and two people standing toward the edge of the roof. There was no fence. Merely a two-foot-tall cement wall between them and a thirty-story drop.

Walid walked a few steps closer and immediately recognized them. *No,* he thought. *Not this.* Grace's hands were bound behind her. She tried to keep a straight face as a tear rolled down her bloodstained cheek. Walid could only imagine she put up a good struggle due to the gash on her cheek.

"I've been expecting you!" the man said to Walid. He was really getting sick of that phrase today. It was difficult to feel any love for this man, though he tried and prayed for grace. Walid looked into a pair of evil snakelike eyes, the same look he saw in Fatima several stories below.

"My old friend," the man said sarcastically.

"Emir…" The Libya-based emir held Grace by her collar; his old boss, the very man who tasked him to prove the Bible wrong. "Sounds funny, doesn't it…" Walid said, realizing he didn't actually know the emir's name. *How narcissistic.*

"Shut up!" the emir said. "We…well, *you*…are running out of time. And we have much to discuss."

CHAPTER 23

Trapped

Stephen and Gilles removed their hoods and scanned the room. They stood in the middle of a one-bedroom hotel room, and nobody had stayed behind to guard them.

"Why would they just leave us here?" Gilles asked.

Stephen walked quietly to the door; part of him expected someone to appear from a dark corner of the room. He looked out the peephole and spotted two men facing the opposite direction. "They didn't. Two guards," he whispered to Gilles, who was opening the window on the other side of the room.

"Come on, man, what are you gonna do?" Stephen said.

"I'm just looking," Gilles said. He stuck his head, and most of his upper body out the window. "Come here. What's that, fifteen stories maybe?"

"It's high, too high for whatever you're thinking!"

"Look at the construction here." Gilles pointed to a pipe running vertically along the wall, merely a foot from the window; sporadic handle-shaped bars encased the pipe. "Steve, this is completely doable! How are you even scared? Weren't you special forces?".

"Yeah, I was, and we're taught to survive!"

"You think they'll let us live if we stay here? We have a better chance if we climb! We'll just go down one floor."

Stephen looked over the edge again and considered his options, or lack thereof. He scanned the room quickly, looking for anything that could work to their advantage. Gilles was already walking to the king-sized bed and threw the comforter off. He looked up at Stephen quizzically as though asking his opinion.

"Stop thinking what you're thinking," Stephen said. "That only works in the movies."

"How do you know? Have you even heard of anyone trying it in real life?"

"No, probably 'cause they didn't live to tell about it."

"Come on, man."

Stephen paused for a moment and smiled in defeated acquiescence. "Fine, what else are we gonna do?"

"Yesssss!" Gilles said, like a child who was about to try something stupid. Stephen helped him remove all of the sheets from the bed and tie them together with climber's knots. "This is totally gonna hold!" Gilles said.

Stephen laughed at his enthusiasm. "And if it doesn't, what a way to go out!"

They brought the sheets over to the window and looked down again. "What if the window's locked?" Stephen asked.

"This one wasn't."

"Yeah, so no other window in the hotel should be either," Stephen said sarcastically.

"Come on, man, help me tie this down." They fastened one end of the sheet-rope to the metal bar closest to them, letting the rest hang down. Gilles gave it a good tug and nodded in approval. "Well, who's going first?" he said.

"This was your idea."

"Okay good, help me over." Stephen had never seen Gilles more excited. Gilles was incredibly smart for his age, though as he learned on their long car ride, his inexperience prevented his agency from sending him on any complicated missions. This adventure was clearly fulfilling a deep passion within his soul to live the mission-impossible dream.

Gilles tied the lowest portion of the makeshift rope tightly to his wrist. Stephen braced himself as he held one of Gilles' arms with a death grip, lowering him as far as he could before Gilles' weight tested the sheets. Stephen's arm became fully extended. "Okay, I'm gonna let go," he said.

"Okay! The window isn't too far!" Gilles hollered. Stephen let go, and the sheet seemed to be holding fast. For around ten seconds at least. As Gilles started to lower himself down he heard a tear and felt a slight bounce as the torn sheet lowered him another inch.

"Hurry up!" Stephen yelled.

Gilles lowered himself to the window and tried to open it. "I can't, it's locked!"

"Well, get it unlocked! I can't pull you up, it's tearing!"

"No kidding!"

Gilles heard another ominous rip and felt himself lowered another inch. Though he had never been afraid of heights, he refrained from looking down to avoid developing the fear. He grabbed the pocket knife from his back pocket and held it tightly in his hand with the knife retracted. He hit the glass once and it cracked. He hit it again with more rigor and the crack started to spread. Another rip.

"What kind of glass is this?" Gilles yelled to Stephen, who watched helplessly from above. As Gilles hit the glass a third time, the crack spread again. As did the tear.

Gilles hit the glass one last time with every ounce of his strength, causing it to shatter. "I did it!" As though following the window's lead, the sheet tore all the way through. Gilles grabbed the metal U-shaped rod framing the top of the window as the sheet fell, trying to hoist himself into the room.

"Gilles! Hang on!"

"I wasn't planning to let go!"

Stephen prayed for God to assist. Gilles' right arm was covered in blood from punching through the glass. After a few seconds, he felt himself being pulled into the window by a pair of strong arms. Stephen listened intently from above but could see nothing else.

Inside the hotel room below, Gilles and the man fell to the floor. His instincts screamed at him to fight, but he was starting to feel dizzy from blood loss and overexertion. The man had a good six inches on Gilles, slightly overweight but muscular still. He stared at Gilles as though trying to determine whether he could trust him. Gilles noticed a woman standing near the closet pointing a gun at him. "Don't move," she said, looking terrified. Gilles wondered if she had ever used a gun before.

Stephen yelled from above, but nobody responded. He searched the room for anything he could use against the guards. He peered out the peep hole again, but this time he saw nothing. He opened the door a few inches and heard voices moving toward him. He shut the door and listened to the two men, who were deep in conversation.

"We need the French one alive," one said.

"This isn't going to work!" the second man sounded irritated. "He doesn't even look like the original one."

"He doesn't have to! He's only the secondary trigger in case something goes wrong."

"Yeah, I guess…Man…what a way to go."

"Oh please. Don't get all sentimental on me. He deserves it! They're trying to derail everything the emir set in motion!"

"It's still pretty sick."

"He won't feel a thing," the first man laughed.

"So what about the American?" the second returned.

"Don't need him. Use the silencer."

Stephen stepped back. He grabbed a lamp for a makeshift weapon in a moment of panic. The door handle turned. He felt as though he was watching everything in slow motion. Would this be one of his last moments on earth? He felt powerless, as though he was waiting to be killed. "Jesus, help," he said aloud. The door creaked opened. Just as he saw the faces of his would-be killers, the room was filled with darkness.

— — — — — — — — — — — — — — — — — — — —

The light wind Walid felt nearly forty-five minutes ago when he entered the building was picking up. He saw a massive storm cloud several miles away. He hoped this wasn't an omen like the rainstorm in New York, though at least now he understood the power he had over such things.

"What do you want from me?" Walid asked the emir.

"I want you to pay." The emir's voice shook with rage; there was something unnatural about it. "You really thought you could deceive me? Stop what I've put in motion?"

"None of this is about you," Walid said.

"Fool! You know nothing!" the emir exploded. Walid prayed for the right words to say, surprised that he felt no anger toward this man—someone who wanted to take everything from him. Though his heart ached for this man.

"Enlighten me then," Walid said.

The emir smiled. Walid felt uneasy about his confidence. "You can't stop it now, Walid. After today, the world will have no choice but to take action. And you know better than anyone where they'll find us."

Walid and Grace looked at each other knowingly. It was finally starting to make sense. The emir *wanted* retaliation. And he wanted it to happen in Dabiq, the location of ISD's worldwide headquarters. Walid knew from years of not only studying but strategizing ISD's playbook that their end-time beliefs were deeply rooted in their attack strategies. According to ISD's theology, multiple countries will come to Syria to fight against the Muslims during the final battle in Dabiq; the clash of Armageddon that will usher in the coming of the Messiah. If ISD attacked the leaders of several nations at such a crucial time in history, they would naturally retaliate. And Walid could only surmise that ISD would "retreat" to Dabiq, forcing an attack there. He hated to admit to himself what a clever plan it was.

"You're getting it now, aren't you," the emir said, watching Walid turn his wheels. "I bet you think we rigged this place with explosives. Such conventional thinking!"

"No, I'm sure you have something far more crooked in mind."

Just then, he heard the rooftop door open from behind him. He turned and gasped. It was Eli! And he was pointing his gun at the emir, who was directly behind him. "Eli, wait," Walid said, as though expecting him to shoot the emir on sight.

"Yeah Eli, wait," the emir mocked. "Join the discussion! I must say, I thought you'd fail, Eli." Walid looked at Grace, her eyes wide with shock. "But here you are. Well done!"

Walid kept his eyes on Eli. He walked to Walid's side, and it was now clear that he was pointing his gun directly at him. "Eli! What are you doing?"

"I'm sorry," Eli said. He looked torn; Walid didn't see the same hatred in Eli's eyes that he saw in the emir's.

"Sorry?" the emir yelled. "You of all people, Eli…you've been with him for weeks! You know how hard he's tried to undermine everything we're doing. You are *not* sorry." The emir addressed Walid. "From the very beginning, when I gave you a simple academic task, you've tried to undermine me."

"I just realized something," Walid said. "I have *you* to thank for my conversion!"

"How dare you!"

"You yourself tasked me with reading the Bible! Have you forgotten? It was that very task: reading, doing a thorough comparative study, praying…all things you tasked me with…that made it impossible for me to deny the truth any longer. Have you even read the Bible?"

"Of course not! That's blasphemous."

"Then why would you charge your best strategist with doing so? Is that not blasphemous too?"

"We are not discussing this!" The emir tightened his grip on Grace's collar, causing her to gasp for air. Walid was cognizant of his need to protect her but more concerned with following the leading of the Lord. And he knew that more needed to be said.

"You must read it!" Walid pleaded. "You are a respected scholar. Any thorough academic would compare books before adamantly declaring one's inaccuracy. And you believe in prayer! We do it five times every day, often more. So what are you afraid of? Ask God to reveal himself to you as I did."

The emir was visibly seething. "Are you trying to convert me?"

"I didn't ask you to convert. Nothing I asked you violates your religion in any way."

"So you've completely disowned the religion now! I knew you were a traitor to ISD, but this warrants death. Fortunately, that was already on today's agenda."

The emir moved closer to the edge of the building with Grace. She looked at peace, seemingly unafraid that he was about to kill her. Walid wanted to charge them, attempt to grab her before the emir could even react and fight it out. This idea made him uncomfortable, and he quickly discarded it. Tears started cascading down his cheeks.

"Good, take a moment," the emir said callously. "Say goodbye to your girlfriend." He held her closer to the edge until a moderate push would have sent her spiraling to her death. Walid felt peace, though he didn't know whether God was giving him peace because He would save them, or because Walid was about to see Him soon! Though he wasn't afraid to die, he prayed for the former option.

"I'm not sad about our circumstances," Walid said. "I know where we'll be when we die. Do you?"

"Lies! Nobody can know that."

"Yes, they can. And what I'm sad about is where you're heading. Your refusal to even ask God to reveal himself…You're afraid that you're wrong. And you can't accept that." As he was speaking, Walid noticed a long electrical cable lying haphazardly across the rooftop. For a moment, he considered using it as a tripwire, though it would be too dangerous with Grace there.

"Stop it!" The emir's voice was now a mixture of anger and emotion. "Don't pretend you're being a saint! Trying to rescue me from something."

"I'm not pretending." If Walid was faking his sincerity, he could have fooled anyone. "I don't hate you. I feel sorry for you."

Suddenly, the emir lost the emotion in his voice and resolutely declared, "I will never believe in your God! And you will never stop this attack. Time's up."

He pushed Grace toward the edge of the building. She screamed and tried to regain her balance, but there was nothing to hold on to. Then Walid heard the deafening blast of a gunshot. He expected to feel searing pain at any moment, falling to the ground in puddle of his own blood. Or perhaps to see Grace shot straight off the building. But instead, he saw the emir recoil after a bullet penetrated his left shoulder. The emir looked at Eli in shock and betrayal as blood started seeping through his shirt. He tried to regain his bearings but tripped over the electrical wire and staggered right over the side of the building, bringing Grace along with him.

———————————————————————

Amin watched Fatima carefully as her bodyguard led him to the circle of gagged people. *Who are these people?* he wondered, assuming they were probably hotel staff. The hotel would have been largely emptied of customers prior to an event like this with high profile visitors. *Could ISD have gone so far as to replace the staff with their own people?* It was certainly doable; he already knew the receptionist and busboys had been replaced, after all. Amin prayed for wisdom, but nothing came to his mind except to keep talking.

"Is this your plan?" Amin asked. "Kidnap the staff, try to fool the international community while your own people conduct business today flawlessly? Come on, Fatima...we both know ISD isn't that good."

"You know nothing about us!" she said. She started to laugh yet again, which sounded forced. Amin listened. *Words, Lord, insight, anything!* Fatima wasn't giving him any useful information.

"What have you told them, Fatima?" Amin asked, referring to the circle of people he sat with. "That you'll shoot them if they move?" One of the men sitting next to Amin nudged him, warning him to stop with his expressions. "I don't buy it. You would've done it already. What're you hiding?"

Fatima was visibly growing impatient. Amin's idea was working. Though he didn't know her as well as Walid, he had met and interrogated people like her in his military days. People like her hated feeling marginalized, and more often than not were fairly braggadocios. Yet still she said nothing, looking away from Amin and fuming. Finally, it hit him.

"You're stalling," he said with an expression of revelation, which nearly pushed her over the edge. "You can't kill us right now. Not yet. What are you waiting for, Fatima?"

"Shut up!" she exploded.

"Oh, I see…You don't know what you're waiting for. They haven't told you. The most important mission for ISD to date, and they have you babysitting."

That was it. Fatima broke into a run and nearly leaped onto Amin, trying to strangle him. He fell onto his back and tried to force her grip open. One of her bodyguards yelled from across the room in a panic. "We need him alive!"

She pulled a knife from her wrist strap and threw it at her bodyguard in a rage, missing by only a few inches. Just then, Fatima pushed herself back from Amin and looked at him in amazement. One of her bodyguards had the same look in his eyes and swiftly ran out of the room. Two bodyguards remained; Amin hadn't noticed before that one of them held a video camera. His pulse quickened as he realized that they were planning to film the group. This wouldn't be a new tactic for ISD but an effective one nevertheless. Filming hostages for ransom, or worse, filming their deaths and broadcasting them to the world would produce immense fear.

"How did you do that?" Fatima asked.

Amin looked around in confusion. Nobody other than the ISD members appeared frightened. "Do what?"

"You know what! That thing with your eyes. They shot out light!"

Amin smiled again; this could only be the Lord working on his behalf. "Light will always shine in the darkness."

"What the hell is that supposed to mean?" she said. Amin sat up and stared at her. "Don't look at me!"

"Fatima," he said, his voice calm and reassuring. "I don't hate you, you know. In fact, I pray you will have an encounter with the one true God. What you just saw was the tiniest display of his power, I think He wanted you to see it so you'll believe."

"What do you want to know?" she asked, seemingly ignoring what he just said. He tried not to look shocked.

"What's ISD planning here?"

"I don't know…those idiots didn't tell me! ME! And I was tasked to lead this!"

"You must know something."

"I know that your friends on the rooftop are probably dead by now," she said. He struggled to keep a straight face, trying to ignore the comment. "I know that despite your opinions, this is one operation you really can't stop."

"Why not?"

"Because it goes much deeper than you think. This isn't some simple bomb we planted. Of course not! This one can't be seen. Nobody will find it until it's too late."

"Where is it?"

"It could be anywhere." Amin started to realize she might really not know. "Now that's enough!" she said as though coming to her senses. "We must wait until everything is in place."

Amin's mind spun with possibilities. Had ISD secured some kind of chemical or biological weapon? Even then, the bomb itself would be visible until it exploded. Where had they hidden it so well that nobody would find it? Despite his confusion, Amin had learned a lot in the last few minutes about this operation. He sat there silently, thanking God for this new information, and wondering how on earth he would escape to warn his team.

— —

Gilles fixed his attention on the woman pointing a gun in his direction. "Okay, this probably looks bad," he said. She nodded in agreement. "But I'm not trying to hurt you."

"Are you with them?" she asked suspiciously. Gilles tried to read her, which was difficult given she wore a black niqab and he could only see her eyes.

"If you mean ISD, then no. Actually, I'm here to stop them," he said, quickly wishing he hadn't said anything. For all he knew, they could be ISD members.

"How do I know you're telling the truth?" she asked.

"Look, lady, I don't know what you need to hear, but I don't have a lot of time. One of my partners is still upstairs, and it's only a matter of time 'til ISD realizes I'm gone. Please put the gun gown."

Her hands were shaking; Gilles was nervous that she might accidentally squeeze the trigger out of sheer nervousness. She looked over at the man who sat next to Walid. "I believe him, Faruq."

"I'm Gilles," he said, throwing his hand out to Faruq.

Faruq grabbed his hand and shook it hard. "Well, thank God you're here. Maybe we can help each other. I'm Faruq, this is Nastia."

She put her gun down and took off the niqab, revealing short black hair, jeans, and a purple blouse. "Thank God I can take this thing off!" she said.

"Why are you in here?" Gilles asked.

"We're on staff here," Faruq said. "I'm the general manager, and Nastia here is the best pianist in Syria. She plays here."

Nastia rolled her eyes and smiled. "And why are you here?"

"I'm here with a team. We're trying to stop ISD from pulling off an attack, though we still haven't figured out what's going on."

"Well, God will lead us," Nastia said.

"You're Christian?" Gilles asked.

"Don't sound so surprised," Faruq laughed. "You are as well."

"How could you know that?"

"Just a hunch."

"We should get down to business," Nastia said. "Your friend…do you know which room he's in?"

"No, we were blindfolded. Maybe he can hear us!" Gilles leaned out the window and called Stephen's name, but there was no response.

"Woah, look!" Faruq pointed at the horizon. There were dark storm clouds in the distance covering what looked like a massive tidal wave, though it appeared to be moving somewhat slowly.

"What on earth is that?" Gilles asked.

"Kinda looks like a sandstorm," Faruq said. "Though it would be the biggest one I've ever seen!"

"Guys, come on!" Nastia said. She had propped the door and was looking down the hallway. "Looks clear."

Nastia motioned for the men to follow her down the hallway. Gilles was both amused and suspicious about a concert pianist's use of military-style hand signals. They found the stairwell and walked up to the next floor. Nastia opened the door and peered down the hallway. "All clear," she said. Gilles wondered where the bodyguards had gone. And why hadn't Stephen responded to his calls? Something didn't sit right. Nastia got on the floor and started low crawling down the hallway. *OK, so she is just a pianist,* he thought.

"What are you doing?" Gilles asked.

She hushed him and kept crawling. Gilles ignored her and ran down the hallway full speed to the room he and Stephen were in. The door was ajar, and the lights were off. He turned the lights on and kicked the door in like he was conducting an urban breach.

He didn't know how to react. Out of all the scenarios that played in his head, this wasn't one of them. Stephen sat on the floor, exhausted, while the two bodyguards laid motionless on either side of him.

"Well, this is awkward," Stephen said. "They're not dead, if you were wondering. I don't think so, at least…We should probably leave in case they wake up."

Gilles shook his head as Nastia and Faruq caught up with him. "They're helping us," he said quickly as Stephen looked ready to fight again. Stephen nodded and led them toward the stairwell.

"Seriously, what happened?" Gilles asked.

Stephen tried to open a few of the hotel rooms but each door was locked, so they entered the stairwell. "This'll have to do," he said. He pointed at the couple with his head as though to question their trustworthiness.

"Um, you know we can see you," Nastia said.

"We work here," Faruq explained. "We want them out of here just as badly as you do."

"Sorry, guys, a little on edge here," Stephen said. "Before those two clowns came in, I overheard them speaking. Gilles, they said they needed you alive. That you were gonna be a secondary trigger in case something happened to the first one. The person arming the weapon must be a Frenchman. Maybe he's part of their delegation, like an insider or something."

"How many are in the French delegation?" Gilles asked.

"I don't know, man, but I bet there won't be many. We need to find the others. I think some of them may be on the rooftop. Those guards had terrible OPSEC!"

"OK, let's go," Faruq said.

"Don't leave us hanging…what happened with the guards?" Gilles asked as they started ascending.

"It was epic, man," Stephen said. "The second they opened the door, the room became pitch-black. I heard one shot fired with the silencer. No idea what he hit. Then I heard a clunk like one of them hit the other with brass knuckles; guess they thought he was me! I wrestled the second guy down to the floor, and he fell unconscious too, though I have no idea how. I didn't even hit him. Maybe I hit a pressure point or something. No way I can make this stuff up!"

"That's so God, right?" Gilles said.

"At least we learned something out of all this," Stephen said.

"I can't believe they want me to be a trigger!" Gilles said. "What's up with that?"

"Yeah well, they were gonna use a silencer on me, so count your blessings."

CHAPTER 24

Smoke Screen

"No!" Walid screamed as he rushed to the side of the building. He looked over the short cement wall, afraid of what he might see. To his astonishment, both Grace and the emir were only a few feet away, hanging on to the metal bars that framed the rooftop perimeter.

"Hang on, Grace! I'm coming for you!"

"I'm slipping!" she yelled.

Walid hoisted one of his legs over the wall. "It's okay!" she said. Though his eyes were welling up with tears, she looked beautifully strong and peaceful. "We'll see each other again, Walid."

He knew it was true but wasn't ready to let go. Something within his spirit rose up like a roaring lion, and he grabbed on to the side of the building, lowering himself below the wall. "I'm not losing you yet," he said. He grabbed her wrist just before her grip was ready to fail, but he wasn't prepared to support their combined weight. He felt himself slipping despite his death grip. Just then, Eli grabbed on to his arm! Eli anchored himself with the electrical cords lying on top of the building, braced himself against the wall with his legs, and held on to Walid.

"You fool!" the emir said to Eli. "How dare you!" Now the emir was losing his grip. He clung to a separate cord, dangling over the edge with all of his might.

"I'm so sorry, Walid," Eli said. "I'm the one who's been feeding them intel. Please forgive me! They threatened my entire family."

"I forgive you, man! Now help me pull!"

"It wasn't real to me at first, but it's real now!" he continued.

"Okay, I believe you!" Walid said, and despite the desperation in his voice, he really did believe him. Eli and Walid pulled Grace up with all of their might and adrenaline. Just as she had half of her body back onto the ceiling, a metal pipe a few feet away from them started bending. "Look out!" Grace yelled as pipe broke. They pulled her the rest of the way up and simultaneously heard the emir screaming something. As they peered over the wall, it became clear that the pipe had been holding his weight.

"Oh no…" Eli said, sitting back against the wall. He couldn't bear to watch as the emir fall, despite all the pain he had caused. "I never wanted this to happen."

"You didn't do this, Eli!" Walid said. "We couldn't have saved him. He chose his own fate."

"I really meant it you know, Walid. About God being real to me."

"I know," Walid smiled.

"Grace, I'm so glad you're OK," Eli said. "I don't know if you can ever forgive me. I know I'm responsible in part for you being here." His voice sounded more confident and genuine than Walid had ever heard it before.

"Eli, of course you're forgiven." She touched his shoulder to reassure him and laughed, as though it was the only way she could release her emotions at the moment.

Caught up in the moment, nobody realized that the pipe Eli was still attached to was also bending. In his haste, he had tied the cord around his waist and anchored it to a standalone pipe. The pipe, however, was no match for the gale-force winds howling on the rooftop. Suddenly, the pipe broke and was blown completely off the edge of the building. By then, it was too late for Eli to react. He called out to Jesus as he tried futilely to grasp for the metal framing the rooftop. Walid dove toward the edge but was too slow. In less than five seconds, Eli was gone.

Walid and Grace ran to the cement wall and looked over. They were completely still for a moment, as though their senses stopped functioning. All they could hear was the worsening vacuum-like sound of the storm winds rushing around them. Walid didn't know what to do; it seemed like this was a bad dream. They both averted their eyes before Eli reached the bottom.

Despite Walid's excitement about seeing Grace again, he couldn't bring himself to show her. He just sat against the wall, quiet and expressionless. He found himself getting frustrated with God. Grace threw her arms around him, remaining admiringly strong after everything she had been through. It made him like her even more. Here she was, after a near-death experience, comforting Walid instead of focusing on her own grief. He wished he could show her how much he respected her but found himself unable to move.

"Walid?" Grace said.

"I'm sorry," he said, finally forcing himself to speak.

"Sorry for what?"

"If I had gotten here earlier…"

"Then I'd be dead! We'd all probably be dead, Walid! Don't do this to yourself."

He pulled her in again for a tight hug as tears streamed uncontrollably down his face. He didn't feel ashamed; in fact, he didn't feel much of anything. He loosened his grip and looked up to the sky. "He had just changed his life! Why now?"

Grace pulled away and grabbed Walid by the shoulders. Her countenance was empathetic but bold, more so than he had seen in her before. "Listen to me, Walid." He pulled himself together, encouraged by the strength in her voice. "I know this may sound insensitive, but we can't focus on Eli right now. This isn't the time. If you're gonna get mad at God, do it later, 'cause we need to trust Him right now, more than ever! There's still a bomb in this building somewhere and we just lost our best lead!"

Walid knew she was right. He closed his eyes firmly and took a deep breath. Walid was thankful for his operational training in times like these. He had never been one to struggle with emotions when it mattered most.

"You're right," he said. He briefly described what happened since they entered the hotel as they walked to the stairwell. "Gilles and Stephen were in the lobby last I saw, though I'm sure they've been moved by now. Amin was still with Fatima when I left him. We should get to him first."

Grace smiled at him as they entered the stairwell.

"What?" he asked.

"It's just good to see you, that's all."

He smiled and squeezed her hand. "You too, Grace."

— — — — — — — — — — — — — — — — — — — —

Stephen and Gilles stopped abruptly around the twenty-first floor after hearing footsteps coming from above. Stephen motioned for Gilles to follow him through the door, but it was locked. "Who locks a stairwell door?" he whispered. They stood motionless, ready to pounce on whoever they might meet. The steps grew louder until Gilles took it upon himself to jump out in plain sight, throw his hands up, and yell "Stop!"

Walid and Grace stopped, laughing upon realizing it was Gilles. "Very intimidating indeed," Walid said. "Oh man, I can't wait to tell Amin about this."

Gilles ignored the taunt and threw his arms around Walid. "You're okay!"

"Grace!" Stephen hugged her. "Are you okay?"

"Yeah, I'm okay," she said. "Boy have I got a story for you guys later."

"This is Faruq and Nastia. They work here and wanna help," Gilles explained. "Where's Amin?"

"Twelfth floor, last I saw him," Walid said. "Fatima was there too with at least two of her cronies. They have a group of hostages."

"How are we gonna get in without getting shot?" Gilles asked.

"Dunno yet," Walid said.

"I might," Grace said. "Any of you gents have a weapon?"

"Not anymore," Stephen said. "You gonna charge in there, guns a-blazin?"

"You know me so well," she said sarcastically. "No, we need to create a diversion! Maybe we can use something else."

"I like where you're going with this," Walid said, stopping to think for a minute. "What about smoke?"

"Smoke? How?" Stephen asked.

"There were vents in the room, coming from the wall facing the adjacent room," Walid explained. "We can easily reach it from that room."

"So you're thinking we pump smoke into the room…make them think it's an attack or something," Grace said.

"Exactly!"

"I can make the smoke!" Gilles said excitedly.

"Of course you can," Stephen laughed. "Everyone knows how to make smoke!"

"It's easy. I just need a pillowcase and CO_2 extinguisher. I saw one in the hallway. Can you guys help?" he said to Faruq and Nastia.

"Of course," Faruq said.

"I'm in too," Nastia said. "My fiancé works here. He's probably in there with the other hostages. I'll do anything you need." Gilles nodded sympathetically.

"Chances are, if ISD thinks this is an attack, they'll run out," Walid said. "We just need to catch them the second they reach the hallway."

"Yeah. We got this," Grace said unconvincingly.

– – – – – – – – – – – – – – – – – –

Down on the second floor, a large, opulent conference room was filling up as dignitaries from several countries found their assigned seats. Most countries involved in the evening's discussions provided one diplomat and no more than three additional delegation members. Many of these additional members were special security forces due to the poor security situation in Syria. Though the specific location of this meeting remained a mystery to the public, the publicity it was receiving due to the leak had many on edge. Drinks were served while the crowd mingled and conducted their obligatory diplomatic activities, feigning positivity and hope for the future of the country.

One man interrupted the commotion with the clanking of a fork against a glass of expensive merlot. He was dressed in a black pinstriped suit worth enough to provide a small family in Syria with meals for a month. "Ladies and gents. Thank you for coming. Your time is most valuable. We will be getting started shortly. In the meantime, enjoy the hors d'oeuvres, the booze, and the company."

He walked off stage and handed his wine glass to a server. Once he was out of sight, he moved behind a curtain, which led to a separate green room and consulted with a man dressed in a navy Dolce and Gabana suit. "Is everything in place?" he asked.

"Almost," the man responded. "Thirty minutes max."

"Hurry…up…," the announcer said through gritted teeth. "We need him here in fifteen."

— — — — — — — — — — — — — — — — — —

Gilles, Faruq, and Nastia worked hastily in the room next to the presidential suite. Faruq had already unscrewed the vent and attempted to clear the ventilation system of any obstructions. At the same time, Gilles and Nastia made dry ice by spraying the CO_2 fire extinguisher into an airtight pillow case.

"It's a small opening, but it'll do," Faruq said.

"Great," Gilles said. "Grab a container of hot water and anything you can find that's long and skinny. We'll have to move fast."

Nastia placed a cylindrical container of hot water directly at the opening while Faruq brought Gilles a curtain rod.

"Okay, here goes something…," Gilles said excitedly. He poured the dry ice in the hot water, causing smoke to immediately emanate from the container. He then pushed it as far as it would go toward the vent and waited to hear the reaction.

— — — — — — — — — — — — — — — — — — —

"I can feel you looking at me," Fatima spat, whirling around to face Amin. She sat for the last ten minutes looking out the window, as though waiting for a signal from someone. "What? What do you want from me?"

"Nothing. I'm just filled with compassion for you," Amin said.

"What?" she said in disbelief. "What are you talking about?"

"You know ISD will leave you," he said. She turned her head to the window again, though her livid façade was fading. "They'd probably try to kill you the second you messed up. And you know their God allows that. The one true God would never do that to you. Nor would I."

"How could you not want me dead after what I've done to you?" she asked.

"I told you, God's given me compassion for you, Fatima. All you've experienced in ISD is hatred, revenge, warmongering…I want you to experience more than that."

Fatima's face softened, but she said nothing. The people sitting around Amin were staring intently at him, as though he was speaking life into their souls.

A strange peace had swept throughout the room, but it was broken quickly by one of the staff members sitting in the circle. "Gas!" she yelled, pointing to the gray smoke pouring into the room from the ventilation system. "He was right!" another yelled. "They're trying to kill us!"

Amin expected Fatima to look furious. Her face, though solemn, rather expressed disappointment and betrayal. She exhaled deeply. The very group she had spent her entire life serving was giving up on her, or so she thought. "I'll kill them," she said under her breath as she bolted for the door. Her security guards were already gone.

Fatima ran to the stairwell, throwing the door open with a power that only adrenaline can proffer. The moment she entered, she collided with Walid. "Hello, old friend," he said, dodging a punch and returning one, which knocked her out. Walid had knocked out one of the guards only moments earlier. Stephen helped him carry the two of them into the room Gilles and the others were in. "Dude, you just knocked out a girl," Stephen said with a smirk, looking at Grace with feigned concern.

"Oh, come on, man," Walid said. "You think diplomacy would have worked in that rage?"

"Touché," Stephen said.

Amin joined them in the room and was welcomed with warm embraces. "That was you guys?" he said in reference to the smoke. "Genius!"

"It was all Gilles," Walid said proudly as he zip-tied Fatima's wrists together.

"Guys, I hate to spoil the bromance, but we need to get goin'," Grace said. "What does everyone know? Maybe we can start putting together the puzzle."

"Well, they wanna use me as a secondary trigger," Gilles said. "That's the term they used. Guessing the guy pulling the trigger is from the French delegation."

"Fatima told me the bomb couldn't be seen," Amin added.

"So did the emir!" Grace said. "He said we'd never find it, that it wasn't just a conventional bomb."

"Oh no," Walid gasped.

"What?" Grace asked.

"Remember New York?" he asked.

"Yeah…You think it's inside someone?" Grace asked.

"It makes sense," Amin said. "Can't be seen, unconventional, and they needed someone else who looked similarly in case it failed. Why else would appearance matter?"

"Maybe they wanna pin it on the French," Grace said. "Maybe their primary is a double agent from the French delegation."

"Oh wow," Gilles said, finally comprehending what this meant for him. "They wanna put a bomb in me…"

"But they won't!" Walid said. "Something doesn't add up. I get that they'd want a fallback, but why would they wait so late? Something must have gone wrong."

"Okay so there's what, three or four Frenchmen here," Grace reasoned. "It won't be the leader, so that narrows the field. How are we gonna grab the guy? If they so much as see us approaching, they'll detonate."

Amin smiled. "I think I have a plan."

_____

Sweat dripped from the announcer's forehead as he took his place in front of an increasingly restless crowd. "Ladies and gentlemen. Your time is precious to us. Please, take your seats and we'll be getting started."

The crowd slowly moved to their seats, trying to secure last-minute deals or make their final empty promises in this rare opportunity for world leaders to mingle. As the announcer stepped down, the UN Secretary General walked confidently to the front of the room, holding the lapels of his black satin suit. His insincere smile greeted the crowd, who clapped tepidly as he took his place at the podium.

"This is a momentous time in history. 'Nations gather from the far corners of the Earth as one in solidarity.'" He painted the headline with his hands, causing some to snicker under their breaths. "But who cares about the headlines?" he laughed. "We're here for business, and we must not waste another moment. First on the agenda: an overview of the current intelligence picture. Then we will focus on postconflict stabilization efforts. As you already know, we will spend the majority of our time on this effort as we lay the groundwork for a better future for Syria. Now…without further ado, we will begin with an overview of the situation on the ground from three of Syria's opposition groups—excuse me, *tribal groups*. Please welcome them to the stage, together for the first time since the beginning of the civil war!" Three men walked slowly to the stage, far less enthusiastic than the Secretary-General.

As they took their places, Walid and Amin stood a few paces beyond the second-floor stairwell, peering into the opulent lobby adjoining the conference room. Two gunmen stood at the conference room doors, while two additional gunmen stood at the lobby entrance. Amin was wearing a guard uniform complete with sidearm that he stole from one of Fatima's guards upstairs. "Wait here," he whispered.

Amin ran out into the lobby toward the two men guarding the conference room, who immediately drew their AR-15s. "Woah, what the hell guys?" Amin said in a more callous tone of voice than Walid had ever heard from him. Walid smiled; his acting skills were on point. "Hands up!" they said firmly but quietly, trying desperately not to disrupt the negotiations. Amin wasn't as concerned; he knew they would be ending shortly one way or another.

"All right, that's enough!" Amin said. "Surely you've heard from Fatima by now."

The men looked at each other in confusion. Amin was banking on two key facts: that ISD operatives, particularly the more expendable guards and triggermen, did not know each other prior to most operations, similar to Walid's experience in New York. Second, given Fatima was a senior operative in this mission, they almost certainly should recognize her name, thus increasing his credibility. However, their blank stares were doing anything but reassuring him.

"I'm your replacement," Amin said to one of the guards.

"Get out of here before you ruin things!" the guard said.

"They're already ruined," Amin said with urgency. "The place is breached! Walid and his filthy infidel friends are in the building right now. Are you getting this? Or have you not heard of him either?"

The guard's faces grew concerned, almost frightened. If they didn't know Fatima, they certainly knew a former ISD leader wanted for death.

Still no movement. "All right, okay, let's play it your way," Amin said. "Call up yourselves and explain that you don't feel like moving from your cushy spot here. Or better yet, I'll call." Amin put his hand up to press on an earpiece that didn't exist.

"Wait," the guard said. "Fine, I'm goin'." The man took off in a light jog, and Amin took his place. Walid didn't like what was coming next, but he saw no other option. Time was running out.

CHAPTER 25

Storm of the Century

Several minutes earlier, Gilles and Grace approached the conference room from the rear. Directly behind the stage was a small greenroom, and behind that a massive kitchen. The kitchen looked like a masterpiece in itself: stainless steel fixtures and appliances, blue mosaic tile mimicking ocean waves, and metal cabinets dispersed throughout the expansive space.

Gilles and Grace split up. Grace hid beneath a large cabinet toward the rear, hoping to come within reach of an armed ISD guard. Though she had been well trained in martial arts from the time she was a teenager, this plan made her uneasy. Still, she figured ISD was unlikely to shoot her and risk a panic in the conference room. She prayed silently as she waited.

Gilles had moved toward the front of the kitchen where appetizers were being skillfully prepared. He too hunched behind a cabinet, thankful that they offered plenty of space to hide.

Gilles wondered whether these were ISD members or unwitting hotel cooks. *No way ISD has this many skilled cooks,* he thought. Suddenly, it all made sense as Gilles' spotted a guard pacing behind the cooks with a standard-issue 9 mm pistol. The cooks' faces showed a mix of terror, fury, and dejection, undoubtedly torn by what they were being forced to do. The Syrians had just barely tasted freedom after the fall of a brutal despot merely a few weeks earlier. Now everything they fought for was being threatened once again.

Gilles moved stealthily to a closer cabinet. The gunman was close, but not close enough for him to make a move. He spotted another cabinet within paces of the chefs and prepared to run. With any luck, or grace, he'd be able to force the weapon from the gunman's hands. As he prepared to pounce on his unwitting prey, he felt the cold tinge of metal on the back of his neck and heard the portentous clicking of the gun's charging handle.

"Well, well," said the man standing behind him. "Just how many of you little urchins are here?" Gilles remained still and silent. The gunman he planned to charge moments earlier dismissed them from the room with his head.

"Start moving. And don't try anything stupid. Don't think I won't shoot." The gunman led Gilles to a separate room adjacent to the kitchen. The room looked like something straight out of a horror film; parts of cows, chickens, and who knows what else hung from metal hooks ready for butchering ahead of food preparation. "We have a special treat for you today," the gunman said as he ushered Gilles to the back of the room.

Two other armed men burst through a door near the back of the butcher's shop looking concerned. "He didn't make it," one of them said, causing the gunman to grunt in dissatisfaction.

"Fine then," he said, turning to face Gilles with a crooked smile. "Looks like you're not the backup anymore."

"This will never work!" Gilles protested, his voice panicked. "I'll never help you!"

"Yes, you will," the gunman said. "You can't save your own life, but you can still save theirs. The people you came with, your family back in France…don't you care about them? We'll hunt down every last one if you give us any trouble."

"Muhammad," one man said to the gunman. "We can't open him up. What if he dies too?"

Muhammad thought for a moment. "Take off your vest. We'll have to improvise." The man took his shirt off and unfastened a thin bulletproof vest. The men went to work carefully attaching the bomb to the vest. Gilles was surprised at how small the bomb appeared. Unless they had some new technology he had never seen before, there's no way it would impact more than a twelve-foot radius.

"This will never work," Gilles repeated.

"Shut up," Muhammad said.

"First of all, you won't kill more than ten people with this thing. And also, I'll warn everyone the second you get me to the door."

Muhammad smiled as they kept working on this makeshift suicide vest. "Who said we wanna blow up the whole place? There are surprises in store for everyone tonight."

Gilles could think of nothing else to say, so he sat there and prayed. He wanted nothing more than to run and warn the others that this wasn't the only attack planned for tonight.

— — — — — — — — — — — — — — — — — —

Grace squatted with her body hunched over in the metal cabinet, trying not to make a sound. She watched a corner of the shiny cabinet, which provided her with a reflection of the perpendicular walkway. When the coast was clear, she grabbed a knife and started moving closer to the kitchen. Just then, two men hastily entered the room and stopped within five paces of her. She flattened herself against the cabinet and sat utterly still.

"Change of plans. Secondary device is now the primary. Muhammad's guys are building it now."

"How long's that gonna take? It should've been ready by now," the second man said.

"It would have been if the Frenchmen hadn't died!"

Oh no! Gilles… Grace thought.

"Relax! There's still time. They'll be so preoccupied with saving the country they won't notice anything out of place," the first man laughed.

"Anything else changed?"

"Target position. He won't cooperate, so you need to get him directly to the target the moment you enter with the entrees. You've seen the layout—far left-hand side of the room."

"The drinks been prepared?"

"As we speak. Final ingredient's about to go in."

The two kept talking as they moved farther away from Grace, who darted out of the room to find Walid and Amin.

— — — — — — — — — — — — — — — — — — — —

"Helloooo?" Fatima heard the sound ringing in her ears as she came to. She grumbled at the pain she felt in her head and wrists, which were secured tightly to a wooden support beam standing a few feet from the hotel room door. "Yeah, sorry about that, but you might try to kill me if I loosen it," Stephen said.

Fatima pulled herself into a sitting position. "I'm not gonna kill you," she said unconvincingly.

"Oh, well in that case…"

"Are you gonna kill me?"

"No. Believe it or not, I still think there's hope for you."

Fatima shook her head in disbelief. Stephen tried to read her countenance, which was markedly calmer than before. She looked defeated. Upset, but no longer shrouded with anger.

"You can still change what's about to happen," he said.

"Sure I can."

"God really does love you despite everything, but you need to *choose* to change. You've seen the power of Jesus, Fatima, you *know* you have!"

"So what? You want me to admit this whole enterprise was a mistake? Change my religion and be a wanted woman for the rest of my life?"

"Yes!" Stephen said. "Before it's too late. The emir had a choice too and let his pride overwhelm him, and now it's too late for him."

"He's dead?" she asked in shock. "You're lying."

"No, I'm not, and I'm not happy about it either. Don't wait 'til it's too late. We might go down with this place for all I know. I know where I'm going. Do you?"

"The place isn't going down."

"What about the bomb? You said it was still active."

"It is. And you probably can't stop it at this point."

"So what, it's not powerful enough? Did something go wrong?" Stephen pushed.

"It doesn't have to be. That's not the point."

She kept beating around the bush, and Stephen knew exactly why. If she directly outed ISD, it would be tantamount to committing treason, and she wasn't ready for that. It didn't matter though; Stephen was starting to understand her insinuations.

"ISD's only going after part of the audience," he said, gauging her reaction. "They have something else planned, don't they."

"Yeah, something. Something huge. Look…even if I thought I had a chance of changing, even if you guys stop this attack…you can't stop what's coming next."

"What do you mean what's coming?"

Fatima's face turned red as tears started falling from her bloodshot eyes. Stephen felt overwhelming compassion for her in that moment and silently prayed that she would have the courage to help him. "Go ahead, take your shots at me," she said, expecting him to verbally assault her in her weakness.

"No, I have no desire for that. Fatima…come with us! Nobody can save you if you stay with them."

"Stop it!" she yelled. She closed her eyes for a few seconds to compose herself and released a loud sigh. "Stephen…" He paid close attention to her. This was the first time she had ever used his name. "It's in the drinks. The other attack. They've probably been served already." Stephen's face turned white as he realized she was telling the truth; they might really be powerless to stop the coming war if people had already started drinking.

"So who's the target of the bomb then?" Stephen asked.

"I really don't know. But I know the Iranians are supporting it. ISD got a huge resource dump from them for this job.

Though they'll never admit to that…they've got other allies here too, but I don't know their nationality."

To Fatima's astonishment, Stephen leaned over to her and cut her zip ties. "You're already making things right, you know. Make them right with God now…Oh, and don't kill me," he smirked. He ran out of the room and flew three stairs at a time on his way to the second floor.

— — — — — — — — — — — — — — — — — — — —

"Don't shoot!" Walid yelled, holding both hands in the air to signal his surrender. He kept his body largely concealed by the dividing wall.

"Don't move!" the guard moved closer to him. Amin looked on from the lobby entrance. He and the guard next to him held their positions.

"Not moving," Walid said. "I have a message from the emir."

"What? Who are you? Show your face!"

"If I do, you'll shoot me, and you need to hear this message if you want your emir to survive."

"How dare you threaten the emir! Step out, now!" the guard said.

"You listen to me!" Walid demanded with such authority that the guard complied. "I have a team on the rooftop holding your emir hostage. If you don't send reinforcements immediately, we'll kill him. And if anything happens to me, he'll meet the same fate."

"Why should I trust you? I don't even know who you are!"

"Yes, you do," Walid said as he showed his face. The guard clearly recognized him. Walid prayed they wouldn't risk shooting him right outside of the conference room. "Go ahead, check your emergency channels."

The guardsmen spoke into his radio and, evidently, received no response. "What have you done?" he asked, cocking his weapon. Amin and the guard next to him continued to face away from the lobby—standard operating procedure in case this was merely a distraction.

"I already told you!" Walid said. "What are you gonna do? Ruin everything by creating chaos right outside these doors? ISD will kill you for it."

"Stay here," he said to the other guard. "If you're lying, I'll kill you myself," he warned Walid as he ran past him to the elevator. The remaining guard cocked his weapon and pointed it at Walid's head.

— —

Grace had nearly reached the lobby outside the conference room when she almost crashed into Stephen, who was running from a perpendicular hallway. She grabbed his arm and pulled him into a small coat room, her face furrowed with concern. "Stephen, I dunno if Gilles is still alive! I think they're gonna put a vest on him. They said the target's on the left of the room. And something about the drinks!" she blurted out in a single stream of thought.

"Grace, slow down," Stephen said, placing his hands on her shoulders.

"I dunno where he is, I just overheard ISD talking about it. It sounded like they were putting something in the drinks too. I think more than one attack's about to happen."

"They are, Fatima just told me."

"What? Where's Walid and Amin?"

"I haven't seen them since we split."

"Come on," Grace said as she walked toward the lobby. After a few seconds, Grace held her fist up in the air, signaling Stephen to stop. She pointed through a glass door in front of them, where they could see Walid standing motionless. They stayed low until they reached the door. "I can't see beyond him," she whispered.

"Why isn't he moving?"

"There has to be someone holding him there."

"Well then, good thing we have this," Stephen said, pulling out a 9 mm pistol that he had tucked into his jeans pocket.

"Where'd you get that?"

"Fatima. She was out for a while."

Grace nodded and placed her hand on the door handle. "Okay," she exhaled deeply. "On the count of three. One... two..."

- -

The gunman continued staring at Walid with a masterful poker face. "I'm not going anywhere..." Walid said. "You can relax."

"Say another word and I'll shoot," the gunman said. Walid complied.

The gunman finally averted his eyes from Walid to press a button on his earpiece and strained to listen as though experiencing bad feedback. "Say again?" he said. Walid knew this couldn't be good. It was only a matter of time before the second gunman would discover what happened upstairs. Walid was hoping to buy his team some time, but his plan seemed to be failing. Amin was preparing to help Walid if necessary, praying for the right timing to make a move. He had a feeling he knew what was coming.

The gunman's face grew irate. "What?" he spat. He ripped his earpiece out and threw it on the floor, focusing again on Walid. He raised his weapon again. Walid prayed for the Lord to send his angels to protect him. He battled his emotions, which told him he was about to die.

At that moment, Grace emerged from the glass door and yelled at the gunmen. "Wait! You're about to ruin everything!"

"Who are you? What is going on?" the gunman asked.

"A soldier," she said, keeping her body concealed behind the dividing wall. "And if you pop that gun, you'll ruin our entire plan."

"You're lying! How do I know everything isn't already ruined?"

There was nothing more to say; Grace stood in silence, praying desperately for ideas. "Step out now or I'll shoot him," the gunman said.

"Wait," she pleaded, stepping out next to Walid.

"Please don't," Walid said to her.

"I know you!" the gunman said. "You're a wanted deserter! You're almost as bad as he is!"

The gunman prepared to shoot; Walid and Grace said the word "Jesus" almost in chorus, making their final requests to God for protection.

Without a second thought, Grace dove on Walid and dragged him to the floor as two gunshots simultaneously shattered the atmosphere. Amin hit the guard standing next to him with the buttstock of his rifle before he could react, sending him to the floor. He whipped around and saw the gunman on the floor, grasping his hand and crying out in pain. Stephen kept his 9 mm pointed at the gunman and warned him not to move. Amin was impressed; Stephen had shot the gun straight out of his hand.

"Grace!" Walid yelled as he pushed himself to his knees. Grace lay on her back, and a tear fell from her face as she looked into Walid's eyes. He couldn't tell where she had been shot but saw the blood creating a small pool on the ground. "Don't you leave me." He leaned down to kiss her for the first time, wondering if it would be his last. She held tight to his broad shoulders and smiled up at him weakly.

Walid looked up at Stephen and Amin, who were tearing up as well. "Go! Get Gilles and warn everyone!"

They ran to the conference doors and ferociously threw them open. The situation was chaotic. After hearing the bullets, many had left their seats and hurried to the front of the conference room, seeking an alternate exit. Everyone drew their attention to Amin as he yelled as loud as he could, "The drinks are poisoned!"

His proclamation exacerbated the situation as he knew it would. Some who had already sipped on their drinks cried out in terror while others ran toward the lobby exit.

Amin sprinted toward the back of the conference room and into the kitchen. Within seconds of arriving, a small explosion sent him spiraling backward like a football over a metal cabinet onto the floor behind it. Stephen arrived in a matter of seconds and called for Amin and Gilles. Amin pushed himself to his knees; he didn't feel any major damage. "I'm fine, go!" he yelled to Stephen, who kept running toward the explosion's point of origin at the front of the kitchen.

"Gilles!" Stephen called as he tried to keep his stinging eyes open to see through the smoke. He wondered if Gilles had detonated prematurely to prevent ISD's plans from panning out. Stephen coughed as he walked over bomb remnants and carnage he refused to look at. A lump was forming in his throat. "Gilles!" he yelled again.

Finally, Stephen heard a man yell from a few paces away. "Somebody help!" The smoke was beginning to dissipate, allowing Stephen to see the silhouette of a man trapped underneath a body. "Stephen! Is that you?"

"Gilles?" Stephen said in amazement, pushing the body off of him. "Are you okay? What happened?"

"Story for another time, brother!" Gilles said, sounding worn but remarkably optimistic. "Help me up. I think I can walk." Stephen pulled him to his feet and looked at him in wonder. He was covered with scratches and minor injuries, but other than that, he appeared to be fine!

"Come on, man, let's go. Where's everyone?" Gilles asked.

"Amin!" Stephen called out, incognizant of the fact that he was standing right behind him.

"Woah, I'm okay," Amin said. "Just some bruises. Let's go. Grace was shot."

Stephen sprinted to the lobby, and Amin and Gilles made their way shortly behind him. As he arrived, he stopped in his tracks. He had never witnessed such chaos. Most of the conference participants had poured into the lobby and ran toward the hotel entrance. The sea of people ran over one another trying to get out. He wondered if there would be any casualties from the stampede.

They ran over to Walid, who had ripped his shirt off to create a makeshift field dressing for Grace's shoulder, where the bullet penetrated. The bleeding appeared to have stopped for now, and Grace was still conscious.

Gilles ran past them to observe the open staircase connecting the second floor with the hotel entrance. He looked on in horror as someone pushed on the front door, which then swung open with such gusto that it shattered and nearly sucked him out. The man held on to the door for dear life. Gilles' eyes were glued to the sandstorm. He had never seen such a powerful storm in his life. It looked like a tornado.

"Guys!" he called back to the group, but nobody responded. Walid had his hands on Grace and was praying boldly for God to heal her. One by one, Stephen, Amin, and Gilles laid hands on her as well and prayed for a miracle. Nothing happened right away. Then Walid heard a commanding voice. "Go to the rooftop."

"She can't move!" Walid protested. The guys looked at him in confusion; nobody else had heard the voice.

"Don't tell me what she can't do. Now go!" the voice commanded.

Walid felt a shift in his spirit. Hope started to spring up in the midst of the storm. "Guys, help me get her up. We're going to the roof."

"Have you seen what's happening outside? We'll be sucked off!" Gilles said.

"I don't care. I'm going. Someone help me get her up."

Amin leaned over without hesitation and helped Walid carry Grace to the elevators. They placed her gently on the floor and cruised to the rooftop, bracing for whatever apocalyptic sand winds would greet them. Walid stood completely resolute. He was certain in what the Lord instructed him to do and thus reasoned that God wouldn't lead him out just to be killed.

When the doors opened they stood amazed at what they beheld. The deep-blue sky was littered with small burnt-orange clouds. The movements of the wind caused the clouds to dance in a melodic way; it was like night and day from what they just witnessed below. Stephen threw his arm out to catch the closing elevator door as the group stood there transfixed. Amin and Walid carried Grace to the ceiling platform as they heard the sound of a helicopter approaching.

"Look!" Grace said, pointing at the chopper coming in from the distance. "How did you know it was coming?"

"I didn't!"

"What's that noise?" Stephen asked. Nobody could make out the sound, but it reminded them of the terrifying, suctioning sound of a tornado. As Stephen and Gilles approached the side of the building, the sound grew louder.

"You guys have to see this!" Stephen yelled.

"This is goin' on the website," Gilles said, filming the unbelievable site beneath them with an iPhone that he swiped from an ISD member in the kitchen. Walid helped Grace to the edge at her insistence. The ground was completely obscured by the sandstorm, which was swirling so powerfully that it had created a funnel-type shape, moving in circles around the hotel. In what they could only describe as an act of God, the sand twister remained two floors below them and failed to rise any higher.

As the chopper neared, two separate elevator doors opened, and at least twenty people from the lobby poured out. It was clear from their clothing that Saudis and Europeans were among the group. Amin exchanged greetings with them and quickly learned that these were US and British choppers that were on standby due to the event.

Grace grabbed on to Walid's hand and pointed him to a familiar face in the crowd. It was Fatima! Walid stood on guard as he watched Stephen walk over to her. They exchanged a few words that he couldn't hear, and both of them smiled.

"Um, what did we just witness?" Grace asked.

"No idea!" Walid said.

Stephen came over to help lift Grace into the chopper. "You're not gonna tell us anything?" Walid asked.

"Long story...I'll tell you later!"

Grace winced in pain as she was lowered onto a seat in the helicopter. She appeared to be growing weaker. Walid sat next to her and tried to get her to drink some water.

Gilles sat next to Walid and yelled to the pilot over the deafening sounds. "What about everyone else downstairs?"

"We've got more on the way!" the pilot said. "We'll get everyone we can."

As they left the rooftop, they watched two US soldiers who stayed behind to help gather the other leaders. Walid had so many questions, though all he could do was marvel at everything that had just happened. How God directed him to the rooftop, foiled ISD's plans to bomb the conference, and seemingly tamed the sandstorm. No words could describe his awe as he continued staring at the sandstorm, which was starting to die down. What a mighty God he served!

CHAPTER 26

The Speech Heard Around the World

The next morning, Walid and the guys sipped steaming cappuccinos from the tenth floor of a hospital in Beirut, overlooking the Mediterranean Sea. Walid watched the sun create a beautiful reflection on the water as it rose from the horizon. He smiled. For the first time in his life, he had found a family. More importantly, he knew he was part of God's family, which brought with it an unspeakable peace and joy. Despite being in a hospital room, he wouldn't dream of being anywhere else right now.

The guys had barely slept as they waited for Grace to wake up from her overnight surgery. Nobody had spoken a word about the events of the previous evening. They napped sporadically throughout the night but mainly talked, prayed, and worshipped. And, when reaching utter sleep deprivation, dared each other to do stupid things.

"Amin, don't be lame," Stephen said. "If Gilles can suspend himself eighteen stories by a sheet, so can you! I'll give you five dollars."

Amin laughed and threw an empty water bottle at him from across the room.

"This is what I've been missing?" Grace said quietly.

"You're awake!" Walid said.

"This is your doing, Grace!" Stephen winked. "We care about you too much to fall asleep, so we've been staying awake with caffeine and tomfoolery."

Grace laughed and cringed at the pain in her shoulder. Walid sat on the bed next to her, taking her hand in his. "You saved my life, Grace," Walid said. "I wanted to thank you earlier…"

"It's okay," she said.

"But why would you risk your life for me? I don't want anything happening to you."

"Because you're worth saving! And besides, you would have done it for me."

"You're amazing." He felt love growing in his heart for her. Was it even possible this soon?

Stephen took a breath as though preparing to say something, and Amin blocked his mouth with his hand. "Hey!" Stephen said.

"You were gonna ruin the moment," Amin said. Stephen looked at him incredulously. "Tell me you weren't gonna deliver some awkward joke!"

"You don't know me, Amin, you don't know me"

The group heard a quiet knock on the door. Grace's doctor entered, looking carefully at his clipboard. "Well, good news," he said. "You're gonna be just fine. I've never seen anything like this before."

"Like what?" Grace asked.

"The bullet missed your heart by less than an inch. It entered from such an odd angle, like it was pushed off course by something. If it hadn't penetrated from that exact position, it could have gone right into your heart."

"Dude, you're like a hero now!" Gilles said to Stephen.

"Seriously, that was some incredible shooting," Amin said.

"That's not the strange part," the doctor interrupted. "In the surgery, you flatlined momentarily. When your heartbeat returned, you started healing before we even finished closing you up. And this morning, your vitals are almost completely normal. Grace, at this rate you're going to be healed quicker than anyone we've seen before."

"Praise the Lord! That's great," Grace said.

"Well, whatever it was…"

"It was Him," she insisted.

"It's normal to feel things like this after coming out of a major surgery," the doctor said. Amin shook his head as though frustrated by the doctor's disbelief.

"He'll heal your daughter too," she said.

The doctor's face became gravely serious. "What?"

"He told me. Lupus, no?"

"What's this all about?"

"The Lord told me when I was under. He wants to heal her."

"I…I'll be back with your release paperwork."

Just as quickly as he left, a nurse hustled into the room and took a good, long look at Walid. "What?" he asked. After hearing his voice, she gasped and looked frightened. "I think you should leave."

"What? Why?"

"Turn the news on," she said, turning to the others in the room. "Do you know who you're with?"

"Which news?" Walid asked.

"All of them. It's on all the news channels." She returned to the front desk, where they could see her whispering to her coworkers through the glass.

"This can't be good," Gilles said as he flipped to CNN. A female news anchor was speaking as words highlighted in red flashed across the screen: Breaking News: Times Square Bomber Speaks Out. In the upper right-hand corner of the screen was a picture of Walid.

"Oh, come on!" Walid said after reading the headline. "I'm not the bomber!"

"Turn it up, Gilles," Amin said.

The anchor continued speaking. "Our sources have gathered critical footage of one of the terrorists involved in the Times Square attack. Listen to his message." Suddenly, the screen flashed to a video of Walid in the safe house in Libya, though nobody on the outside would have known its location.

"Their sources? It's from a public website," Amin laughed. "Way to stretch the truth."

Walid looked down for a moment and tried not to get choked up. "You know, Eli actually convinced me to film myself after I did the same thing for him. I hope he's getting a kick out of this in heaven right now."

Grace squeezed his hand to comfort him as they kept listening. Walid never thought he would see his face on the news, and certainly not from every available news station! Though he was proud of the message he recorded, he had a feeling another storm was coming soon.

Walid had just described his involvement in the Times Square attack on CNN. "I had already left ISD at the time, though I was working undercover to try to stop the attack. ISD changed the plans on me at the last minute, and I failed as a result. I did everything I could to stop it. To the families who were impacted by this attack, I am truly sorry and pray for God's grace to rest upon you. There are at least two more attacks planned: one in Syria and one in Europe. I am doing everything in my power to stop those last two attacks. I would ask anyone viewing this message to pray for me and my team. This may sound confusing coming from a former terrorist. You see, before I left the group, ISD tasked me with writing a paper to disprove the Bible and help them acquire more legitimacy. Turns out, that was an impossible task. The more I studied, the more I came to realize that Jesus Christ is the son of God, and that…" CNN cut off the video before he could finish his message. The scrolling headline changed to "Terrorist Seeks Prayers from Victims."

"You did the right thing, Walid," Amin said.

"It's like they didn't even hear what I said," Walid said. "They cut off the whole part about what Jesus did for me!"

"It's the news, Walid, it's what they do," Stephen tried to reassure him. "People who want to hear the rest of your message will seek it out, and they'll find it."

"He's right," Grace said. "People will see your authenticity."

"Yeah, I guess," Walid said. He directed his attention to Amin, who started pacing. What's up?"

"I dunno, just wondering what's coming next." The emotions of the previous evening were finally starting to hit him. "I think we need to talk about what happened. This isn't over yet."

"I don't wanna talk about him," Walid said quickly. "I just...I just feel kind of responsible. I mean he gave his life for me! I never imagined anyone would risk everything to do such a thing."

"I know," Amin said. "But I can pretty much guarantee he's not regretting his decision from heaven. And you'll get to thank him someday."

"Yeah...So what do we do now?" Walid switched gears as quickly as possible. "A few of those guys may have drank whatever ISD put in the champagne. And the attack in Europe is supposed to be the biggest one yet. We *barely* stopped that last one!"

"So we'll get a bigger team then," Gilles said.

"Yes!" Amin agreed. "We have to expand. And we need to stop focusing on how difficult this looks or what went wrong in the last operation."

Walid felt frustrated but thankful for their constant optimism. "You guys don't feel the least bit discouraged?"

"Sure, a little," Gilles said. "But I refuse to yield to it."

"Hey, what happened back in the hotel, anyway?" Wald asked him. "How does one survive a suicide bomb?"

"Ahh, I knew you'd ask," Gilles said. "Well, ISD was running out of time after they killed the other Frenchman, so they tried to make a quick suicide vest instead of risking my death too. Problem is, it was completely unstable, so instead of attaching it to me in the adjacent room, they walked it into the kitchen while one guy held my elbow with a death grip. This is pretty much like something out of a movie, right? So one of the cooks throws a ladle—a ladle!—at the guy holding the bomb, causing him to drop it, and the rest is history."

"You're kidding me, man," Stephen said.

"Can't make this stuff up!" Gilles said.

"You must have been within arm's reach of the bomb," Grace said. "How did you survive?"

"There were two things between me and the bomb: another ISD guy and one of those cabinets. Both took the brunt of the explosion. I felt the heat, like being in the middle of a bonfire or something, but no major damage."

"Amazing," Walid said.

"There's something else though," Gilles added. "I dunno what they put in the drinks or if it was just some lie to cause fear, but I have a feeling it was the former. We have to warn them somehow."

"Those are some powerful people...how are we gonna reach them?" Stephen asked.

"Same way Walid did," Amin said. "Our website. After Walid's global coverage, you can bet they'll be monitoring it."

Grace's doctor came back into the room and handed her some paperwork. "As your doctor, I'm required to tell you that physically, you should stay here at least another day. But you did something for me, and now I owe you a favor."

"You don't owe me anything."

"Well, I just spoke with my daughter. She has more energy now than she's had in years. I don't know about all this, but maybe there's something to what you said."

"That's great!"

"Anyway, you'll wanna hear this. One of our nurses spooked after seeing you on TV," he said to Walid. "But something tells me you're not that bad."

"Well, thanks, I think I'm all right," Walid smirked.

"She's called the General Security Directorate. Not sure how long it'll be, but you can bet they'll be here soon. Do you have anywhere to go?"

"We'll figure something out," Walid said. "Thank you for the warning."

"Hey, Doc," Gilles said. "Did you see a Syrian man come in here with a Frenchwoman 'bout two days ago? They were with us."

He thought for a moment. "Yes, though they're gone now. Transferred to Paris for surgery." Gilles nodded.

"Thanks for everything," Grace said as she signed her paperwork and wrote the URL of the website on his copy. "If you ever need a helping hand."

The doctor shook everyone's hand. "Good luck to you all. Now don't waste any more time. They'll be here soon."

CHAPTER 27

The Coming War

"See the guy on the far-right-hand side?" Amin said to Walid as they waited to show their passports at Beirut's international airport. Walid nodded. "Go to him if you can. He doesn't check documents carefully."

Walid was thankful Amin had been through this airport multiple times. Ten minutes earlier, he purchased burner phones for everyone in the group and handed Walid and Grace their IDs. Walid had used several fraudulent IDs in years past as an ISD leader, but never imagined he would need one after leaving the group! He felt uneasy not knowing the guy who made the ID, but given it was one of Amin's many contacts, he felt somewhat assuaged.

As Walid inched closer to the front of the line, he glanced at his friends. They were scattered throughout the line to avoid associating with each other in case anyone recognized them. He prayed for peace despite feeling somewhat paranoid that the entire world might recognize his face.

"Next!" the desk receptionist called.

Walid stepped forward. "One thirty p.m. to Tunis."

It was Amin's idea to fly to Tunis, which was still a tourist spot despite the increasing unrest. It would appear less suspicious than Tripoli. More importantly, it was far less dangerous. The woman barely looked at Walid as she typed something on her laptop. He could hear the boarding pass printing. "Business or pleasure?" she asked, finally looking into his eyes.

"Business," he smiled. He cringed on the inside, feeling as though his lying skills had waned.

"No luggage?" she asked.

"No, quick trip," he said. *Stop asking questions*, he thought.

"Hmmm." The woman looked at him in confusion. Walid looked away to avoid her gaze, noting that Amin, Gilles, and Grace, who was on crutches, had made it through the line. "You look so familiar. Like a movie star or something."

"Suppose I just have one of those faces."

"I suppose," she said, handing him the boarding pass. Walid exhaled in relief as he started walking away. The feeling of relief, however, would soon pass.

Walid avoided his group and continued straight toward security. Before he was even close, someone yelled from behind him. "You there! Hold on!" Most people in the terminal, including Walid, turned to watch the commotion. His heart dropped when he realized that two airport guards were looking directly at him. He tried to act natural and walk slowly toward them, a confused pretense painted on his face.

"There a problem?" Walid asked.

One guard raised a picture to his face. "What is this?" Walid acted insulted and inconvenienced, glancing at the picture. *Oh no*, he thought. It was him! There was no explaining this away.

"It's him," one guard said.

"Gotta run," Walid said. He sprinted in the direction of the airport exit, not knowing what else to do.

"Stop!" the guards yelled as they took off after him, though they were no match for Walid's speed. If ISD did anything positive for him, it was getting him in excellent shape for moments just like these.

Some people yelled in fear at the commotion, though nobody understood what was happening. Still, the appearance of chaos is all it took for panic to ensue.

Walid ran out the door and ran across one of three wide lanes of incoming traffic, barely dodging a public transportation bus that slammed its breaks to avoid hitting him. It created a natural barrier between him and his pursuers. The moment he stopped at the median, a car pulled up beside him and someone yelled from within, "Get in!"

Though this seemed like a stupid idea, he saw no other choice and surprisingly felt at peace in his spirit. Still, he hesitated.

"Quickly, Walid!"

Walid jumped in and immediately recognized the person sitting in the driver's seat.

"Go, go, go!" Walid yelled as the guards reached the car. One of them ran alongside the vehicle and managed to open the backseat door, hanging on as the increasing acceleration caused his feet to drag. Walid jumped into the back seat and pushed him out the door, sending him rolling on the asphalt. "He'll be fine," Walid said as he hopped into the front seat.

"Undoubtedly," the driver agreed.

"What are you…how did you…why are you even here?" Walid struggled for words, shocked to see Bashir again in the most unlikely of locations.

"To help you, of course."

"Come on, Bashir, why are you really here? And slow down! We have to go back."

"Your friends will be fine."

"How'd you know I was traveling with them?"

"Why else would you wanna go back to that mess?" Bashir said. "They're not associated with you, Walid, not in Beirut. Nobody will go after them."

"You don't know that."

"I do. My people will watch them 'til they leave. Man, Walid, I forget how impressive you are sometimes until I see you in action."

"Are you messing with me?" Walid asked. This whole encounter felt surreal. "Who are you working with? I don't even know who's side you're on anymore!"

"We have a lot to discuss, Walid. But I promise you that I am on your side."

"Where are we going?"

"Somewhere safe, for now. You have a phone? You should call your friends, let them know you're okay, or they'll try to follow you."

Walid called Grace and assured her that he was OK, urging her to fly to Tunis. Though she protested, he convinced her he would meet her there soon.

"You like her, huh?" Bashir said after Walid hung up.

"Can we not talk about women?"

"Sorry."

"Bashir, I'm happy to see you. Just give me some time. This whole situation is just weird. Please tell me where we're going."

"There's an underground base on the outskirts of Beirut. We can VTC to Tunis from there, and you can call your friends again."

"OK. So why did you come?"

"To save your life, Walid, I told you that. They're under orders to kill you, not detain you. Those weren't airport guards back there."

"How do you know? How does anyone even know where I am right now?"

"Closest airport that makes any sense. Damascus international is under ISD's control right now, and the eastern roads are too dangerous for anyone to risk. We've been tracking ISD's comms, so I knew you'd be here. I'll introduce you to my team soon." He paused for a moment and took a deep breath. "By the way, I'm a wanted man now too. They figured it out after I met you in Tripoli. ISD perceives you as a real threat to their existence. They'll never admit it, but they're afraid of you!"

Walid sat back in his seat and smiled for the first time in hours. "Well don't get all cocky now!" Bashir laughed.

Walid looked out the window, watching the beautiful Beirut skyline roll by. He thanked the Lord for a moment of beauty in the midst of chaos. It made him consider whether he'd ever be a free man again, free to take a vacation or visit a beautiful location like this. Though he knew God had forgiven him and that he was truly a new man, he knew some wouldn't see it that way.

"Do you know anything about Damascus?" Walid said.

"What do you wanna know?"

"I just can't make sense of it. Why bother with some minor bomb if they were just going to poison everyone?"

"Oh, that…" Bashir said gravely. "It wasn't poison. It was a viral biological agent."

Walid finally started to understand. "So they *wanted* them to go back and think nothing was wrong! And the bomb?"

"Did you notice who was sitting at the target table?" Bashir asked.

"No, Gilles never told us."

"Well, I only heard the initial plan. It was supposed to be Iran, Russia, and a few others."

"I thought Iran was working with ISD."

"They were."

Walid felt a lightbulb turn on. "And they wanted to blame it on the West, that's why they chose Gilles."

"They wanted this to seem like a failed attack," Bashir said. He paused for a moment before continuing. "So…another thing…ISD has another insider. Someone high up, a leader. Heard them talking about it before they set a bounty on my head."

"Who?" Walid asked.

"I don't know," Bashir said. "Whoever it is, I think they're from one of the countries at that table."

Walid turned to look out the window again, pondering.

Bashir drove over a hill and started the descent into a valley near the Mediterranean. "We're getting close now."

– – – – – – – – – – – – – – – – – –

"You think this was a good idea?" Gilles asked Stephen as they stepped off the plane in Tunis.

"Guess we'll find out soon."

"Just hope we're not too late."

"What happened to Mr. Optimism? If we're too late, then we're too late," Stephen insisted. "At least we have a plan."

"Well yeah! Obvs!" Gilles said with feigned enthusiasm.

"Dude…nobody says that," Stephen said. "We should call the others."

Stephen dialed Amin as they walked toward a taxi. Amin finally picked up after four rings. "Hey, man, everything cool?" Stephen asked.

"Great!" Amin sounded energized, ready for the next adventure. "We're on our way now. You?"

"Same, bro," Stephen said. "Just landed. Call us when you arrive."

"All right. About to call the other one." Both knew it was too dangerous to speak with any further details in public.

Amin looked at Grace in the backseat of a taxicab in Beirut and smiled. "Family's well."

"Good," Grace said. "This is fine, thank you," Grace said to the taxi driver, who pulled over to a seemingly abandoned bus stop on the outskirts of the city. The driver raised an eyebrow in confusion as they exited the vehicle. The two breathed a sigh of relief, thankful to be sitting safely in the middle of nowhere, at least for now. They sat on the bench, basking in the sweet silence and serenity that would soon come to an end.

— — — — — — — — — — — — — — — — — —

Hours earlier, the team followed contingency protocols after Walid ran out of the airport. Gilles and Stephen went straight to the security line while Amin and Grace walked to a coffee shop in the main terminal. Grace would call Walid and go through security with Amin after ensuring he was all right.

After five or ten minutes of waiting, Grace and Amin spotted the security guards walking back inside, looking frustrated. She smiled at Amin, realizing he must have escaped. "Amin...I don't think we should get on this plane."

"Oh, and why's that?"

"There's more we can do here," she urged.

"I think you just don't want to leave him again."

Grace ignored the insinuation, though she knew it to be true. "You've got contacts everywhere, Amin. You must have some here, no?"

"I might..."

"Amin, stop being coy! There must be a safe house here."

"Keep it down!" Amin said, worried that someone might overhear. He sipped his coffee and stared at the table, asking the Lord for their next steps. He looked back at Grace, who was staring intently at him, waiting for his response.

"Well...it'd be one of the least crazy things we've done in the last few weeks," he rationalized.

"I knew it!" she hit his shoulder playfully in excitement.

"You know I'm always up for an adventure," he said.

"Amin, listen, we've already said we need to recruit more people to stop the next one," she said, trying to choose her words wisely. God forbid she even whisper the word *bomb* in an airport. "We need to spread ourselves beyond North Africa. I really think this is a good thing."

"Me too. I like the sound of this. Come on, let's go."

— — — — — — — — — — — — — — — — — — —

"Where are you, man?" Amin asked Walid over the phone from the deserted bus station. "You just ran out on us," he joked.

"Forgot my keys," he laughed. "I'm safe, I'm with Bashir, believe it or not! How's Tunis?"

"About that…We're not there. Well, two of us are."

"What? What happened? Is Grace with you?"

"Yeah, one sec." Amin handed the phone to her.

"Walid, we're still here!"

"Grace! How are you feeling?"

"I'm OK. Doctors gave me the good stuff."

"Where are you guys?"

"Well, middle of nowhere right now. You know Amin, he's got people everywhere."

"But why are you staying? I mean, I'm happy you're here, but what's the plan?"

"We figured we'd have better luck splitting up. We've had a lot of hits on the site since you aired your message. It's time to build a nontraditional army of sorts!"

"That's perfect," Walid said, enjoying her enthusiasm. "Why don't you call when you get to Amin's hideout? We shouldn't be on an open line for long."

"All right, we'll talk soon."

Amin observed a black vehicle approaching quickly from a distance. "This should be us," he said. "We'll be at the safe house in no time."

– – – – – – – – – – – – – – – – – – – –

"Where are we?" Walid asked as he looked out at a gated community near the ocean.

"We're in Sidon," Bashir said excitedly. "Feels like going back in time, right?"

Walid felt the excitement too. Jesus preached in Tyre and Sidon during the peak of His ministry, though Isaiah and Ezekiel prophesized the city's destruction due to its corruption. The history certainly was rich. "Whose place is this?" Walid asked.

"I know the couple who own it—they're great! Strong Christians, and both work high up in the government. God's really given them strategic placement here. I knew the guy before he got the position, way back before I joined ISD. We've only recently reconnected."

"Well, praise God they're so forgiving," Walid said, referring to their recent positions in ISD.

"About that," Bashir added sheepishly. "They don't know *you* are coming—just that a friend was going to stay here for a few days."

"Oh…well, here's hoping they don't watch any news," Walid sighed.

"It'll be fine. Like I said, they know someone's coming."

"Ah, someone."

"They want to help us, Walid."

Bashir walked Walid around to the rear of the house and let himself in with a key he had in his wallet. "They won't be here for a little bit."

Walid followed Bashir through the entry hall to a spiral staircase. The house was a classic Mediterranean-style home with beautiful arched windows, columns, and a stucco finish. The couple living here was clearly well-off. Walid listened to the sounds of laughing and singing coming from upstairs. Bashir hesitated before walking up.

"Thought you said they were gone," Walid said.

"They are. You trust me, right?"

"I guess."

"Well, maybe one day you can fully trust me again. 'Cause I wanna work with you and your team! I've made a lot of connections the last few months. I think we both have a lot to offer each other."

"Bashir," Walid touched his shoulder and smiled. "You don't have to sell me. I do trust you, and you know I've already forgiven you. I've just been through a lot lately."

"Me as well," Bashir said. "We'll get through this together. God will help us."

"We have a lot of catching up to do."

"Yes. In the meantime, there's some people here I want you to meet."

Bashir led him upstairs into a large, open room where ten people sat in couches around a rustic coffee table. "It's him!" one person said as the group turned to face Walid. "Praise the Lord!" another said. Some got up to shake his hand or kissed him on the head, a common greeting in Middle Eastern culture.

"Uh, hey!" Walid said. "What's going on?"

"They saw you on the news," Bashir explained. "Found your website and listened to the entire message. You'll never believe this! They were in ISD's Syria branch before defecting and fleeing the country. It's really quite amazing how they found this couple."

"I must have watched at least ten of the videos posted by former ISD members!" one of the men said. "Walid, Jesus visited every one of us. For me it was in a dream. For some it was a vision or just a sense of knowing or prophetic word."

"We traveled in groups of two or three and met up at a large souk in Sidon," another said. "Well, this couple was there and walked right up to us, saying the Lord told them they'd meet us at the souk today!"

"That's amazing!" Walid said.

For the next hour or so, the group exchanged stories and enjoyed each other's presence. Though Walid was exhausted from the last several days, he felt completely recharged.

— — — — — — — — — — — — — — — — — —

Two hours later, Walid watched the sun set on the terrace, marveling at the beautiful Mediterranean view. He was reminded of the view from his villa in Tripoli. Though he was there several weeks ago, he felt like it had been months. *God, look how far you've brought me.*

Bashir walked outside, and Walid embraced him. "Bashir, I didn't think my message would reach anyone. Not to the extent that it has."

"He's about to do even greater things," Bashir said. "I can just feel it."

"Critical times we're in. So exciting, isn't it?"

"Yes! There's a pretty big storm ahead, and we're about to chase it," Bashir said.

"You know, for the first time, I'm not worried about it. Look at how far God has brought us in the last several months! Can you imagine what He will do in the next year?"

Bashir shook his head. "So what's your plan if things ever calm down? Can you imagine such a life?"

Walid thought for a moment as he looked out again at a deep-orange sun setting over the ocean. A big smile grew across his face as he looked back at Bashir. "You know, I think we've got a book to write that we never finished."

ABOUT THE AUTHOR

Julianne Hale is a consultant working in the Intelligence Community. For more than ten years, she has served as a policy and counterterrorism expert focusing on the Near East region. Julianne wrote hundreds of reports for the US government analyzing world events, terrorist operations, and radical Islamic ideology, resulting in national intelligence and impact awards from several agencies. She has collaborated with more than fifteen nations and traveled to three continents in support of her work. Above all, her passion is in advocating and developing solutions for people in global conflict zones. She is partnering with international ministries to bring both humanitarian aid and the greatest gift of God's love and grace to people in the Near East region.

CPSIA information can be obtained
at www.ICGtesting.com
Printed in the USA
BVOW09s0713290517
485402BV00001B/151/P

9 781640 280120